DAVE RUDDEN

Random House New York

To Eilish, because I promised

This is a work of fiction. Names, characters, places, and incidents either are the product of the author's imagination or are used fictitiously. Any resemblance to actual persons, living or dead, events, or locales is entirely coincidental.

 Published in the United States by Random House Children's Books, a division of Penguin Random House LLC, New York. Originally published in hardcover by Penguin Books Ltd., a division of Penguin Random House LLC, London, in 2016.

Random House and the colophon are registered trademarks of Penguin Random House LLC.

Visit us on the Web! randomhousekids.com

Educators and librarians, for a variety of teaching tools, visit us at RHTeachersLibrarians.com

Library of Congress Cataloging-in-Publication Data
Names: Rudden, Dave, author.
Title: Knights of the Borrowed Dark / Dave Rudden.
Description: First American edition. | New York : Random House, [2016] | Summary: A young orphan learns that monsters can grow out of the shadows in our world, and there is an ancient order of knights who keep them at bay.
Identifiers: LCCN 2015031377 | ISBN 978-0-553-52297-6 (hardback) | ISBN 978-0-553-52298-3 (hardcover library binding) | ISBN 978-0-553-52299-0 (ebook)
Subjects: | CYAC: Orphans—Fiction. | Monsters—Fiction. | Knights and knighthood—Fiction. |
BISAC: JUVENILE FICTION / Fantasy & Magic. | JUVENILE FICTION / Action & Adventure / General. | JUVENILE FICTION / Family / General (see also headings under Social Issues).
Classification: LCC PZ7.1.R828 Kn 2016 | DDC [Fic]—dc23
LC record available at http://lccn.loc.gov/2015031377

Printed in the United States of America
10 9 8 7 6 5 4 3 2 1
First American Edition

Random House Children's Books supports the First Amendment and celebrates the right to read.

CONTENTS

PROLOGUE

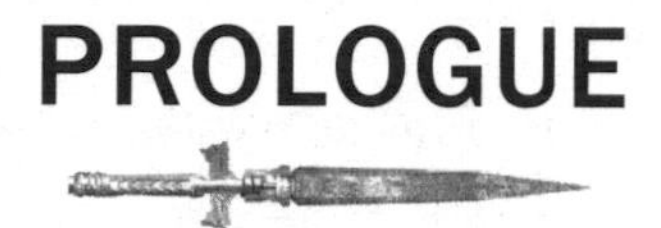

TICK

LOOKING BACK, IT had been a mistake to fill the orphanage with books.

Director Ackerby tapped the rim of his teacup with a finger. *The untidiness of it all,* he thought.

Far below in the yard, children dipped in and out of the shadow cast by his tower office—gossiping in scattered groups, voices raised in excited chatter. All talking about the visitors, of course. This was what happened when you bottled up 250 boys and girls. Last week, a thrush had bounced off a classroom window and the orphans hadn't shut up for days. Had they named it? He wouldn't be surprised.

His gaze swept the buildings below. Crosscaper Orphanage slouched against the mountainside like it had been dropped there—a graying stack of towers and flat, fat dormitories that shuddered when the wind was too harsh and sweated when it got too warm.

It was an uphill struggle for orphanages *not* to be dismal, but Ackerby had always thought Crosscaper took special pleasure in it, as though it knew that the groan of its slumping masonry and the rattle of its window frames were giving entire dormitories of children nightmares.

"Sir?"

His secretary's voice seeped through the intercom and Ackerby stabbed at the button to respond.

"Yes?"

"Your two o'clock is here, sir. Shall I send them in?"

The director barely heard him. He was staring at the newest addition to the orphanage grounds, standing out against Crosscaper's comforting grayness like a healthy man in a hospital ward. Bright white walls. New windows that shone. A door that didn't squeak but whispered open like the sharing of a secret. Children waited outside, as they had every day since it opened.

A *library*. As if the orphanage chaplain wasn't filling their heads with enough nonsense.

The intercom burped again. "Sir?"

Ackerby sighed. He had flicked through some of the dog-eared books in the library and it had been much as he'd feared. His own office was lined with beautiful leather-bound works (the word *book* painfully inadequate—they were *compendiums,* they were *texts,* they were *tomes*), the kind one touched with gloves, if one touched them at all.

Some, he mused proudly, had never even been opened.

The library books, on the other hand, had been read to pieces. And as for the content? Story after story of noble orphans rescued from drudgery—and now every time someone came to visit, hopeful children began packing their bags, ready for their new life as wizard, warrior, or prophesied king.

Ackerby sniffed. *Chosen ones.* If they were wanted, they wouldn't be here.

"Yes, send them in. And bring some tea." He thought for a moment. "Forget the tea."

Director Ackerby did not believe in coddling visitors. There was an art to these things. Inspectors were made to wait ten minutes; it didn't do to annoy them, but you also didn't want to make them feel too important. Solicitors were seen immediately (you never knew who might end up footing the bill), and potential parents had to wait half an hour, as a sort of test of their commitment.

In Ackerby's opinion, if you weren't prepared to drink bad coffee and flick through last year's *Home and Housing* magazine, then you clearly did not deserve a child.

"Mr. Ackerby?"

There were shadows in his doorway.

Ackerby liked to keep the lights low. It shaved money off the bills and he had the vague idea that it might be beneficial to the children—exercise for their eyes, perhaps. The visitors had stopped where the light from Ackerby's desk lamp and the glow from the hallway fell short. Their faces were obscured, indistinct.

For a moment, Ackerby wasn't sure if they were people at all.

"Thank you for seeing us at such short notice," the smaller of the visitors said. "I hate to steal time away from the busy."

The couple stepped forward in unison. The woman was tall and thin, with a spine curved like an old coat hanger, her clothes and skin white as frost, hair chopped short around her neck in a frayed mop the color of chalk. The man beside her was the shape and pallor of a goose egg, with a shock of colorless curls that jigged and bounced as if trying to flee from his scalp. His waistcoat creaked as he offered Ackerby his hand.

Normally, Ackerby would smile firmly (if a little coldly) and grasp the visitors' hands a smidge too hard as he asked their names. Ackerby was proud of his handshake. He had read books on the subject. A firm and painful squeeze—*that* was how you dominated a meeting.

The man in the waistcoat took his hand. "Of course, stealing time from the idle is no crime at all."

Pain.

Distantly, Ackerby noted the throaty *pops* the bones of his hand made as the visitor's grip ground them together—like a plastic bottle reshaping itself. The books he had read on the power of a good handshake were replaced by hazy diagrams from medical textbooks, and then swiftly by nothing at all.

He fought back a gasp of relief when the man in the waistcoat let go. The visitor grinned cheerily up at him and dropped into a seat with a pleased sigh, waving at Ackerby to join him.

An unlit cigarette hung from one side of the woman's mouth. She didn't move. She just stared.

The pain in Ackerby's hand faded and he rallied. *Commanded to sit? In my own office?*

He stalked round his desk and spun on a heel, regarding the visitors coldly. Standing behind the desk made him feel better. He told himself that it was simply pride in the decor and not the comfort of putting a slab of solid oak between him and the man in the waistcoat.

"Good afternoon," Ackerby said, though he didn't mean it and it wasn't. "Welcome to Crosscaper Orphanage. And you are?"

His feeling of unease deepened as the visitors continued to stare blankly at him. He couldn't say what was wrong exactly, but there was something . . . calculated about their looks. As if they were working out something about Ackerby in their heads, an equation he wouldn't enjoy.

"Your names?" Ackerby repeated, and although there was absolutely no need to explain such a simple question, he found himself stammering, "For—for our appointment book. Our files, I mean."

The request hung in the air, slowly starving to death.

"Names?" the man in the waistcoat said after an eternity. "Ah. Yes. Names. Sorry. We are new." His dark eyes flicked over the office before settling on Ackerby like flies. "I like the name Ellicott. A pleasure."

It hadn't been so far, but you couldn't leave a statement like that hanging. Ackerby forced a smile. "Yes, of course. Nice to meet y—" His brow furrowed. "What do you mean *new*?"

The man's smile deepened. "I understand that you must be busy, so we will take as little of your time as possible. We are looking for a boy. Denizen Hardwick."

It took a moment for Ackerby to bring up a mental image. Nothing wrong with that—that was what files were for, and you didn't get points for rattling facts off the top of your head. Hardwick was . . . small. Unremarkable. Had . . . hair. Brown? Red?

The director frowned. The only thing he could really remember about the boy was that he had never caused an abundance of paperwork, which was the only trait in a child that Ackerby actually liked.

But there was something else . . . something he couldn't recall . . .

"What about him?" Ackerby asked.

The cigarette made a slow path to the other side of the woman's mouth.

"He is a resident here?" The man popped his knuckles against his jaw, the noise so loud it made the director flinch. "Excellent. We have been looking for him for a long time. We are . . . relatives of his. Cousins."

A knot formed in Ackerby's stomach. This Ellicott character was lying to him. Ackerby was sure of it. He had no idea *why* he was sure of it, but a smile like that wasn't cousin to anything, except maybe a spider.

"I would have to check my records," Ackerby said stiffly. That was his usual phrase when he knew the answer to a question but hadn't liked being asked it. "The name does sound familiar, but—"

"We will not take much of your time, Director Ackerby," the man in the waistcoat said. "We merely wish to know a few things. First, has he turned thirteen?"

Ah. That was why Denizen Hardwick had stuck in his head.

"Yes, actually," he said. "A few weeks ago." He glanced around his desk. "There was a card they wanted me to sign . . . I'm sure I saw it. . . ."

"The card is unimportant," the man murmured. "We have been looking for Denizen for a long time. It is a pity we missed the celebrations." The word skittered from his tongue like a cockroach. "No matter. Where is he now?"

"Now?"

The man fingered the buttons on his waistcoat. "Someone would have come for him on his thirteenth birthday. Another . . . relative perhaps. Come to take him away to a whole new life." His plump lips twisted in a cheerless grin. "Exciting. We would like to know where they went. Where Denizen Hardwick is now."

"Oh," Ackerby said. "He's downstairs."

The man's gaze sharpened. "Excuse me?"

"He's downstairs. In class, I would imagine." The director of Crosscaper drew himself up haughtily. "I don't know where you got your information, *sir,* but no one has taken Denizen Hardwick away to a new life. He is still a resident here, thirteenth birthday or no."

The couple glanced at each other.

"Is that a . . . problem?" Ackerby said, his sudden burst of defiance disappearing as soon as it had come. He didn't know who these people were, and their questions were unnerving him.

"No," the man said slowly, as if tasting the word. "No problem. And he has received no visitors?"

"On his birthday?" Ackerby said confusedly. The conversation had gotten away from him, and he felt the beginnings of a headache behind his eyes. The thrum of his heartbeat in his ears was suddenly very loud.

"Ever," the man said. "But that day in particular. Anyone at all."

Ackerby shook his head. The man's eyes were . . . strange. They glittered with a sort of chill, metallic brightness. Ackerby wasn't sure what was more difficult—looking into them or looking away.

"Good. Now. Did anything strange occur on his birthday? Between midnight and midnight. Anything odd that caught your eye."

Ackerby's headache intensified. "Sir, I would ask you to—"

"It's a simple question, Director. Any fires, disappearances, injuries, spatial or luminal distortion, shadows moving strangely . . ."

Sweat broke out on Ackerby's forehead. His patience, never the most stable thing at the best of times, finally snapped.

"Sir, I do not know to what lunacy you are currently subscribed, but this questioning makes no sense. You cannot simply come in here with no identification, no papers, and start talking to me about *shadows moving strangely*! Who do you think you are?"

The man who had introduced himself as Ellicott sighed, lifting one chubby hand to his temple. His eyes narrowed like a disappointed uncle, and Ackerby was suddenly aware of a noise. It was soft, barely audible above the echo of his own voice.

Ticking.

It underscored their words, as fast and quiet as the heart of a bird. Ackerby glanced down at the digital clock on his desk, taking his eyes off the couple just for a second.

And the woman in white *growled* at him.

The sound slid from her lips like a tide of grime, a rough-static snarl of hunger. Something gleamed between her teeth as she stalked toward him. The man in the waistcoat rose to stand beside her.

His head twitched to the side like a snake preparing to strike.

Her head twitched the exact same way.

Ackerby blinked, and in the darkness between eyelid and cheek the woman in white had vanished behind him. There were hands round his neck, forcing him to his knees. He felt breath, cold and fast, on the back of his neck—

—and Ellicott's voice was a purr.

A pity. Such a pity.

The words were pins of ice in Ackerby's brain as the man in the waistcoat knelt to stare into his eyes. The woman in white held him rigid, her white fingers like a steel trap, and though Ackerby was not a small man, he could no more move than fly.

I thought we would not have to resort to this. Given time, we can be . . . convincing. Imaginatively and painfully so. Regretfully, in this instance, we just do not have the time to spare.

The ticking rose to a roar. It was suddenly very hard to breathe. Distantly, Director Ackerby noticed that when the man in the waistcoat spoke, the woman's lips moved silently in time.

You will tell us about any visitors he has had. Any watchers. Any letters. Any contact in the years since he was left here. Anything at all.

His eyes twinkled.

Family is so dear to us.

He nodded at his companion, one professional to another, and the woman broke the director's collarbone with one smooth twist of her fingers.

Ackerby howled.

HE COULDN'T SAY how long they held him. An hour, maybe less—long enough for Director Ackerby to dredge up every fact he knew about Denizen Hardwick. There wasn't much, but the visitors made him go over it again and again and again.

Denizen Hardwick had been left at Crosscaper Orphanage at the age of two. He had received no visitors and no letters, and his thirteenth birthday had passed without incident. It was only after the director started to sob and repeat himself for the fourth time that the iron grip on his collarbone went away.

Swaying there, delirious and on his knees, it seemed that Ackerby saw the couple more clearly than he had ever seen anyone before.

The pendulum jerk of their heads.

The peculiar hardness of their skin, like fingernails or teeth.

Their bright and empty smiles.

Strange, the man in the waistcoat said when they had finished. *If she didn't come for him on his birthday . . . then perhaps he is of no interest to her, and then of no use to us. No matter. Confusion suits us more than symmetry.*

He patted Ackerby on one tearstained cheek.

Thank you, he said. The woman in white bowed low, mockingly. They made to leave, but then the man turned to Ackerby with a thoughtful expression on his face. *You have satisfied us, Director Ackerby. And I like this place.* He gave the air a sniff. *You are in great pain, and you may wish to take out this pain on young Denizen in turn. We understand. We approve.*

The sound of ticking was fainter now.

Just a little more misery in the world.

Somewhere distant, a door closing.

That's all we ask.

1

ABSENTEE AUNTS

FOUR MONTHS LATER—OCTOBER 2

"I DON'T HAVE an aunt."

Denizen Hardwick stared down skeptically at the note in his hand. That was the way he looked at most things, and he had a face built for it—thin cheeks, a long nose, eyes the color and sharpness of a nail.

The note, left on his bed in Dormitory E that morning, was the object of a special amount of skepticism, so much so that he was surprised it hadn't started to char at the edges.

Your aunt has been in contact. She is taking you away for a few days. You will be collected at 6 p.m. Pack a bag.

Director Ackerby

"I don't have an aunt," Denizen said again. It didn't sound any less stupid the second time round.

"Well, that's not exactly true," said his best friend, Simon Hayes, also staring at the note. "You just don't have any aunts you're aware of."

Dormitory E was a long room with a high ceiling built for spiderwebs. Massive windows invited the weak October sunlight in to die, their frames rattling occasionally with the wind.

There were twelve beds, and at this particular lunchtime ten of them were empty. Most of Crosscaper's orphans were outside because sunlight in October was a rare gift and they hadn't been given a mysterious note to stare at.

Denizen ran a hand through his shaggy red hair. He was small for his age, and barring a late growth spurt, he would be small for every other age as well. The freckles that swarmed his cheeks and nose in summer had now faded in winter to lost and lonely things, all but the one on his lip.

He hadn't been aware you could have a freckle on your lip. Maybe Denizen was the only person a lip freckle had ever happened to. Maybe it was a mark of destiny, singling him out for great things . . . but he doubted it. Denizen Hardwick wasn't the kind of person to believe in special circumstances—in distinguishing freckles or meaningful birthmarks or fortuitous aunts.

Denizen Hardwick was a skeptic.

"I don't have a— Look, if I do have an aunt, where has she been for the last eleven years?"

"Can you get any clues from the paper?" Simon asked. The new library had a collection of detective novels, and Simon was very interested in what one could learn from the smallest details.

Gamely, Denizen inspected the note. Unfortunately, all he could see was that it was on yellow paper, which meant it had come straight from the director's desk and was therefore not to be argued with, in the same way you didn't argue with gravity. Apart from that, it was inconsiderately devoid of clues.

"No," he said. "Sorry."

Simon's and Denizen's beds were beside each other and had been since they were both three years old in Dormitory A downstairs. That had started their friendship. Furtive book trades at night, an inquisitive nature in common, and a shared dislike of sports had continued it.

There were a lot of things Denizen liked about Simon, but first and foremost was how he radiated calm the way the sun radiated heat. It was impossible to be annoyed at Simon. It was impossible to be annoyed *around* Simon. A conversation with Simon had the soothing effect of the cool side of the pillow.

Through either blind luck or best-friend osmosis, Simon had snagged all the height Denizen lacked. His giant winter coat did little to bulk out his slender frame, and splayed as he was across his bed, he looked like a crow in a scarf.

"But why now?" Denizen said. "Why is she getting in contact now?"

"Maybe it took her ages to find you," Simon said. "Or she was waiting for you to be older?" He thought for a moment. "Maybe she travels a lot and you have to be old enough to travel with her. Or to be left on your own in her giant house."

"Giant house?"

"You never know."

"I doubt she has a giant house."

"It's not impossible. She could be a super-rich spy. It would explain where she's been all this time. Or maybe she's a chocolatier."

Denizen rolled his eyes.

"A spy-chocolatier," Simon insisted, grinning. "Solving international crises through the subtle application of nougat."

Part of Denizen knew that he should probably be more excited. A relative appearing out of nowhere to take him away? Most of the other children and teenagers in Crosscaper had spent their entire lives dreaming of something like this.

That was what worried Denizen. Dreams were tricky things. He'd only ever really had the one, at least until the past couple of months.

Since the summer, his sleep had been haunted by Crosscaper's dark corridors, a figure in white drifting down them like a moth made of glass. In the dream, the figure had lingered, its milk-skinned hands caressing the door of each dormitory in turn before finding his and slipping in. . . .

He shook his head. Definitely not a dream he wanted spilling over into real life.

Maybe Simon was right. Maybe his aunt was a chocolate-spy. Maybe Denizen's life was about to change. Less skepticism. More weaponized hazelnut creams.

His bed creaked as he sat down heavily on it. Like everything in Crosscaper, it was falling apart. The orphans relied on castoffs and donations, and since neither Simon nor Denizen fell into the realm of average height, they had the worst of it—more hold-me-togethers than hand-me-downs, skewered with a fortune of safety pins so that when the boys moved, they clicked like ants.

The creaking of his bed didn't worry Denizen—there were too many books underneath it to let him fall.

One of Simon's fictional detectives had commented that you could tell a lot about a person from the contents of his bookshelf, but an inspection of Denizen's collection would simply tell you he loved words. *Love on the High Seas* sat next to *The Politics of Renaissance Italy.* (Crosscaper's books were all donations, and it had bothered Denizen for years wondering who donated books on ancient politics to an orphanage.) And while some volumes were more well-thumbed than others, each one had been read until the covers frayed.

My aunt might have books, Denizen thought, and immediately quashed the idea before it had a chance to grow.

He was not going to a new family. He was not going to a new life. He was being brought out so a stranger could have a look at him. If afterward this mysterious aunt decided she wanted to meet him again, fine, but he was not getting his hopes up just to be disappointed.

And the first thing she was going to do was answer his questions.

Simon hadn't brought it up. He hadn't needed to—he knew Denizen too well. Denizen was one of only a few children in Crosscaper who didn't know anything about their parents. Oh, he knew their last name. He knew that they were . . . Well, he knew he was in an orphanage for a reason, but he had no idea what that reason was.

Simon did. His parents had been killed in a car crash. Mr. Colford, their English teacher, drove Simon to their grave on the anniversary of their deaths every year. Michael Flannigan, two beds down from Simon on the left, had lost his parents in a fire. Samantha Hastings's mum had died of . . . Well, she wouldn't say, and the unspoken rule of Crosscaper was that if you didn't want to share, nobody had a right to pry.

But Denizen simply didn't know.

It was the only other dream he'd ever had. A woman—small like him, though it was hard to tell because he was looking up at her. Her arms were around him. She smelled of strawberries. Her song . . . something about the dark . . .

Denizen didn't remember his father at all.

Simon flashed him a faint, sympathetic smile. He knew exactly where Denizen's thoughts were.

"Listen," he said as the bell announced the end of lunch, "I should get down to class. I'll tell Ms. Hynes you can't make it because you have to pack."

"That'll take like ten minutes. I don't need to—"

"You're right," Simon said. "I'll tell her you'll be along shortly. Maybe you could ask for some extra homework to take with you."

"Ah," Denizen said, grinning. "Cool."

They stared at each other awkwardly.

"It's just a day or two," Denizen said. "I'll probably be home tomorrow."

"Sure," Simon said. "Yeah. Look. Enjoy yourself, all right? Have a chat with her. Try not to overthink things. Let her spoil you if she feels guilty about not being around. See what you can find—yeah? Best of luck."

Denizen loved words, but that didn't mean he could always find the ones he needed. Instead, he wrapped his arms round Simon in a tight, quick hug.

And then he was alone, note crumpled in his hand.

Outside, the courtyard quieted. Denizen sighed. As nice as it was to take a few hours off class—he wouldn't have been able to concentrate anyway, the words *absentee aunt* bouncing round his skull like a bee in a jar—he wouldn't have minded some company. Now he was alone with his thoughts, and he couldn't help turning them over and over in his head.

Denizen Hardwick had an aunt. So where had she been all this time?

Maybe she hadn't known he existed. Families fell out all the time—that had been the main theme in both *Love on the High Seas* and *The Politics of Renaissance Italy*—so maybe she was only tracking him down now.

Was she his mother's sister or his father's? What had happened that had made them lose touch?

His stomach knotted. There was so much he wanted to ask her. Would she cry? He wasn't going to cry—that would be terrible. But she might. Were there going to be hugs? Would that be weird?

Denizen tried to imagine what it would be like. The woman would be . . . small, he supposed, maybe with his eyes and hair. His imagination had very little to go on. A hazy image formed in his mind of a chubby woman with red hair, her features a strange mix of his and those of Crosscaper's cook, Mrs. Mollins—the most auntish woman he knew.

In his imagination, the hybrid Mollins-aunt fell to her knees and started sobbing when she saw him. Denizen squirmed. That image just made him uncomfortable. Then again, if awkward aunt-hugging led to answers about his past . . .

As far as Denizen was concerned, six p.m. couldn't come quick enough.

2

NONFICTION

THE SUN DIPPED below the horizon, taking the day with it as it went.

It was 5:45 p.m., and Denizen stood in Crosscaper's great courtyard with a bag at his feet. It had taken him longer to pack than he'd thought. *What do you bring to meet a surprise aunt?*

In the end, he had settled for a few changes of clothes and a winter coat. He couldn't be expected to plan any better, not when he had no idea where he was going. If that inconvenienced his aunt at all, well, that was what you got for going around being mysterious.

Occasionally, Denizen would glance back at Crosscaper's front doors as if reassuring himself that the orphanage was still there. Which was silly. He was only going away for a day or two. He'd have to come back—his books were here. All his aunt wanted to do was take him to dinner and salve her conscience for being absent for most of his life.

That worked for him—Denizen had done fine by himself for years. He didn't need someone showing up now and trying to *help* him.

He'd cooperate, though, just as long as she answered every question he could think of about his parents. Eye color, hair color, favorite food—he'd been tempted to make a list, before deciding that it might come across as crazy. Or maybe not. There probably wasn't a standard on what was crazy or not. *I mean, how often has this situation come up?*

He looked back at Crosscaper again. It hadn't always been an orphanage; the classrooms were of new, bright stone, whereas the dormitories with their peaks, towers, and scowling buttresses looked much older. Also, why the high stone walls? It struck Denizen as a bit excessive. Orphanages had to have walls for runaways, he supposed, but these walls had definitely been designed for another purpose, unless orphans used to be a lot bigger and breathe fire.

There was something castlelike about the gates as well—monstrosities of black oak and iron, their surfaces pitted and scarred from centuries of wind and rain. When he was younger, Denizen had run his fingers over every notch in the wood, imagining ancient battles, the furious pounding of enemy swords.

Those gates marked the borders of his childhood, the beginning and end of what he knew.

Without a word, Director Ackerby strode past Denizen and unfolded one long arm, pointing a black remote at the gates. Whirring, they parted on massive electronic hinges—bright and shiny against the age-darkened wood—to reveal the bay and a great sweep of sea.

Crosscaper Orphanage was the westernmost building in Ireland. Denizen's geography teacher, Mr. Flynn, had always been quite proud of that for some reason, as if the world wasn't a globe and *westernmost* didn't just mean "until you got to the next bit."

Farther up the hill were the cliffs of Benmore and the hooked finger of Moyteoge Point (cursed by generations of bad spellers), and west of that was just ocean—half a gray world of it, all the way to the east coast of America. Their class had scaled the cliffs once to look out at the iron cast of the sea, the breeze tasting like salt and emptiness.

Most of the students had preferred to face east toward the fat little pocket of Keem Bay, the villages and the bridge to the mainland—Ireland laid out in fading shades of green—but Denizen had been transfixed by the sea. It was hypnotic. All that space, that desolation. A birthplace for storms.

He stole a glance at Ackerby. That was how

everybody looked at the director—it was like dealing with a gorgon. Meeting his eyes meant he was meeting yours.

Now the director just stared out into the evening, a frown on his long face. Carefully, Denizen allowed himself a proper look. It was odd, staring fully at someone you'd only ever seen from the corner of your eye. It made Ackerby . . . smaller somehow.

Without the mystery of an averted gaze, the director looked like a heron rescued from an oil-slicked beach—hunched and slow and miserable. Up until a month ago, one of his arms had even been bound up winglike in a sling. With any other member of the staff, Denizen might have asked what had happened, but not Ackerby. Ackerby didn't speak to children. On the rare occasions he did, they were referred to as *boy* or *girl* as if he were struggling with the Latin name of some exotic insect. He'd barely been seen outside his office recently. All sorts of rumors had been flying about as to why.

They both stared out into the darkness in silence, which meant Denizen heard the car before he saw it.

This far from civilization, the countryside was deathly quiet, though in the summer you could hear the faint sound of holidaymakers at Keem Bay, driving fat, waddling cars that sang like bumblebees.

This car sounded nothing like that. The noise of its engine rose up through the darkness like the breathing of a big cat—not a lion or tiger but something older, something prehistoric. He felt the growl of it vibrating in his chest.

It gleamed even in the darkness as it slipped through the gates, a continent of glass and night-black metal, huge and old and rich with the smell of oil. Its windows were tinted, shrugging away the light from Crosscaper's windows. As the car growled to a halt, its headlights switched on with a sound like lightning hitting a cushion. *Brrssh-shik.* They were so bright, they annihilated everything else. Both Denizen and Ackerby took a step backward as motes of dust spun, trapped in the twin spears of light.

Denizen squinted, confused, into the glare. *It drove up here with its lights off?*

The door opened.

His vision still adjusting, Denizen's first impression of the visitor was made up of sounds: the snakish rattle of a seat belt sliding back, the squeak of a pair of leather shoes meeting gravel, and a long and contented sigh as a face was tilted to the winter cold.

The visitor smiled. "Evening."

Denizen frowned. He had a lot of frowns. This one was No. 13—the Questioning Frown. He'd never had an aunt before, but he'd sort of expected them to be female.

A chauffeur, then? It fit with the car, but weren't

they supposed to have a uniform? Peaked caps and coats that buttoned up the side, spine straight as a soldier.

This man wouldn't be let within a hundred meters of any military unit, formal or not. Denizen couldn't have said exactly what made him think that—the mane of long dark hair that fell to his shoulders or the expensive suit the color of coal—but as the man stepped closer, Denizen decided it was his smile.

You couldn't be in the army with a smile like that. The man smiled like a cat burglar.

"Jensen Interceptor," he said, and his smile widened as he saw the look on Denizen's face. "The car, that is. I'd never get away with a name like that." He wrapped gloved fingers round Denizen's hand and shook it vigorously.

"I'm Graham McCarron."

"Er," Ackerby said.

Denizen had never seen him lost for words before. It might have been McCarron shaking Denizen's hand first—adults existed in a secret club, and you weren't supposed to break ranks by treating a kid with equal respect—but it could just have been McCarron himself. He came across as the kind of person who often left people lost for words. Perhaps his smile stole them.

The two men shook hands.

"Director Ackerby. A pleasure."

"Is it?" McCarron said, and then turned back to

Denizen as if Ackerby hadn't said anything at all. Denizen felt a tiny smile inch its way onto his face. It gave him the courage to speak.

"Are you . . . Is my aunt in the car?" Movies had taught Denizen that when you became important enough, you didn't have to get out of cars to greet people. People got into your car to talk to you.

"She's at work," the man said, "so she sent me to collect you. I'm a colleague." He looked up at the half-hearted slump of masonry that had been Denizen's home for eleven of his thirteen years.

"Well, this is nice," he said brightly. "Sort of a"—he seemed to be searching for the right words—"bleak, hopeless charm about it. Good place to be sad, I imagine."

Denizen's eyebrows rose. The children at Crosscaper weren't treated with kid gloves. It was recognized that a *bad thing* had happened to you, and that *bad thing* was the reason you weren't at home with a family, but the *bad thing* had happened to every kid there and that had knocked a lot of the edges off. Denizen could count on two hands the number of people he'd met in his life who had parents. It was just something you had to live with.

With all that in mind, however, Denizen had never before heard someone point out so blithely that

Crosscaper was miserable. He gave Ackerby a sideways glance, just to see if he was going to try to defend the orphanage, but the director looked like he had no intention of arguing.

In fact . . . Ackerby looked worried. More worried than Denizen had ever seen him. The director always had a kind of sour look on his face, the put-upon glare of a man who disliked the world. This was something else entirely. Ackerby looked frightened.

"Sir? Is everything—"

"You two probably want a moment," McCarron said, whipping a handkerchief from his pocket and scrubbing at an imaginary stain on the Interceptor's flank. "Tearful farewell and all."

Ackerby didn't look at Denizen. Instead, he spoke quietly and quickly out of the corner of his mouth.

"I'm sorry, boy. I don't . . . I don't . . . Maybe it'll be fine. Yes. Yes. Family."

The director never took his eyes off McCarron.

"Family is so dear to . . ."

He winced.

"Folks?" McCarron was staring at them, the handkerchief swaying from his hand.

Ackerby blinked and passed a hand over his face. He looked positively ill.

"Go on, then," he said in a faint voice.

The No. 13 Questioning Frown was replaced by the No. 8—I Am Missing Something Important Here, Which Is Unfair Because It Concerns Me.

Unfortunately, the only real course of action seemed to be to go along with it. So when McCarron eased open the front passenger door, Denizen got in, settling his bag in his lap. The interior of the Jensen Interceptor was white leather and wood paneling—pleasantly warm compared to the cold evening—and lived up to its name. If the door had been closed, Denizen could have easily believed himself in a spy submarine or fighter jet.

Ackerby and McCarron were talking.

"Do I need to sign him out or . . . ?"

"No, no . . . just . . . just go."

Absurdly, Denizen felt a little annoyed at how quickly Ackerby was handing him over—*You'd think he was being held up at gunpoint*—and then McCarron slid in beside him. He ran gloved hands across the steering wheel the way you'd ruffle the head of a beloved dog and sighed happily before turning to Denizen.

"Ready?"

There was something very final in the way he said it, and Denizen paused before he answered.

Home can mean a lot of different things.

It can be the place where you feel safest. The place where you know that, no matter what, there'll be someone to look out for you. It can be a place you know so well you could navigate it in total darkness—a place you know like the shape of your own face. It can be a duffel bag. It can be a city.

For Denizen, home meant a place where there weren't any surprises. A place where he knew how everything worked. Granted, *familiar* didn't mean *enjoyable,* but predictability had its own comforts.

Denizen knew Crosscaper. He knew how it worked. The gates ahead led only to uncertainty. There might have been comfort in the predictable, but the unknown was exactly that—a mystery potentially full of the answers to all the questions he had been wondering about his entire life. Who he was. Who his parents had been.

He'd never find them here.

"Let's go," Denizen said quietly.

3

BAD-DREAM ANGEL

FOR A LONG time, they drove in silence.

The road looped round the shoulders of the mountain like a tailor's measuring tape. On one side loomed the great stone face of the mountainside, on the other a sparse verge of grass—grazed by strutting, fearless sheep—and then the dizzying drop to a moonlit sea.

McCarron let out a long, low whistle as they passed.

Denizen was deep in thought. How long should he wait before asking why McCarron had driven up a cliff road in a black car at night with the headlights off?

The lights were on now; otherwise Denizen's heart would have climbed out of his chest entirely. Maybe he just hadn't seen them. Maybe they'd been on low . . . but that was the thing about the darkness of the countryside—it was *dark*. If someone had walked up the road with a lit match, he would have seen it.

Villages darted by them one by one—Dooagh, Keel, Achill Sound—then the bridge to the mainland, so long that for a moment the car felt suspended in space, the lights behind not quite meeting those ahead. The car's purr rose to a throaty growl as the countryside folded up behind them.

Denizen was counting kilometers in his head. Achill Sound was the farthest he'd ever been from home. Everything before Crosscaper didn't count—that was a different chapter of his life, one where the pages were stuck together and unreadable.

Despite himself, he felt an odd shiver of excitement with each new kilometer passed. Every sign added more distance and more names to his internal map. *Lough Feeagh, Newport, Castlebar . . .*

"It'll be another few hours to Dublin," McCarron said eventually. "Feel free to take a nap."

And miss something? No thank you. Instead, Denizen tried to sneak a proper look at McCarron.

He was maybe thirty, or a very rough twenty-five, and whatever he did for Denizen's aunt must have paid well. Both McCarron and Ackerby had been wearing suits; however, whereas Ackerby's was as ill-fitting as every other piece of clothing in Crosscaper, McCarron's fit him like a second skin. There was a silver sword pin on his tie.

And he had scars. Denizen was trying to time

surreptitious looks with the street lights they passed. It wasn't just one scar—there was a fine tracery of silvery lines on one side of his face, culminating in a bloom of raw white tissue on his cheek. It looked a little like the scar on Simon's hand from the car accident that had killed his parents, all the color and life drained from the skin to leave it bleached and dead. That meant the scars were old. Really old.

It took a moment for what McCarron had said to catch up with him. "We're going to Dublin?" Denizen said. "Is that where my aunt lives?"

McCarron nodded. *Well, that's one question answered.* Denizen tried to shake off a treacherous shiver of excitement. Not knowing anything about his family had left him very appreciative of even the smallest iota of new information.

And a city. I've never seen a city before.

He coughed and Frown No. 4—the Give Nothing Away—slid down like a steel trap. He was going to interrogate his aunt. He would not be deflected. This wasn't a school trip. This was a fact-finding mission.

Denizen lay back in the seat, the leather creaking.

"Go on, then," McCarron said as they left another town behind.

"What?" Denizen said.

"Go on. Ask."

"I don't know what you're—"

That cat-burglar grin returned to McCarron's face. "If I were you, I'd be asking all sorts of questions about your aunt. Walk in armed, so to speak."

"Do I need to?" Denizen asked. "Walk in armed, I mean." Worry crept into his voice. "I don't actually know anything about her."

Was this why she'd stayed away? It would be just his luck that the family member showing up after all this time turned out to be some sort of crazy person. That might explain why he hadn't been sent to live with her all those years ago.

"What's her name?" he said suddenly. *Start with the basics.*

"Vivian," McCarron said. "Vivian Hardwick. Though I wouldn't start with Vivian. You sort of have to *earn* Vivian. Aunt Vivian? Auntie?" A strange look passed across his face. "Definitely not *auntie*."

"Oh," said Denizen. "What do I call her, then?"

"I suspect she'll be doing most of the calling," McCarron said, "but you can't go wrong with a good *Ms.* Ms. Hardwick."

They drove in silence for a few more minutes until what McCarron had said sunk in. "You've worked with my aunt for a while?" Denizen's voice was hesitant. "Did you . . . did you know my parents?"

It took McCarron a long time to respond. "Sorry, kid. Up until this morning I didn't even know you existed."

Denizen couldn't stifle a disappointed sigh.

Gloved fingers drummed on the steering wheel. "Look, the next few days are probably going to be hectic, but if there's one thing I do know, it's that you Hardwicks are tough. You'll see your way through it."

You Hardwicks. That was strange. He'd never thought of his name as a plural before.

"Thanks, Mr. McCarron."

McCarron grinned at him.

"My friends call me Grey."

DENIZEN WATCHED THE countryside slip by through half-closed eyes. Rain was pounding the windows, but inside the drowsy shell of the car there was nothing but heat and the firefly glow of the dashboard lights.

They passed through clusters of houses huddling together for warmth, through towns and forests and fragments of dreams. It was the same dream Denizen always had—his mother, the warmth and strawberry smell of her. The familiarity of it comforted him.

He shifted in his seat, somewhere between sleep and waking. She was saying something. He'd dreamt of the words so many times, but he'd never known what they were. . . .

Abruptly, Denizen woke. He had . . . There had been something important, but it drifted away from him, vanished like mist when he tried to grasp it. A bad taste had collected in his mouth. His stomach roiled. He shook his head to clear it.

"We're not far," McCarr—*Grey* said. "I got a call to check up on . . . a work thing." His tone was cheerful, but there was an edge beneath it.

The landscape around them had changed—fields and forests replaced by neatly trimmed grass on man-made slopes, the dirty gray concrete of overpasses and the grimy steel of safety rails. Bridges passed over them in stripes of shadow. Denizen could see a tunnel ahead, its mouth lit by golden lights.

They flickered. Twitched in their sockets.

Sweat broke out on Denizen's forehead. Another bridge swept shadow over them. The speed of the car, the way it drifted smoothly over the asphalt, made it feel like the Interceptor was falling, that any moment the wheels would gently lift away from the road and the car would plummet, tumble forward end over end—

He swallowed. "Do you . . ." Nausea burned at the back of his throat. There was a sick tug in the pit of his stomach, greasy sweat on his forehead. He fought to get the words out. "I feel a bit—"

"Denizen?"

He clawed at his seat belt. "I don't feel very well. I feel a bit—I feel—"

"Don't unbuckle that," Grey said sharply.

"What?" Panic was mingling with the nausea. He'd never felt like this before. "Why?"

Hard to focus. His breathing was ragged. The lights of the dashboard blinked and smeared, the voice of the singer on the radio rose to a scream. . . .

Grey's voice sounded a million miles away.

"Because I feel it too."

The mouth of the tunnel collapsed.

Stone gave way with a sound like giant bones snapping. Grey slammed on the brakes and wrenched the wheel sideways. The car spun—the landscape a dizzying blur—before skidding to a halt as the mouth of the tunnel caved in on itself with a roar of tortured concrete. Dust wheezed out from between the cracks. The car rocked on its wheels. Silence was a long time coming.

The world returned in pieces. First, the *tink-click* of the cooling engine. Then the croaking of Denizen's breath. A stripe of fire across his chest where the seat belt had cut.

"You all right?"

Denizen blinked blearily. Grey's hand was on his shoulder. He tried to focus through the ringing in his ears. The car . . . The tunnel had . . .

Grey's face was twisted in concern. "Denizen. Are you all right?"

"Yes, yes, I'm fine," Denizen said finally. He eased the seat belt away, hissing at the pain, and twisted to look down the road in front of them. Stone dust painted the air white. Another hundred meters, another few seconds of driving, and the tunnel would have come down right on top of—

Denizen shivered.

Grey had already opened his door and eased out of his seat, standing with his hands in the pockets of his pants. The tunnel walls ended raggedly before him like the gaping collar of a headless man. Grey clucked his tongue, as if this were a minor inconvenience rather than an actual brush with death.

"Oh dear," he said to no one in particular.

Denizen got out of the car. It took him a moment to see what Grey was staring at amid the exposed steel rebar and the broken concrete slabs, but when he did, the cold feeling in his stomach deepened to a frozen ache.

Something *moved* in the murk. A shadow—trickling from cracks and crevices, seeping from the fractured rock.

For a moment, Denizen thought it was oil, some kind of leak building behind the collapse, but liquid would have obeyed gravity. Here the rivulets darted *up* at each other, trickles becoming streams, growing fat and webbing across the stone.

A street light went out. Then another. The bulbs popped as they died, and with each dying, the night marched up the road toward them. Denizen barely noticed. His eyes never left the tunnel mouth. It was pitch-dark now, blacker than the starless sky above.

Something within let out a wet, burbling growl.

"Denizen, I need you to listen very carefully." The warmth had left Grey's voice. "There's a bag in the backseat of the car. I'd like you to bring it to me."

Another rumbling growl. Insistent. Hungry. Stone rasped on stone.

"*Now,* Denizen."

It was awkward walking backward to the car, but nothing in the world could have made Denizen take his eyes off the tunnel mouth. It stared back—he felt it, the unblinking regard of old and terrible eyes. Every breath he took felt too loud. His heartbeat pounded in his skull.

Prey. That was it—he felt like prey. This was the moment the snake swayed. This was the moment the cat blinked before pouncing. Denizen knew it as surely as he knew his own name.

He forced his fingers to move, and the door opened with a throaty click, as loud as the end of the world. Denizen winced.

And the thing in the darkness stepped into the light.

It was massive. That was the first thing Denizen noticed. Its sheer size was an assault on his senses, a weight that forced him back. Its limbs hung asymmetrically from vast and jagged shoulders, badly wrought wings rising to scrape the tunnel mouth—stone scarring white in its wake.

It dragged short and violent gasps through the mouthless thumb of stone that served as a head. The shadows of the tunnel came with it, hanging from its throat in cobweb curls, snaking like veins through its lumpish chest.

Each shuddering step it took drove home to Denizen how *wrong* it looked.

As if you'd been asked to sculpt an angel, but you'd never seen one before, and there were people to tell you what one looked like . . . but they hated you.

Its roar blew out the last of the street lights.

"Denizen," Grey said. "The bag?"

Turning his back on the creature took every bit of courage Denizen possessed. The beast was stalking toward them. The notched blade of a girder was clutched in its hand, half covered in lumps of concrete, and Grey looked so tiny and fragile before it.

Fragile and utterly unconcerned.

"Thank you," he murmured as he took the bag from Denizen's unresisting hands. He casually opened it and rummaged through, humming to himself like he'd forgotten his keys.

The angel snarled and the sound beat against Denizen's ears, making his head ring. There was something fundamentally wrong about it, in every line and detail. At moments it was blurred as if he were looking at it through dirty glass, and at others its shape was painfully sharp.

It was . . . it was *inconsistent.* His head ached just looking at it.

The concrete slopes around them were bisected here and there by railed staircases. The more Denizen looked at them, the more he was reminded of an old arena, like the Colosseum—a place where duels were fought to the death, where great beasts circled little men. . . .

All Grey needed was a sword, Denizen thought dumbly, and the image would be complete.

Grey drew a sword from the bag at his feet. Denizen couldn't even bring himself to be surprised. The weapon gleamed in Grey's hand, an elegant piece of sharpened steel, and all Denizen could think of was that they still used those safety scissors shaped like ducks at Crosscaper.

The angel bellowed and Grey nodded in return, the blade in his hand scribing a circle in the air. The stone head swung to follow the movement as though

Grey were an old-time hypnotist with a watch. Denizen didn't dare breathe as the thing took one more staggering step toward them, dust sloughing from its shoulders.

The moment broke. The beast charged. Grey laughed and leapt to meet it.

Pavement cracked under its feet as it launched itself into a lumbering, apelike run. Half wings beat uselessly at the air, shadows racing across its bulk like a time-lapse photograph of a sunny day.

The first swing of the girder-blade hit only air. The second dug a meter-long furrow in the surface of the road, and the third smashed a signpost to a drunken angle. The creature raised its blade again, roaring like a rockfall—and Grey lifted his hand and spoke a word.

Just for a moment, Denizen felt sunlight on his face.

The angel came apart with glacial slowness. Dust bled from its joints, shadows retreating like paper touched to flame. Flash-charred steel and stone clattered sizzling to the ground, and Denizen blinked spots from his eyes, turning his face from the sudden heat.

One by one, the street lights returned.

4

Doors

"Well," Grey said, emptying a bag of crisps into his hand, "that was unfortunate."

Denizen laced his fingers round his cup of tea, as much to stop them from shaking as to warm them. He couldn't remember if he'd taken a sip or not.

Rain pattered against the windows. They'd found a café a few minutes from closing—the lights low, tealight candles flickering on each table, kittens staring blindly from an ancient print on the wall.

"I do understand, you know." Grey idly moved crumbs around his plate. He didn't look like he understood. He was still wearing that cat-burglar smile, wider now that he had made a pot of coffee, three sausage rolls, and two bags of chips disappear.

He might have been suffering inner trauma, though. *Does inner trauma make you hungry?*

If so, it hadn't worked on Denizen. He'd gotten as far as adding milk. Everything else was beyond him at the moment.

"Denizen." Grey dabbed at his lip with a napkin. "Stop being broken. I can't deliver you to your aunt if you're broken. Say something. Ask a question. Yes, it will be a stupid question. Ask it anyway."

He'd cut right to the heart of Denizen's silence. It wasn't that Denizen had nothing to say—in fact, the questions were tripping over each other in his head. Grey was offering to answer them too. All Denizen had to do was ask. And, like unraveling a shirt by pulling a single thread, answer would follow answer and he'd suffocate under the weight.

Statements. Maybe statements were the way to go.

"That was an angel," he said in a haunted voice. "That thing—it was an angel."

Grey picked up one of the empty packets of crisps and spread it flat with his fingers. "What makes you say that?"

Frown No. 6—Insistent. "Because it looked like an angel."

Grey folded the packet neatly into a square and then reached for another. He seemed entirely and maddeningly focused on the task.

"Did it?"

Well, now that Denizen thought about it . . . it

hadn't. Angels were graceful and beautiful, weren't they? At least they were in stories, and after this evening, Denizen was both a little more ready to believe in stories and a lot more skeptical all at once.

His stomach still churned as he thought about how abnormal the thing had been—the glitchy, headachey *wrongness* of it. The creature might have had the basic shape of an angel, but it had jarred his senses the way a crack in a mirror distorted a face.

"Look," Grey said, flattening the final crisp packet, "if it helps at all, I had the same conversation at your age. It didn't make much sense to me either. Honestly, this could have gone better, but you know what they say: no plan of action survives first contact. I'm not supposed to be telling you anything. Your aunt was pretty clear in that regard."

"Why not?" Denizen's eyes narrowed.

"Because she . . . she wanted to talk to you herself. But that was then."

"Grey," Denizen said, leaning forward. The last of his reservations had vanished; he'd just been told he wasn't supposed to know anything, and that made him immediately want to know everything. "What did I see tonight?"

Grey glanced around. The café was empty and the owner had disappeared into the back, but Grey still leaned forward, resting his chin on his palm. He hadn't removed his gloves to eat, and crumbs dotted the black leather.

He must be cold, Denizen thought. He had to keep squeezing his own hands into fists to stop them from shaking, though that wasn't due to the cold at all.

"OK," Grey said. "Where do I start?"

He lifted the tall plastic beaker of sugar and put it in the center of the table. Next he moved the tealight candle until it was parallel with the beaker. Shadows shifted as he set the candle down.

"What you have to remember," he said, "is that we don't understand a lot of this ourselves. And when people don't understand something, they build stories up around it. We're dealing with theories here, not specifics. Exact answers are difficult. Keep that in mind."

Denizen nodded nervously. Grey flashed him an encouraging smile and then carefully and deliberately placed his finger in the middle of the shadow the sugar beaker had cast.

"What's this?" he asked.

Denizen frowned. "It's a shadow."

"No, it isn't," Grey said. "It's a door."

He withdrew his finger, and the shadow of his hand followed it. "And the thing about doors is that they go both ways. People go in. And things come out."

"Things like the . . . whatever it was?"

Grey nodded.

"But people would . . . people would notice." Denizen looked at the shadows under his hands, the darkness that lurked behind or in front, all the places where the light didn't fall. Were creatures like the bad-dream angel lurking behind all of them? He shivered. "If things like this happened, we would know, wouldn't we?"

Something dark and sad passed over Grey's face. "I grew up in a place like Crosscaper, Denizen. We both know people disappear all the time."

He ran a hand through his long dark hair. "I want to say more. I do. But your aunt will explain when we get to the house. She'll want to . . . There's something we have to do before you can be told the whole story."

"You fight them. Is that it?" Denizen said. "You did something. Destroyed it. You didn't even use your sword. Also, you have a *sword*."

"I do indeed," he said. "And yes, I have experience with these sorts of things. Your aunt does too. And that's as much as I'm willing to say without her here. We were going to put you up in a hotel, but after what's happened I think she'll want a longer chat."

"Well, that would be nice," Denizen said a little bitterly.

Now that the shock had worn off, anger was rushing in to fill the gap. Say what you liked about the orphanage—and he did, a lot—it certainly lacked towering stone monsters lumbering around trying to kill him. Denizen would have been quite happy never knowing they existed at all.

Now he was entitled to a bit more disclosure. The thing was, he knew none of this was Grey's fault and it was stupid to be angry, but that just made him even crosser.

Grey raised an eyebrow. "Excuse me?"

"Oh, it's fine," Denizen said. "I could have died back there, but that doesn't mean you should actually tell me what happened instead of spouting vague stuff about shadows being doors and—"

"Stop," Grey said suddenly. His gaze had sharpened, his lips a thin line. Denizen was abruptly reminded that, nice guy or not, Grey had faced down a nightmare not half an hour before without batting an eye.

"I get that you're a little on edge at the moment. Really, I do. And yes—you do deserve to know more. But right now the words you're looking for are *Thank you, Grey, for saving my life.*"

He placed both hands back down on the tabletop, but not before Denizen noticed that they were trembling.

"I know I make it look easy, but these things carry a cost. The least you could do is be patient."

They sat in silence for a few moments until Denizen sighed. "Sorry. And thank you."

Grey grinned. "Good. Now drink your tea."

5

Caper Dark

The sky fell as rain.

It sounded like Crosscaper was under siege—bullet-drops bouncing off the windows, ancient gutters rattling like machine guns, all underscored by the artillery roar of the thunder. The storm had started small—a rising wind, a leaden heaviness to the sky—but now it shook the stones of Crosscaper like all the wars of history come at once.

Simon loved it.

He laid his forehead against the cool glass of the dormitory window, angling his head so he could stare at the sky. Storms came to Crosscaper a lot—this was the house at the end of the world, as their geography teacher, Mr. Flynn, liked to say—and every time one swept in off the Atlantic to batter against the orphanage walls, Simon would slip out from under his covers with a silly grin on his face.

There was something comforting about them—all that power and rage ending just centimeters from his nose. It would have been absolute misery to be caught out in the torrent, but here in his pajamas, with a blanket over his shoulders, Simon was snug and safe.

The other students snored behind him. They were well used to his habits. Simon had been here nearly his whole life—he was part of the furniture by now. As long as he avoided Ackerby and some of the spikier teachers, he was mostly left to his own devices.

Rain moved in great drifts across the courtyard. *Tea in a bit,* he thought. Technically, the doors to the kitchen were supposed to be locked, but Mr. Baxter the caretaker only locked doors when he remembered to, which wasn't often. Usually, Denizen would go down for him so Simon didn't miss any of the storm.

He was missing that tonight. Not the conversation—half the time, they didn't even talk, Simon staring at the rain and Denizen reading—but Simon just liked knowing someone else was there.

Lightning arced between the clouds, and Simon looked away from the sudden light. It was strange, that empty bed at his back. He and Denizen had been practically inseparable since the day they'd met. *What if his aunt takes him away for good?* The note hadn't said when Denizen might return, and it was Simon's birthday at the end of the month, and . . .

No. Simon shook his head. There was no sense in worrying about these things. He'd be back when he was back. Besides, Denizen needed this.

Simon stood up, stretching to work the kinks out of his muscles. The longer you lived in Crosscaper, the more it changed you. Some students looked for attention—acting out, getting into fights—and others threw themselves into their studies so they'd get scholarships after they turned eighteen.

Simon and Denizen had found refuge in books.

Simon had learned a lot from the crime novels he read. Disguises, research methods . . . He wasn't sure when he'd need to tail someone, but he was certain he could do it.

Denizen was different. He read fantasy novels. And eleven years of living in Crosscaper with that kind of reading material had made him into a fortress. Nothing went in; nothing came out.

It was like he was determined to wait out his childhood, staring skeptically at anybody and anything that came close to him. The only reason Simon knew this at all was because he had bunked next to Denizen for so long, and he hadn't so much besieged as camped outside the gates and waited for Denizen to come out.

Lightning flashed again in a crooked spiderweb, painting the world in lurid green and white, the rain a million mirrors all cracking at once. Simon had lived here almost all his life, but the eerie glow of the storm painted everything differently, like he wasn't looking at Crosscaper at all but at some other darker place.

And as if responding to that unpleasant thought, the gates of Crosscaper trembled. With a snarl of distressed hinges audible even over the roar of the storm, they began to creak open. Simon leaned forward. Usually, the gates swung open smoothly, hissing apart on well-maintained electronic hinges.

Now they screamed.

The thick storm-chain round the gate handles twitched and pulled taut. Metal groaned—the gates stopping, straining—until it gave with a broken-neck *snap*. The ruined padlock fell to the ground with a clatter, the chain slithering free after it.

Behind Simon, one of the orphans cried out in his sleep.

A light flickered on below in the porch and someone ran out toward the gates, a coat over his shoulders to protect them from the rain. It might have been Ackerby or Mr. Baxter, Simon couldn't be sure, but the man paused in the middle of the courtyard, rain-battered and uncertain.

There was a sense of something about to happen.

Simon felt it—a crushing nausea in his chest. Obligingly, lightning bit dramatically at the sky, illuminating the courtyard.

Three figures, painted in white. A short, round man in a waistcoat stood between the open gates, face held up to the rain. A woman dressed all in white loomed over him, ragged hair slicked to her scalp, her eyes holding the lightning just a moment too long.

Between them there was a . . . Simon squinted. No matter how much the lightning flashed, it did not reveal the third figure. Instead, the light just defined . . . a shape, a hole in the air, a distortion that made Simon's eyes water and the back of his neck go cold.

It was the shape of a little boy.

The person with the coat over his shoulders shouted something that was swallowed by the thunder. Simon's breath fogged the glass, and he scrubbed at it with his sleeve.

The three visitors didn't respond, though the woman in white sank to her haunches, eyes gleaming. The child-shape cowered as the man in the waistcoat stepped forward, rain glistening on his stub of a nose, lips split in a vicious smile.

Run. The thought came from nowhere, and yet it was all Simon could do not to shout it out loud. *Run.*

Lightning struck the courtyard.

Heaven and earth were connected just for an instant

by a bar of writhing light. The window frames jumped in their settings. Simon jerked back from the window, his vision suddenly seared white, the world full of the choking taste of ozone—the stink of tortured air.

For too long he just sat there, vision returning in spots and blotches. Like spider legs, every hair on his body stood on end. Finally, he got to his feet.

The courtyard was empty.

Fear curled down Simon's spine when he saw the coat lying abandoned on the muddy gravel. Something animal rose in him. Panic, the adrenaline-addled need to run, to get out of there—that a terrible thing was happening and the darkness was coming in—

He took a deep, ragged breath.

No. Simon Hayes was not prone to panic. Denizen had always said it was the books he read, that he'd inherited the unshakable calm of a hardened detective. Simon liked that. It was far cooler than the truth.

The simple fact was that Crosscaper had changed him. It had taught him one lesson: panic never solved anything. Getting angry or upset was a waste of time unless it let you change the situation you were in.

This was no different.

He ran to Michael's bunk and tried to shake him awake. It didn't work. Each orphan just moaned and squirmed against his hands, unresponsive, their heads lolling in a deep and unhappy sleep. He stared into their faces, whispered to them as loud as he dared, but their eyelids simply flickered frantically as if trying to see in the dark.

There was no reason to freak out, Simon told himself—though having to tell himself that wasn't a good sign. Nothing had actually *happened.* The gates had swung open with a noise like all the snarling in Hell. Someone had gone out in the rain to see what the racket was.

That was all normal. Of course, then there was the lightning . . . but lightning had to strike somewhere, didn't it? That was just a coincidence. Made things a little more dramatic than usual.

The boy-shaped hole in the air was a little more difficult, as was the strange sleep somehow affecting everyone but him, but Simon was sure there was an explanation. He just didn't know what it was.

Maybe it would be wise to take the precaution of fleeing in terror first and trying to explain things later.

There was nothing he could do here. He should go to get help. Simon wasn't sure exactly what he'd say—*The gates are screaming, and no one will wake up* didn't exactly sound useful or sane—but it was better than waiting here.

It didn't take long to consider his options. If he made it down to the third floor, he could cut across to the classrooms to the right. From there he could go downstairs and get out of the side door of Mr. Colford's room and then head to Dooagh, the nearest village, roughly a half-hour panicked run away.

This was doable. Completely doable. He had no idea where the strangers were, but the whole plan and his continued sanity depended on not thinking about that.

I'm not fleeing, he told himself. *I'm just giving myself an opportunity to come to the rescue later.*

Simon dragged on a pair of socks and shrugged a coat over his pajamas. He picked up his shoes and, taking one last look at the empty bed beside his, slipped out into the dark.

6

Seraphim Row

"Here we are. Seraphim Row," Grey said, easing the Interceptor to a halt.

Here was a narrow street with tall houses of gray brick nestled shyly behind thick green hedges. Street lights glowed in patchwork, choked out by the spreading shoulders of trees. So far the city had been alive with noise, but this felt like a place removed—silent but for the rustle of fallen leaves. There were no other cars parked on the street.

Denizen stared at the house as they walked up the driveway. It was a grand old monster—the architect had obviously wanted a castle, and by the looks of it had possessed the budget but not the space. None of the buildings on the street were new, as far as Denizen could make out, but this one looked like it had been there for millennia.

The windows were arrow slits, the door wide enough to accommodate a company of soldiers. It was two or three times the size of all the other houses. In fact, they seemed to shrink away from it. Denizen could see why; the mansion looked as if, with the slightest provocation, it would lunge at the others and swallow them up too.

A pole rose from the lawn, its flag fluttering half-heartedly in the breeze. Denizen looked around: there were flags in front of every other house as well.

"What do they mean?" he asked.

Grey threw his bag over his shoulder, tugging down his suit jacket to straighten it. "A flag outside a building means that it's an embassy. We passed the American one on the way here—remember that big circular building? British, Japanese, Mexican . . . all just round the corner."

Denizen knew quite a lot about flags. He'd often thought about what would happen when he was old enough to leave Crosscaper. Maybe he'd teach in foreign countries, or just travel, wander from one strange city to the next, collecting stories and adventures and scars. Reading atlases had become like research to him. He'd learned what the colors and symbols of each country meant, like a promise to himself that he'd someday go there.

He didn't recognize this flag at all.

It was white—whiter than snow or milk or any of those comparisons people use for describing colors. It was the white of a flag—the kind of white that people fight for.

In the center of the white there was a hand, palm outward, as if to stop or ward off. It was the deep black of an unstarred sky. Behind it were two crossed hammers in the same funereal shade.

Denizen looked closer. The hammer was a symbol too—an important symbol. Hammers were just about the oldest tools humanity had. They built things. They raised up homes. These looked a little like sledgehammers—long-handled, with blunt, massive heads.

There was an iron plaque beside the door marked with the same hand-and-hammers symbol. Underneath were the words EMBASSY OF THE KINGDOM OF ADUMBRAL in flowing golden script.

"Adumbral," Denizen said. "Where's Adumbral? I've never heard of it."

"I'd be very surprised if you had. The whole country's about four kilometers across." Grey was rummaging in his pocket. "Nice place, though. Maybe you'll see it someday."

He slid a long iron key into the lock. It turned with a rough click.

"So my aunt lives in an embassy?" Denizen said,

the No. 13 Questioning Frown making a brief appearance.

"Well, this isn't really an embassy. Not exactly. Not at all, in fact."

"So what happens if someone from Adumbral comes here looking for help?"

Grey paused. "You know, it's never come up."

The door swung open, and they stepped into candlelight.

Heat washed over Denizen. There were candles everywhere—arrayed over the mantelpiece, on plinths by the walls, even on the floor—carving the carpet into geometric lines. A massive chandelier hung overhead, lit with so many little fires that it glowed like a composite sun.

Grey stepped over the lines of candles as if they weren't there, and Denizen followed, picking his way carefully. He squinted, but between the winking, dancing flames there was only darkness. It was like standing in the middle of a constellation.

Denizen had never really thought about the difference between electric light and candlelight. Electric light was stark. It was constant. It forced the dark back with a snap of a switch—one state or another, on or off. This was true of even Crosscaper's dim bulbs, which didn't so much light up a room as show off its dirt better.

Candlelight was something different. It grew from the head of a match like something alive, pushing back the darkness in fits and starts, luring it in and burning it away. It breathed and it danced and it ate what you fed it.

Grey appeared utterly at home in the gloom. He tossed his bag into a corner—it disappeared, black-on-swallowing-black—and beckoned Denizen to follow him up a great set of marble stairs that suddenly loomed out of the darkness, a candle glowing on each step.

As his eyes adjusted, Denizen could make out maps on the walls, old charts in gilded frames, banners and shields that looked like they belonged in a museum. Each one was marked with the hand-and-hammers.

They passed portraits. Denizen looked at them as he went by, the briefest glance before moving on.

An old man in armor with a beard like a rain cloud, one eyebrow raised as if daring you to comment. A hammer hung at his waist, twin to the ones on the flag outside, and the plaque below the painting read:

MALLEUS EDWIN ROOK 1765–1811

Another man in the same armor, this one with a great mass of scars down one side of his face. Denizen couldn't tell if he was grinning or if the scars had just pulled his face that way. He wore a hammer too.

MALLEUS CASTOR GILHANE 1780–1832

Next, an ancient woman with a hard jaw and silver hair. She held her hammer close, gauntlets resting on its battered iron head. Maybe it was the same weapon, handed down from warrior to warrior, from century to century.

MALLEUS SOROPHINA DEVRENY 1810–1900

"Grey?"

There was someone waiting for them at the top of the stairs.

Candles painted the girl out of the darkness, turning her round, tinted spectacles into dazzling mirrors. Denizen saw her dark blue frock coat, her mass of unfettered black curls, and finally her white teeth, bright against skin the color of milkless tea.

"Are you all right?" Her accent was British, the words clipped and precise, yet softened by worry. She couldn't have been more than a year or two older than Denizen—fifteen or sixteen at most. "Should I have rung D'Aubigny? I had to—"

"Not at all," Grey said. "I was in the area—you did the right thing. And I sorted it. So it's fine." He smiled brightly.

The girl still looked concerned. "Could you identify it? For my notes. Anything you can tell me would be useful."

Grey shrugged. "How am I supposed to know what it was?"

"You're not," she said. "I am. While it's fresh in your head, Grey. Any and all details would be helpful."

"Sorry, Darcie," Grey said, gracefully stepping round her. "It was a thing. I killed the thing. I don't know what else to tell you. Besides, more important things are afoot. Denizen Hardwick, may I introduce Darcie Wright, our resident genius."

The barest of smiles flitted across her face. "I have asked you before not to introduce me that way."

She and Denizen shook hands, and then her expression changed from polite to hawkish interest. "Wait. Denizen *Hardwick*?"

"Vivian's nephew," said Grey.

"Oh," Darcie said. She was still staring at Denizen like he was a particularly interesting laboratory specimen. "I wasn't aware she had a nephew."

"That's all right," Denizen said, feeling vaguely silly. "I didn't know either."

"So a new recruit, then?" Darcie said to Grey.

"That's what we've brought him here to find out."

Her eyebrows rose. "So he's not . . . Grey, if I had known—"

"Darcie," Grey said firmly. "It's fine. I think his aunt would like to speak with him herself."

She nodded. "Of course. Of course she would. Carry on, then. Denizen, it was nice to meet you."

Denizen forced a smile past a No. 8 frown. He hadn't understood half of what they'd said, but it was probably rude to cut in and ask for an explanation. Grey had said all would become clear in time, and if his aunt was somewhere around, he didn't have much longer to wait.

He looked back at Darcie. Just before the darkness swallowed her, she mouthed something at him.

It looked like *good luck*.

"You'll like Darcie," Grey said as they walked. "She's our . . . librarian. Sort of. This way, if you wouldn't mind."

They made their way through shadowy corridors. Candles were everywhere—placed in hanging lanterns, jammed crookedly in wall sconces, sitting on saucers on the floor. There seemed to be no pattern to their placement. One corridor had so many candles that Denizen could make out every detail of the wall hangings that decorated it. Others were lit with so few that all he could do was step blindly after the sound of Grey's footsteps.

There were more portraits in some of the hallways they passed, but Denizen didn't get a chance to look at them. The air was thick with the smell of dust and melting wax.

They passed through a huge room lit by a single candle so it seemed like the darkness fell away forever on both sides. Denizen thought he heard footsteps mirroring his, just for a moment, but when he listened harder they faded away.

Thoughts bit and thieved at him. *What am I going to say to her?*

Up until earlier, Denizen had been quite proud of his plan. He'd been sure his aunt was only contacting him because she wanted some connection to his parents, or to get rid of the guilt of not being around eleven years ago when he'd really needed a next of kin.

She would be upset. She'd be looking for some kind of forgiveness, and he'd grant it—no skin off his nose—but in return he'd want every single thing she knew about his parents. After that, he didn't particularly mind if she wanted him to live with her or not. All he wanted to know was where he came from.

But the bad-dream angel had changed all that. Denizen's plan had existed in a world where there weren't strange shadow-creatures or mansions full of candles. They changed things. They certainly put him off trying to figure out what was going on just in case more horrors emerged from the woodwork.

If his aunt had come to him instead of sending her . . . colleague . . . he would have had whole hours to talk to her. Instead, he'd been dragged from place to place, was nearly killed, and was now tramping through darkened corridors because she didn't even have the courtesy to meet him at the front door.

"Wait." Denizen leaned against a wall and folded his arms. "I've had enough. Sorry."

Grey turned to face him and blinked. "Come again?"

"The rushing about. The *I'll tell you laters*. It's like you're *enjoying* all this cloak-and-dagger stuff. Very little of today has made sense, and I want you to actually explain what's going on. What this is. All of it."

"And you'll get an explanation, Denizen. I've told you. Your aunt will—"

Denizen fought to keep the anger out of his voice. "My aunt didn't even bother to collect me herself. She wouldn't have brought me here had *something* not pulled itself out of the concrete and tried to kill me. Sorry if I'd rather know what's happening." He took a deep breath. "So shove your mystery. I'll wait here."

Grey stared at him for a long moment, and then his

eyes flicked to something behind Denizen. His voice was wry. "You Hardwicks are all alike."

Denizen turned round.

She wore armor. Real armor, the kind that Denizen had only ever seen in the black-and-white illustrations in history books. A cloak as white as snowfall was pinned to her shoulder guards—*Pauldrons,* Denizen's memory offered, *they're called pauldrons*—which gleamed above a chest plate of polished steel. Its center was worked with the same hand-and-hammers symbol Denizen had seen everywhere since coming to Seraphim Row. The backs of her massive gauntlets were carved with it too. A hammer hung from her waist—blunt and brutal and utterly inelegant. A tool of war. Of breaking and death.

It was the softest thing about her.

Her steel-gray hair was scraped back from her skull in a painfully tight knot. Her cheekbones looked sharp enough to cut glass; her lips twisted in disapproval below a long nose and eyes of the palest, coldest gray.

Eyes, he realized, not dissimilar to his.

Vivian Hardwick stared at him and said nothing at all.

7

Twenty-Three Past Midnight

Denizen withered beneath her gaze. It was like being ice under a blowtorch. Butter under a red-hot sword. Vivian's eyes were the shade and softness of a castle wall, and they fell on Denizen with the same unforgiving weight.

After roughly a hundred million years, her gaze shifted back to Grey. It didn't look like the stare was having the same effect on him. Instead, he stepped forward and gave a swift and courtly bow.

"Malleus, I—"

She cut him off with the wave of a gauntlet. "You were to observe him at the hotel."

Grey looked slightly sheepish. "There was little point in keeping up a pretense, Malleus. Darcie caught a Breach coming into the city, and I was the closest to deal with it. Denizen saw everything. I thought it best to bring him straight to you."

"Why?" she snapped.

Grey's brows knitted. "Well . . . you're family. He should hear it from you."

"Hear what?" Denizen asked. Neither Grey nor his aunt seemed to notice he'd spoken.

"The best course would have been to wait until after we were sure," she said coldly.

"My apologies, Malleus," Grey said, his tone excessively formal. "I won't—"

She ignored him. "Denizen. Follow me."

She turned on her heel and strode back the way she'd come. Denizen and Grey followed.

Denizen couldn't take his eyes off her. Vivian Hardwick was tall, towering over even Grey, and her voice was hoarse as if not used to speaking above a growl. And that had been the second time someone had mentioned a kind of test or condition to his being here.

His fists clenched. So, what—there was something he had to do, and if he failed, they'd just send him home? They expected him to ignore everything he'd seen? And Grey had called her Malleus, the same title as the old people in the portraits.

What was this place?

Grey and Vivian were talking quietly. Denizen

tried his best to listen without it looking like he was eavesdropping.

"Is Director Carsing still at Crosscaper?"

"No. A man named Ackerby. Dreadful human. Very nervous. Eager to get Denizen out of the door."

A strange expression darted across her face before she frowned again. "Eager? You didn't think that odd?"

"I just thought you'd paid him a visit. With respect, Malleus."

"Hrmph. And the Breach?"

"Happened when we were coming into the tunnel. Darcie was going to send Jack, but it just fell into my lap. Couldn't have avoided it."

"And the creature?"

"Shrapnel."

"Good."

She pushed open a set of double doors and disappeared into the room beyond.

Torches—real torches, like something from a haunted castle—cast puddles of light across a great wooden desk. It dominated the room like the jutting prow of an ancient ship. One wall was lined with cabinets, another with three cloth-and-plastic mannequins. The floor was polished planks.

More paintings and charts hung on the walls, but they were not what grabbed Denizen's attention. Instead, he stared at a galaxy of swords.

Some were long, graceful curves of steel—the kind that a samurai might carry into war. Others were the classic type of sword you saw in fantasy stories—wide-bladed, single-edged, the hilts topped with a ball of steel. Single-edged swords barely longer than kitchen knives rested beside massive two-handed glaives that looked like they'd hammer rather than cut. There were slender blades that seemed barely strong enough to hold an edge, and flat, wide swords like butchers' cleavers with backswept hooks at their points.

For Denizen, swords were swords. He knew, in a vague sort of way, that for a couple of thousand years the sword was the highest form of military hardware in the world. He knew there were different types. He just hadn't thought there were so many.

They reflected the light like a declaration of war.

Vivian swept into the middle of the room and unclipped her cloak from her shoulders, folding it over one arm. The armor whispered as she moved, steel on leather on steel.

"How was the meeting?" Grey said, taking the cloak from her and hanging it on a hook on the wall. He stepped behind her and undid a strap on her armor, sliding the pauldron free with a practiced motion and putting it on one of the mannequins.

Vivian shrugged a curve of metal from her other

shoulder and handed it to Grey. "Long. And boring. And I look like an idiot."

She didn't. She looked like a long war in silver. The armor was unpainted, though subtle carvings swept across its surface. Denizen had read about knights in finery; they wore their colors proudly, heraldry painted bright on their shields and armor so that everyone knew who they were. This wasn't armor to look at. This was armor to keep you alive while someone tried to kill you.

"Any news from the Palatine?" Grey said. Vivian glanced at Denizen and her mouth pursed.

Grey sighed. "The cat's out of the bag now, Malleus. Even if we tell him nothing else, he's seen one of them. It can't do any more harm."

She said nothing as Grey undid more of the fastenings on her armor. There was a padded jacket under her chest plate, and she dragged out its laces with short jerks until the whole garment hung loose. Her vest underneath was dark with sweat.

"So you do plan to tell me what's happening?" Denizen blurted out, and then paled as that blowtorch stare fell on him again.

His aunt slipped the hammer free from her belt and held it up in the air. It was nothing like Grey's blade or the swords that hung on the wall. Those were beautiful—elegance rendered in cold and shining steel. Whether it was a hilt worked to look like a snarling wolf's head or even just a scrap of tied ribbon, each weapon had a hint of art to soften its killing edge.

The hammer had none of that. Its haft was thick oak, the head a cruel lump of black iron. There were dents and nicks in its surface. It drank the light instead of reflecting it. Whoever forged it had made no attempt to lessen its brutal functionality. Its haft must have been the width of Denizen's wrist, but his aunt held it one-handed. *How strong is she?*

"What do you *think* is happening?" Vivian said, turning the hammer this way and that. The way she said it made anger flicker dully in his stomach. She spoke as if she were talking to a small child or to no one at all.

"Sorophina Devreny."

She raised an eyebrow. "Excuse me?"

"The hammer," he responded. "I've seen it before. In her portrait on the staircase."

"Sharp eyes," his aunt said without a trace of approval.

"I think," Denizen began, "that when things come through from . . . this other place, you fight them. And kill them. I think Grey used something impossible to do it. He used magic—"

"I hate that word."

"Well, *whatever,* but something that shouldn't exist."

Denizen was sweating now. He felt like he had just before the bad-dream angel pushed its way into the world—sick, like nothing fit together the way it should. It made his words come out slowly or wrong, made him feel frantic, out of his depth. Angry. He wanted to show her that he wasn't some stupid kid they'd dragged out of an orphanage. He wanted to prove himself, and he didn't know why.

"I think you're both soldiers. You definitely act like one," he said to his aunt. "But he doesn't." At this, Grey gave an idly mocking salute. "And soldiers don't wear armor and carry war hammers. Not anymore."

"We do if our war predates guns," said Vivian.

Denizen felt a laugh bubble up within him, a laugh born of panic, and he knew if he didn't swallow it back, it would never stop.

"I think that if a war had been going on that long, I'd know about it."

Another piece clattered to the desktop. Vivian still wore her gauntlets and somehow they looked like they belonged there—blunt, clutching things at the ends of her arms, devoid of warmth or humanity.

Grey hung the last of the armor on the mannequin, his eyes never leaving Denizen's face. Vivian was staring up at the swords as though answers were to be found in the play of light on blades.

"Would you?" she said. "Would you know? If I, and

men and women like me, had spent our entire lives preventing it?" She steepled her fingers with a rasp of steel. *"Has today not been a sharp lesson in what you don't know?"*

"You've never heard of our war," Grey said quietly. "There are no big battles, no flags held proudly, no poems, and no heroes. We don't give speeches. We don't hold parades. We die alone, or we die in twos and threes, but we always, *always* die in shadow. Unseen. Unmourned. If our war got into the history books . . . well, that's how we'd know we'd lost."

Swords shimmered in the firelight.

Denizen's head hurt. Just for a moment, his vision swam, the torches smearing until he blinked furiously. "Who's the enemy?" he said. "Who are you fighting?"

"You met one tonight," Vivian said. "What was it?"

A monster. An aberration. The air tearing with every move it made. A sense of wrong, a feeling that the world was sick—

Denizen thought of darkness, of a tunnel like the mouth of an eel, pitch-black and writhing. *That* was the enemy. That had been the heart of the thing.

"Darkness," he said. "Living darkness."

"As good a name as any," Vivian said, still looking at the swords. "What's the time?"

Grey checked his watch. "Twenty-one minutes past midnight, Malleus."

"Malleus," Denizen said. "Like the portraits on the stairs."

"My title," Vivian said. "My weapon. My duty."

Denizen felt as though he was standing in the middle of a storm—the kind that reached down and rearranged the landscape, the kind that tore air from your throat with a hurricane shriek. He just needed a moment. That was all. He just needed a moment to breathe.

"Twenty-one and a half, Malleus."

"Why does the time matter?" Denizen's fingers clenched into fists. "Somebody. Answer. Me."

Vivian lifted her chin. "At twenty-three minutes past midnight, you turn thirteen."

Denizen laughed once, a hard laugh with no warmth in it. "My birthday was months ago. Of course, you can't be expected to know that. I mean, the fact that all of you are clearly *insane* means that these small details might escape—"

"Shut up," Vivian snapped.

There was a long silence. Grey looked away.

"I do not need this," she said. "I don't have time to deal with a surly, untrained teenager. Do you think I like this situation any more than you do? Of course I don't. This isn't a game, and right now you are worse than useless. You are dangerous. *And I do not have time for this.*"

"Twenty-two minutes past."

Denizen shook with rage. His fists were balls of pain from squeezing them so hard. How dare she? Hadn't he held himself together this far? Eleven years on his own and not even the memory of a family to give him something to cling to.

He'd been doing *fine*. In five years, he could have left Crosscaper, and no matter what he did or where he went, at least he'd be doing it himself. He was his own family. No one else mattered.

"Are you even listening?" Vivian's voice was frozen iron. "You think that just because you'd prefer to ignore all of this, it won't affect you? How *blind* are you? How—"

There was a ringing in his ears, the pain was spiking right behind his eyes, and still her voice berating him, calling him useless. All he wanted to do was make her stop—

Twenty-three minutes past.

The torches went out. Another light took their place.

Denizen's mouth opened in a snarl. Not speech—words were useless—this was rage, pure and potent, an animal roar, and light spilled from his eyes, his hands, his open mouth.

You couldn't have called it flame. It was too bright for that. The air writhed round his fingers and ignited with a sound like shattering glass, lancing out to split the dark. In that moment, every shadow in the room wailed and died. Power flashed from Denizen's hands like a hole had been torn between here and the heart of the sun.

Vivian doused the fire with a sweep of her hand.

Stillness descended. The air tasted of soot. The torches flickered back to life awkwardly, as if unable to explain where they'd gone. Swaying, Denizen's vision filled with stars. He felt like something had been broken, as if a part of him had snapped and could never be repaired. He staggered.

Weakness swept over him, like every flu or cold he'd ever suffered had just hit him all at once and the last thing he saw before the floor rushed up to meet him was Vivian's bitter smile.

"Welcome to the family."

8

THE TASTE OF GLASS

THE WOMAN IN white was eating lightbulbs.

Simon couldn't take his eyes off her. It was horrible. She had found a cupboard on the third-floor corridor—six meters from the closet in which Simon was hiding—and had begun rifling through its contents.

Linens had been experimentally sniffed and idly tossed aside, forming lonely snowdrifts on the floor. A first-aid kit had been emptied out, its contents separated with a toe and then methodically stamped apart. Now she was opening boxes of lightbulbs, shaking the spheres out into her palm and peering into them before closing her teeth round their fragile domes.

Crunch.

It was dawning on Simon that she hadn't been searching the cupboard; she was just destroying whatever she found. There was no urgency in her movements, and a strange look of amusement creased her skin. Unfortunately, that meant Simon had no idea how long she might stay there, blocking the corridor—his only access to the classroom wing.

It was pure luck she hadn't seen him. An unexplainable feeling of dread had made him seek refuge in a broom cupboard, cracking the door open a hair just in time to see her appear at the top of the stairs.

Maybe he had heard her without even realizing it. Maybe he'd felt her presence or the air her movements displaced. Maybe the animal part of his brain was taking over—all the prehistoric instincts you didn't use in the modern world.

Simon didn't know or care. All that mattered was that he hadn't been caught.

Suddenly, the woman's head jerked to one side, as if she smelled his relief. She spat out a dry clot of glass and carefully closed the cupboard door, head cocked like a hound's.

Simon froze, taking his hand off the door so it settled back against the jamb, hiding her from view. His heart pounded, louder and louder—*Stop, stop, she'll hear it!*—and the floor creaked as she took a step toward him.

Don't panic.

With the door closed, she was more of a collection of sounds than a physical presence, sounds that Simon had to assemble in his head—a process that wasn't doing anything for his heart rate.

Periodic creaks. *Steps. She doesn't care about being quiet—why would she?* A drawling rasp—breathing roughened by glass. A cascade of stiff, mechanical pops that Simon realized in horror were her fingers clenching and unclenching. Had he not seen her with his own two eyes, he wouldn't have believed it was a person out there at all—just a machine, gaunt and terrible, bearing down upon him.

More terrifying than that, though, were the silences. Silence meant he had no idea

where

she

was.

Creak.

IIsss.

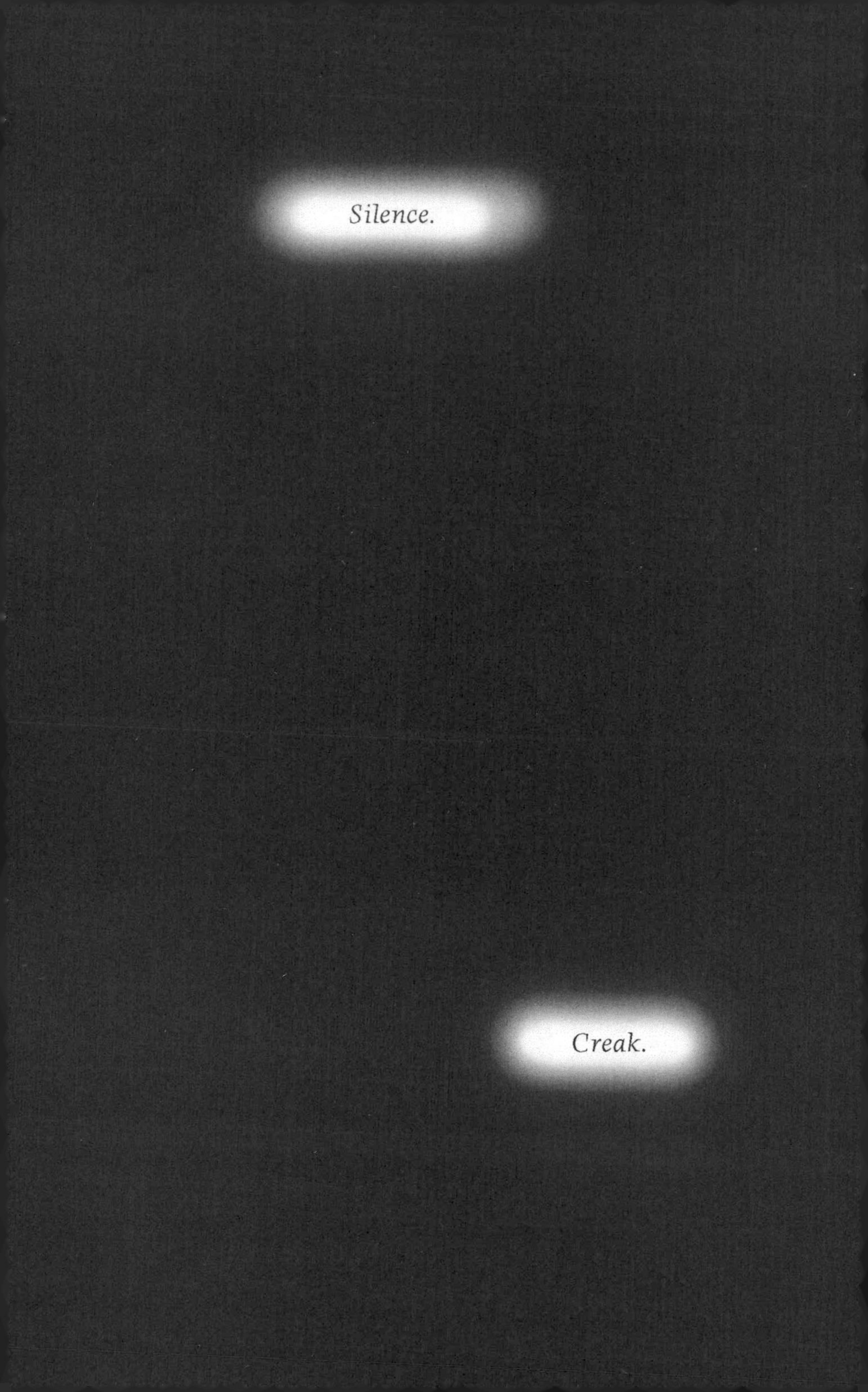
Silence.
Creak.

Hsss.

Silence.

Simon closed his eyes and then opened them, and cursed the sound of both. Everything became magnified. His heartbeat was thunder, his breathing a storm. The moment stretched maddeningly, and Simon became convinced that he could hear the *bzzt* of his nervous system, the *hoosh* of his sweating skin, and finally, beneath it all, the *tink* of the future becoming the present one second at a time.

Silence.

The door handle began to turn. Simon felt his stomach go concave at the thought of being that close to the woman's hand. Somehow, magically, he didn't scream. Entire agencies of fictional detectives would be proud. Most of them would have screamed by now. He was sure of it.

Creeeeaaaaakk—

Maybe just a little scream. It couldn't hurt—

And then she was gone. The handle was released, and footsteps as swift and light as the ticks of a clock rose suddenly and then faded. Simon waited a hundred hammering beats of his heart before allowing himself a single long sigh.

Well, that was horrifying.

It took more effort than Simon had ever expended to touch the handle and open the door, and more still to step into the corridor and expose himself to the night. He wanted to throw himself down the corridor at a flat run, lose himself in flailing limbs and the hot burn of adrenaline. Instead, he walked as slowly and carefully as before. Years in Crosscaper had taught him which floorboards creaked, which doors could be opened silently and which had to be eased open one hair at a time.

An observer might have found his movements strange—hopping left and right, freezing in place, then setting a bare foot down as lightly as possible on a single floorboard before lunging heavily across three more—but Simon was a veteran of nighttime wanderings. In these corridors, he knew exactly where to put his feet. The floorboards hadn't so much as sighed.

Glances into the dormitories he'd passed had told him what he'd already begun to suspect: every other boy and girl in the orphanage was asleep. Some had moaned to themselves in pain or fear; others twitched under their blankets as if jerked by invisible strings.

A bad dream had come to Crosscaper.

But not to me, he thought. *I'm still awake.* Simon wasn't sure whether that was a blessing, or if at any moment he'd keel over himself. Until then, though, he had a responsibility to try to escape and bring back help.

The door at the end of the third-floor corridor led to the classrooms, which had their own staircase down to the ground floor. The familiar shapes of the desks and cabinets had been made new and strange by the dark. He almost wanted the lightning to strike again just so he could see. Twice he had to navigate the blackness with both arms outstretched, tapping the backs of chairs, blindly reaching with the tips of his fingers.

The storm still raged outside, his steps quickening every time the sounds of the rain and wind became louder, slowing each time they faded away. Simon focused on the careful mechanics of where to place his feet, freezing every time a noise, real or imaginary, reached his ears.

One more floor to go. And then . . . Simon had been trying not to think about what came next. There were only two ways out of Crosscaper: the tradesmen's entrance at the back, which was always locked from the outside, or the front gates. He could get outside; that wasn't the problem. The problem was getting *out*.

He would have to cross the courtyard.

Simon crept to a window, pressing his face to the glass as close as he dared. It looked deserted but for the rain hopping off the gravel. The porch light was still on—the warm yellow glow melting the knot in his stomach a little—and for a second Simon thought he was being silly.

He was half-dressed . . . he wasn't going to rush out into the night, was he? Maybe the others were awake;

maybe this was a misunderstanding; maybe this was nothing at all—

Lightning then, the thunder half a beat behind.

The storm must have been right over Crosscaper. There was no other explanation for the thunder being that loud, the lightning so bright. The whole world lit up in sickly green, and Simon flinched from the window as he saw the man in the waistcoat floating in the center of the courtyard—short little legs dangling off the ground, chubby arms lifted to the rain, hair soaked to rats' tails across his scalp. His eyes were closed, a wide smile on his face. The rain didn't fall on him anymore—it swirled round his body, dragged by some invisible current to orbit the man as though he possessed his own gravitational pull.

It was the most frightening thing Simon had ever seen.

The man spoke, the words whispered but perfectly audible, as if the storm were afraid to drown them out.

Too long have we been wanderers. And this place . . . the misery of it . . .

The words slithered through the windows. They poisoned the rain.

We can be strong here. We can grow fat here.

The gates began to swing shut with the same palsied jerkiness with which they had opened, tortured metal squealing as it tried to resist. They closed with a final, dreadful clang.

Simon stepped away from the window. His only escape route was gone and he was alone and—*panic never solved anything.*

Slowly, painstakingly, Simon built a wall of rationality between himself and his fear. That was what Crosscaper did. It taught you that the worst had already happened and all you could do was adapt.

A detective would stay. A detective would take notes, observe, and wait for that perfect moment to save the day. He'd record what he saw of the strangers, look for a weakness, something he could use.

Denizen will come back. I need to be here to warn him when he does.

There was a cupboard on the other side of the classroom. Simon found a pen on a shelf and then squeezed himself in underneath. If he wrapped his arms round his knees, then he just about fit.

Somewhere distant, the storm raged. Simon pulled the door shut, and there in the darkness, he scratched on the cheap wood of the cupboard:

Day 1

9

A Darker Place

Denizen woke, and it was like his eyes were new.

The winter sun shone through the blinds like no other sun had shone before. Denizen contemplated it for as long as he could, resolutely ignoring the question of whether he was going to sit up.

No. Moving wasn't an option. Moving would tell his body—mistakenly, obviously—that he was awake and then the world would start up again, with its stress and pain and unexplainable situations.

He was just going to stay still. Right here. For the rest of his life.

The peace lasted until he blinked. It felt like someone had dropped a brick between his eyes. Denizen whimpered. That didn't feel good either.

Encouraged by the pain, memories began to flood back into his poor, abused head. Just scraps of things—

arguing with his aunt, being *angry,* angrier than he'd ever been . . .

Fire. There had been fire.

Sweat soaked him suddenly, as if he'd just broken the back of a fever, and with it came a ghost of the rage he had felt, the nuclear strength of it, how it had flowed out of him the night before in a tide of white-hot light.

It had felt . . . good. All the worries that had plagued him since getting Ackerby's note had been gathered up and fed to the flames. In that moment, light leaking from his eyes and mouth, Denizen had felt . . .

Pure. Powerful.

Slowly, wincing, he raised his head off the pillow and looked around. Window blinds cut the sun to slants. An old pockmarked desk stood in the corner with an equally ancient chair tucked underneath it. There was a bookshelf against one wall—Denizen immediately logged it for future examination—and a candle sconce on the wall. Aside from the latter, the room was almost aggressively normal. He could have been in Crosscaper.

That was good. Normal was good. There was solace in a room this boring. Nothing exciting could happen somewhere like this.

There was a knock at the door.

Well, it was nice while it lasted. Denizen pulled the covers up over his thin chest. Someone—his aunt?

Argh!—had removed his T-shirt and jeans before putting him to bed. The knock came again, and Denizen looked around the room, trying to savor the boringness before it was taken away.

"Can I come in?" It was his aunt.

I could say no. He had a mental image of Vivian simply booting the door open and sighed. "Sure."

She entered, dressed in a shirt and a pair of dark trousers, carrying a tray in her gloved hands.

Staring at her, Denizen couldn't help noticing the way she moved. It wasn't grace, not exactly, but a sort of mechanical elegance, like the scissoring of gears or the slow sweep of a crane. She moved as if she knew exactly where each part of her was at all times, fully aware of the measurements of the world and how she fit into them. There would never be an iota of wasted effort, nor a finger out of place.

An old burn scar dribbled colorless flesh down the side of her neck. He hadn't noticed it last night. It started behind her ear and swept all the way to her collarbone before disappearing beneath her shirt collar. Another scar—a thin pale line—bisected her lower lip.

Vivian didn't look at him at all. She set the tray on the desk, and it was only when the smell of bacon, toast, and tea drifted over to him that he pulled his gaze away from her scars.

His stomach woke and began to insistently remind

him that he had not eaten since the Middle Ages, and emotional trauma made a person hungry, and everything he had gone through so far was nothing compared to what would happen if he did not *immediately* eat his own weight in toast.

He barely noticed Grey come in—his eyes were fixed on the plate and cup, the faint steam rising from both. This was how they used to torture prisoners. He'd read about it. The guards would leave delicious, beautiful, *captivating* food just out of reach, and eventually you'd tell them anything for one moldy crust. It made sense, in an evil way. Why waste time pulling out fingernails and putting thumbs in vises when all you had to do was let the smell of fried bacon do all the work for you?

"I'm sorry," Vivian said.

She still hadn't looked at him. She pulled the chair out from under the desk and sat, staring down at her hands. "I have not . . ." She seemed to be drawing the words from a great depth. "I have not dealt with this as well as I should."

"The fact is," Grey said, "this is on a need-to-know basis. We weren't sure if you had the potential to be one of us. If you didn't—well, what we're about to tell you is a lot for someone to carry."

"I didn't want to bring you anywhere near this if I

didn't have to," Vivian said. "That's why I haven't contacted you before now."

Denizen didn't respond.

"I had my reasons, Denizen. My work is unforgiving. I travel. I keep strange hours and stranger company. I can go months without seeing home. Or daylight. And there are . . ."

"Monsters trying to kill you?"

Vivian nodded.

"They try to kill me too," Grey said. "You aren't special."

Vivian continued as if Grey hadn't spoken. Somehow, Denizen got the impression that she did that a lot. "The less interest I showed in you, the less chance there was of something else taking an interest in you. If you had not seen the creature last night, if you hadn't proved yourself on the moment of turning thirteen, then we would have sent you back to Crosscaper.

"*That* I will not apologize for. If there was any chance I could have kept this life from you, I would have taken it. I owe it to your . . . I owe it to your parents."

I owe it to your parents. The words sent a shiver through him.

"But you can tell me now, can't you?" Denizen said. "I'm one of you."

"Every Dawning is different," Grey said. "Yours was

a little . . . rougher than most." He pointedly did not look at Vivian. "But yes—you're one of us, or you have the potential to be. So go on. Ask."

Denizen stared at them for a long moment. "All right. Why did you lie about my birthday?"

That surprised her. *Of course it did.* You had to grow up in Crosscaper to really understand.

People were put together from their parents. Long before you made friends or met teachers or were inspired by people you read about or saw on TV, your parents influenced you. They were your model and your makers. This was doubly true of children in Crosscaper. Everyone Denizen had grown up with jealously held on to any connection they had with their parents.

Michael Flannigan still had his father's battered briefcase, rescued from the fire that had taken his parents from him. Simon would point-blank refuse to do an exam if he didn't have ink for his mother's silver fountain pen—and the teachers in Crosscaper always kept some handy because they understood that the most sacred possession an orphan could have was a memento from his parents.

Denizen didn't have anything. Just the birthday in his file. It was something you couldn't lose or forget, the way he had forgotten what his father looked like or the words his mother sang in his dreams.

And it had been a lie all along.

"Anonymity is protection, Denizen," said Vivian. "And anyone watching you with sinister intent would have seen your thirteenth birthday pass without incident. It was the only shield that could be afforded to you."

She actually did seem sorry, or at least uncomfortable, but Denizen didn't care. He was about to ask her flat out what her involvement with him and Crosscaper was when something she'd said suddenly struck him.

"What do you mean, *watching me*? Who?"

"We call them the Tenebrous," Vivian said, and Denizen could have sworn he heard a touch of relief in her voice at the subject being changed.

"Or the Obscura," Grey continued, "the Stygian or Those Who Walk Under Unlit Skies, depending on what century you're from and how poetic you want to be. They seep into this world from a darker place. You felt it last night in the tunnel. As if the world had ripped along a seam."

The memory almost killed Denizen's appetite. It had felt so *wrong*—reality grinding against itself, trembling at the intrusion of something that shouldn't exist. An angel that moved like a nightmare.

"That was a Breach," his aunt said. "A violent crossover event. Tenebrous claw their way into this world—hunting, reaving, pursuing their own deranged ends.

They pull a body together out of whatever they can find. Stone, sand, flesh, metal. Some are like the beast last night—just animals, vicious but barely aware. Others are as smart as any human and infinitely more dangerous. We deny them where we can."

"Deny them?"

"Some people are born with a link to the Tenebrae," Grey said, "the shadowy realm where the Tenebrous come from. We don't know a whole lot about it—whether it's one world or a thousand or a whole universe half a breath away. But we have a connection to it, and with that connection comes power."

"Like you used on the Tenebrous last night."

Grey nodded. "We have a fire in us, Denizen."

As if woken by his words, Denizen felt a slow heat unfurl within him, like embers suddenly kindled in the cathedral of his chest. It didn't feel new—it felt like it had always been there, surging from some hollow he hadn't known existed.

"Maybe it comes from the Tenebrae," Grey continued. "Or maybe it's something born in us to hold that darkness back. We don't know. We just know it works."

Denizen breathed out. The memory of how the power had felt still made his fingers tingle. He had used it only once. He didn't even know how he had done it, but he knew that he wanted to do it again.

"You have a gift," Vivian said. Her tone didn't make

it sound like he had a gift. She made it sound like he had a skin condition.

She's probably disappointed I turned out to be like them. If I wasn't, she could just send me back to Crosscaper. The harshness of the thought surprised him.

"But it comes with a Cost." She pulled off her gloves.

It took Denizen a moment to understand what he was seeing. At first, he thought she was wearing a second pair of gloves—the material wrinkled, shineless and black, so thin he could see the play of muscles beneath, the outline of fine bones—fingernails.

"We have had many names," Vivian said, her voice full of terrible pride. "We rode away from dying Rome to haunt the courts of kings, to counsel emperors and guard the world from shadow. We wind through history like a serpent—hidden, always hidden, keeping safe the kingdoms of humanity. I am a Malleus, a Knight Superior of the Order of the Borrowed Dark, and my hands are marked by the price of power."

Denizen stared at them. They were iron, and yet they moved more fluidly than any machine or prosthetic; they were *alive,* clenching and unclenching as smoothly as his own. There were old scars on the knuckles, places where the metal was notched and dented. Across her palms the metal had run like wax exposed to some great heat. With a start, he looked down at his own hands—

The Cost had marked Denizen as well.

In the very center of his left palm there was a black spot, as if someone had pressed a coin of dull iron into his skin. He ran a finger over it, then dug in a nail. It hurt, but barely, the pain coming from far away.

"It's the price we all pay for the power we wield," Vivian said. "A way of keeping us humble, stopping us from becoming too powerful. We use our gifts sparingly, when we use them at all."

There wasn't a seam where the iron met the skin of his hand. It didn't feel wrong—it felt like it had always been there, like the fire in his chest. The Cost had spread all through Vivian's hands, rising up her forearms in threads of black. How long had it taken her to change that much?

"So what happens now?" He looked from Vivian to Grey.

"We offer you a choice," Grey said. "No one should be forced to put their life on the line for people they've never met. So stay with us for a while. A week or two. See what your training would be like. Then you can join us as a Neophyte or you can go.

"Whatever happens, you'll have to receive some education—make sure there are no . . . accidents . . . should you lose your temper."

"Accidents?"

"The power is awake in you now," Vivian said. "It's not something you can just ignore. You'll need to learn to control it. If you don't, then it might come when you're not expecting it—when you lose your temper or feel strong emotion.

"That's why we had to bring you here. Your power could have Dawned in a crowded classroom or dormitory. Not only would that have jeopardized the secrecy of our Order, it could also have proved very dangerous."

"You're worried I might freak out and accidentally burn someone's face off?"

"Yes," Vivian said simply.

"This," Denizen said with a bitter smile, "is the worst recruiting pitch ever."

Vivian stood abruptly. "There are more important things here than coddling you, Denizen. Our family and the Order are intertwined. It's the highest honor for a Hardwick to serve. Do you know what the motto of our family is?"

Denizen had offended her, but he was too angry to care. "Yes, actually. I looked it up. I thought it would be comforting, you know, in the absence of an actual *family*. It translates as *safety through caution*."

Denizen would be the first to admit that as mottoes went, it wasn't the most rousing, but he had still taken pride in a connection to his family.

"Different Hardwicks," Vivian said with a grim smile. "Our family have been in the Order for a thousand years. Our motto is *Tu ne cede malis, sed contra audentior ito*. 'Yield not to evil, but attack all the more boldly.' I have seen terrible things in my years of being a Knight. I have shed blood on four continents. I have fought creatures so potent they have warped the very world around them."

She tugged her sleeve up farther to reveal long claw-mark scars in the iron, white and wrinkled like furrowed snow.

"Mongolia, eight years ago. The Wry Bile had nested in the sand and was preying on nearby villages until I walked out into the desert and burned the sand to glass. One of its many forms flung itself out of the firestorm, all madness and hunger, and it might have torn my throat out if Grey hadn't taken it apart."

"She got me back, though," Grey said, smiling wryly. "Ukraine, six months later. The Hounds of Vox—all spines and teeth, they're awful—had gone to ground in an abandoned Soviet base and of course I stroll in like I'm buying the paper. Ten minutes later and I'm dragging myself out of the wreckage with two broken legs and Vivian storms by me with this irritated look on her face—yeah, that one—and—"

"And I did my duty," Vivian said. "This is a calling, Denizen. We swear an oath. And I . . . I understand that you feel like nothing makes sense anymore. I felt the same."

"I didn't," Grey said. "I knew exactly what was going on all the time."

"And that makes you a unique and special person," Vivian said without the slightest change in tone before addressing Denizen once again. "You have to learn enough to control your power. If you wish to leave after that, then we will not stop you."

"Although we could use all the help we can get," Grey said hastily, shooting a glance at Vivian.

Is she trying to get rid of me? Denizen thought, his eyes narrowing. *One minute she's talking about how important it is to be a Knight, the next she's telling me she doesn't care if I leave or not.*

His mind was already reeling with what he'd been told. There was only so much space in his head for revelations about how the world was put together, and he felt like he needed an hour in a dark room just to sort through the pieces and make sense of them.

And there was another question, the one that had brought him here. Now that Denizen had the chance to ask it, he was almost afraid to, in case the floodgates opened and a thousand other questions came out.

"My parents," he said finally, his voice hesitant. "Were they Knights? Is that how they . . . is that how they died?"

Vivian didn't say anything. Her face didn't move, not a muscle.

"Your parents were good people," she said eventually. "They were . . ." She took a deep breath. "I have to get back to work."

"What?" Denizen said. "You were just going to—"

But she'd already left, sweeping imperiously through the door. Denizen stared after her incredulously.

"She's . . . uh . . ." Even Grey seemed taken aback. "She's under a lot of stress."

"A lot of stress?" Denizen repeated, shock and hurt warring in his voice. Something cold bloomed in the back of his brain, and he looked up at Grey. "You said this was a war, right?"

Grey raised an eyebrow. "Yes?"

"So who's winning?"

10

Three Days

On Denizen's first day in Seraphim Row, Fuller Jack beat a sword into shape with his bare hands and told him there was no such thing as magic.

"I don't like the word," the huge man said, lifting a fist of scarred black iron. "It's lazy."

Bald and massively muscled, Fuller Jack was from a tiny island off the coast of Scotland—so small that lying down would have required two boats, as he put it—and had a voice that filled the forging shed like a cheerful thunderstorm.

With a bushy, gray-streaked beard and arms thicker than Denizen's legs, he looked like a blacksmith from a bygone legend—which was exactly what he was, though nothing else about the forging shed was remotely medieval. The art had moved on a lot in the last few centuries, apparently, and the shed looked more like a mechanic's garage than something you'd find in a castle.

"What do you mean *lazy*?" Denizen asked.

He stood back as far as the shed walls would allow. Swords were being quenched in barrels of oil and water, and when the red-hot metal was dipped, droplets could hiss and splatter, burning flesh and skin like wax. Occasionally, a drop would pop and spit against the iron of Jack's forearms, fizzling out as if disappointed.

"What the Knights do is the same thing as making a sword. You put in what's needed—materials, time, energy—and you get a result. It's not free, and it's not easy. Magic?" He snorted.

"Magic's the unexplainable. The say-a-word shortcut. You never want to think about the Tenebrae's power like that because then you'll start using it to get out of scrapes you could have avoided if you'd been thinking straight. Power should never be used lightly. There's always a Cost to be paid."

Denizen nodded, trying not to stare at the notched iron of Jack's forearms. By the looks of it, he'd been paying for a while.

"Then why do you do it?" Denizen asked.

"Someone has to," Jack said, shrugging his massive shoulders. His gaze once again dropped to the tools in his hands, and Denizen suddenly had the feeling he'd only been given part of an answer, a thought Jack didn't want to finish. "And I have an easy time of it compared to the others. I like making things, and it's for a good cause."

Jack made swords. He made axes. Occasionally, he made maces, morning stars, and other, stranger weapons. He fed power into their forging, made them more potent against creatures without real blood to spill. *Spoken steel.*

When Grey broke a blade in combat or Vivian needed a dent beaten out of her armor, Jack made a fist and fixed it.

There was a shelf above Jack's head laid out with tiny statues of carved wood and steel. From where he stood against the wall, Denizen couldn't make out all the detail, but their delicate, artistic curves were very much at odds with the blacksmith's bulk.

"Oh yeah," Jack said, noticing where Denizen was looking. "Keeps me sane. Can't be sharp objects all the time, you know."

Denizen didn't, but he nodded anyway.

"Listen to me," Jack said, shaking his head. "Getting *philosophical* on you. As if your head wasn't melted enough already. All I mean is that jumping into things without thinking is dangerous. Especially when it comes to this. You should question everything. Ask *why* before you act."

"I like asking questions," Denizen said with a rare smile.

The Knight laughed. "Then you'll be more than fine around here. If, of course, you decide to stay."

Denizen looked at the ground. "I don't know. Grey said that you guys need me."

"Weeeeell," Jack said, "there aren't many of us. A cadre here in Dublin, another in Paris, one in Munich, one in Sofia . . . People born with a connection to the Tenebrae are rare. I'd understand if you wanted to run for the hills, though. I did at first."

"Really? I thought . . ."

"You thought someone pops out of the shadows with a sword and a lifetime contract to fight the hungry dark and everyone just says, 'Grand job, where do I sign?' "

Jack grinned. Denizen found himself grinning back.

"No, sir. I took enough training to keep a lid on it, worked my way round Europe for a couple of decades, and then one night I stumbled into an alleyway fight between three howling ghouls and the most beautiful Frenchwoman I'd ever seen."

"You saved her?"

"Hell, no. She saved me. Stung my pride so much, I signed up the next day."

Denizen's grin faded. "And my aunt? What can you tell me about her?"

Jack was silent for a moment. "Your aunt is a Knight through and through," he said. "I've fought beside her for eight years, and I doubt it took her two minutes to make up her mind. Don't . . ."

"Don't what?"

"Don't try and live up to Vivian Hardwick." His face was serious. "Make your own choice."

Denizen nodded slowly and then frowned. "Wait! You joined up because of a girl?"

Jack's heavy brows furrowed. "You got a problem with that?"

ON DENIZEN'S SECOND day in Seraphim Row, he opened a door and nearly lost the tip of his nose to a throwing knife. It whirred by his face—so close he saw his own shocked reflection in it—and buried itself in the wall.

The Knight who had thrown it rolled from a cartwheel into a perfect aikido *ai hanmi* stance and told him that what they did wasn't war.

"It is pest control."

Corinne D'Aubigny was a petite switchblade of a woman with wolfish blue eyes and a colorful tattoo inked across both shoulders. Denizen couldn't work out exactly what it was; the elaborate image rippled with the movement of her muscles, and he didn't want to be caught staring. Another tattoo—a black rose—began on her stomach and disappeared beneath her tank top.

He stepped awkwardly onto the edge of a soft

rubber mat and tried not to rub the end of his nose. He wasn't sure if this was D'Aubigny's bedroom or her gym; wooden racks lined a wall, holding weapons far more exotic than the ones in the Room of Swords. Training mats were spread over the floor. There was a cot in the corner. Arrayed in a neat line between it and the wall were more of the carvings Denizen had seen in Jack's forge; these were finished and gleaming with varnish. Some were large; some were tiny and delicate. No two had the same shape.

They were Tenebrous, Denizen realized. Trophies.

"In a war," she said, her French accent as delicate as cobwebs, "one never stops. One never leaves the job half done. There is a thing. It is called total warfare. You do not chase the enemy to his border and then go home and have a brandy. You understand?"

There hadn't been a whole lot about total warfare in his classes at Crosscaper. Perhaps it was more of an advanced subject.

D'Aubigny turned to a rack, made a clicking noise with her tongue, and selected a katana—a long, curved Japanese sword. It parted the air with a hiss as she made a few practice cuts.

"The Tenebrous, the Obscura, they come with little warning, but when they do, we are ready. Every time the shadow rears its head, we are there to—"

Snick. The katana cut the air.

"Pest control. You see?"

She brought up her sword in a guard position, the blade held diagonally down across her chest. It moved and she moved with it, one position to the next, faster and faster until she was surrounded by a whickering cage of steel.

Denizen tried to follow her movements, but D'Aubigny was a blur, bare feet flashing, the sword a silver tongue that cobra-flicked at imaginary opponents, slashing and thrusting and blocking avenues of attack that existed only in her head.

It was terrifying, Denizen thought. And beautiful too, in a strange way.

"That's why this will never be over," she said as she twirled. "We do not fight. We do not *war*. We react. We stamp on the ants when they appear. And we are very good at it."

The blade stopped, its point shivering in the air.

"But we never burn out the nest."

Her blue eyes held his. He swallowed. "I understand."

Iron climbed D'Aubigny's arms in jagged streaks, wrapping her muscles in filaments of black. She tossed her blade upward and slapped the hilt so it spun, carving a perfect circle in the air before her fingers darted out to catch it by the blade. She stared down the length of the quivering sword for a moment and then lowered it, the hilt pointing at Denizen.

He took it from her. It was very heavy.

"Do you plan to stay?" Her tone did not indicate any preference in the matter.

"I don't know yet," he said. "My aunt . . ."

"Do you know what *Malleus* means?"

Denizen shook his head.

"'Hammer,'" D'Aubigny said. "Only the greatest of us carry such a weapon, such a title. Your aunt is . . . impressive." Her accent made the word music. "If she led us to war, I would follow.

"I am not saying it would be easy—we would need every Knight, every man and woman out there with the iron in their palms. But if any of the Mallei could do it . . ."

She paused, thoughtful. Denizen felt his hand start to tremble from the weight of the sword.

"This is not a war. There is no glory. We are . . . border guards. We are a watch with no end in sight. It is hard. She is hard."

Respect thrummed through her voice, as it did when anyone spoke of Vivian. No affection . . . but definite respect.

D'Aubigny took the blade from him. "I suppose Jack told you how we met?"

Denizen nodded.

"They were only ghouls." A smile played round D'Aubigny's lips. "He could have taken them."

Denizen suppressed a smile and turned to leave. Just as he opened the door, she spoke again.

"Would you like a piece of advice? This is important."

He nodded. "Of course."

She looked from him to the throwing knife embedded in the door. Her smile disappeared.

"Next time you come in here, knock."

ON DENIZEN'S THIRD day in Seraphim Row, Grey took him for a walk in St. Stephen's Green and told him that the Tenebrous were not monsters.

"*Monster* is too easy a word," Grey said, flicking some foam from the plastic lid of his coffee cup. "It's too fairy tale. In stories, the monsters are big and hungry and stupid, and all you need be is small, quick, and smart. Or else they're smart but *chatty* monsters, the ones who tie you up and then explain all their plans and weaknesses instead of doing the smart thing and biting your head off." He snorted. *"Fairy tales."*

"So what *are* the Tenebrous, then?" Denizen asked.

"Ask ten Knights and you'll get ten different answers," Grey said. "We know they cross over from the Tenebrae—our word, by the way. I don't even know if they have a word for it, let alone one I'd be able to pronounce. We know they make a body from whatever's on hand—hence your angel being concrete and asphalt."

"Why did it look like an angel?" Denizen asked. He still got shivers thinking about the thing, the . . . *Tenebrous.* The angel had been distortion itself—a strangeness like static that had made Denizen's eyes hurt and his stomach twist.

It had moved like a wound in the world.

"It didn't do a great job, did it?" Grey said thoughtfully. "They usually don't. They look . . . *wrong,* even the really old ones that try to pass as human. It's the little things. The face. The eyes.

"Maybe it picked up the shape somewhere before, saw a statue of an angel and liked it. Who knows? We've written down every scrap of knowledge gained over centuries of war, and there are still some pretty serious gaps."

The afternoon was cold and bright. Frost hadn't given up its grip on the grass and kids Denizen's age crunched their way across it, laughing and chatting on their lunch break. Bundled in a coat, hat pulled down over his ears, Denizen envied the students their lessons in English and math. They didn't have to juggle a whole new secret world full of monsters—*not*-monsters—only to find out that the experts didn't know anything either.

"The Tenebrous are . . . complicated," Grey continued. "The one you saw? A low beast. A crazed, starved thing. There are many others. Thousands of them. Part of Darcie's work is cataloging them for our Order. They have their own courts, their own nobles, even their own . . ."

"What?" asked Denizen.

Grey's lip curled. "The Endless King. Not something you need to worry about right now. Some things are best kept dark." He took a long pull of his coffee. "Point is, they're not monsters. Monsters are simple. The Tenebrous are like us—complicated, ever-changing—and that makes them much worse. If you choose to take the oath and lift a blade . . ." Grey hesitated. "But you're not sure yet, are you?"

Denizen shook his head.

"Well, if you decide to join us, that simple fact will keep you alive."

They watched the students in silence. A young couple giggled on a nearby bench. Birds flitted from branch to branch.

"I was curious about something."

"Oh?"

Denizen picked at his cup. "When you got the call about the angel, you could have told Darcie that you had me with you. If I hadn't seen it and had turned out to be normal, Vivian mightn't have bothered meeting me at all."

Grey gave a catlike shrug.

"But you put her on the spot. She *had* to talk to me then. Right?"

"Couldn't say," Grey said. "Maybe. Who knows? I certainly don't."

His tone made Denizen smile. "Why, though?" he asked. "Why jeopardize the big secret?"

Grey sighed. "OK. With regards to the secret, people have found out before. Werewolves, sea monsters, dybbuks, chimeras . . . and the stories get retold, but you'd be amazed at how hard it is to actually *prove* they exist. Tenebrous aren't any easier on cameras than they are on the eyes.

"Secondly—and don't take this the wrong way—your story isn't exactly unique. This is a dangerous calling, and orphans and war go hand in iron hand." His voice was soft. "A lot of people never get the answers they're looking for. Maybe I wanted to make sure you got yours."

"Thank you," Denizen said. "Really." His expression soured slightly. "Except my aunt doesn't seem to want to talk to me at all."

"Well, there is that," Grey offered. "But that's what I get for trying to put Vivian Hardwick in a corner."

"Do you think she wants me to stay?"

Grey shrugged. "I have no idea. The list of things I claim to know about—and that's a long list, mind you—does not include your aunt. I've fought beside her. That's as close to knowing her as anybody gets."

"I've noticed," Denizen said a little bitterly. "She hasn't spoken to me since the first day. Since she explained . . . well, whatever." He played with the plastic lid of his cup. "I wanted to ask her about my parents. I don't even . . . I don't know if they were Knights, or how they died, or anything really."

Grey nodded. "I understand, kid. The Malleus is a hard woman to reach. She'll tell you in time. This can't be easy for her either."

That thought hadn't occurred to Denizen, and he didn't like thinking it; it was much easier sulking at someone when you didn't stop to consider their point of view.

"This isn't about heroes and villains," Grey said. "Blades flashing, fires roaring, a great sweep toward death or glory. It's day after day of danger and fear. That changes a person. We live on borrowed time, Denizen. Our flesh turns to iron the longer we fight, but there's a change on the inside too."

There was a quiet sadness in his voice. "I honestly don't know which is worse."

He stared into the distance for a long moment and then sighed. "Laugh a minute, aren't I? There are perks, though."

Grey lifted his cup high and, when he was sure

Denizen was watching, whispered under his breath. A single coil of smoke began to rise from under the lid. Denizen's eyes widened as a spot of scorched plastic spread like a bruise across the white lid. Grey's lips moved again and light pulsed from somewhere inside the cup, the lid collapsing inward.

Denizen inched backward on the bench—he could still feel the heat of the fire. If the couple sitting across from them looked in Grey's direction, if someone happened to pass by . . .

"Grey, what are you—Grey, someone will *see*."

Grey didn't seem to hear. Reflected light flashed in his eyes as he whispered a third time and the cup crumpled, eaten from within by the flame. His wrist flicked and the cup spun away, exploding into cinders and smoke.

The girl a bench away yelped in surprise, her boyfriend threw Grey a dirty look, and Grey turned to Denizen with a mad little smile.

"Jack told you that this wasn't magic. A great man, Fuller Jack, and a solid Knight, but he lacks imagination." He shook ash from his fingers.

"I'll show you real magic."

11

Real Magic

"Seventy-eight Cants. Seventy-eight ways to change the world."

The last time Denizen had made the journey to the Room of Swords, he'd made it blind—following the sounds of Grey's footsteps through a murk of darkness and candlelight. Even now, at noon, the light didn't reach far, choked out by winding corridors and dusty windows. But Denizen strode through the gloom as if under a summer sun. The iron in his palm had been the first change he'd seen in himself since his thirteenth birthday, but it hadn't been the last.

Denizen Hardwick could see in the dark.

He'd only noticed one night when he had been woken by . . . he couldn't remember what. A dream, a memory, some unknowable, unnameable thing that had jerked him out of sleep with his heart pounding and sweat on his brow. Eyes widened in the dark—though all the lights were out, the details of his room were perfectly clear, the colors washed out and dim as if he was looking at the world through moonlight. The bad dream had been instantly forgotten. For a long moment, Denizen had just sat up in bed, amazed, a wide smile on his face.

Now he sat cross-legged on the cold stone floor of the Room of Swords, watching Grey go from torch to torch with matches.

"Intueor Lucidum," the Knight said. "The Shining Gaze." He shrugged. "I think. My Latin's woeful. And as superpowers go, it's not flight or anything, but I'll take what I can get."

"Why do you even need lights if our powers let us see in the dark?" Denizen asked.

"Habit, mostly." He frowned. "And I'd miss colors. Now pay attention—what did I just say?"

"Seventy-eight . . . Cants? So magic words?"

Grey winced. "Don't let Vivian hear you say that. They're phrases. Concepts. Words so powerful, they're almost alive. They give shape to the fire within us. Like a flood channeled by the banks of a river. The power can be snapped without them . . . but it's incredibly dangerous, requiring an almost impossible effort of will. The Cants are safer." He frowned. "Moderately safer."

Denizen remembered the weakness and pain that

had swept over him after he had first used his gift. He had absolutely no desire to feel it again.

"And there are exactly seventy-eight of them? That's pretty precise."

Grey turned from the torch he was lighting. "Any soldier should be able to tell you the number of arrows in his quiver or how many bullets are in his clip. These seventy-eight Cants are all we have to work with, and each Knight must know their strengths, their weaknesses, how they can be combined . . . and the Cost they'll exact."

The torches glowed. Shadows twitched across stone.

Removing his jacket and laying it across the table, Grey stretched. Denizen could see dark shadows of iron through his white shirt.

He'd begun to notice that all the Knights moved in a certain way—careful but not stilted, thoughtful but not hesitant. D'Aubigny flowed like molten glass. Jack had the unstoppable momentum of a siege engine. Grey slipped from moment to moment as if he ran the world and everyone else was just a visitor. They all moved with their own particular type of grace.

They moved like they knew a secret.

"Most Knights focus on becoming proficient at a select number of Cants," Grey said, sitting down opposite Denizen, "the way a warrior might choose the weapon best suited to their hand. Jack, Darcie, your aunt—they all have their specialties, their ways of making war. But it all starts with this."

He pushed his hair back from his face. "I want you to close your eyes."

Though he had seen as much in the last few days, this request still caused a skeptical look to flash over Denizen's face before he complied. Next thing Grey would produce an old-fashioned watch on a chain and ask him to stare at it.

"Can you feel your connection to the Tenebrae?"

Denizen sat there, staring at the lights that played across the back of his eyelids, and waited. How *did* one feel a connection to the Tenebrae? There was the beginning of an ache in the back of his head, but that wasn't it. His knees were already starting to hurt from being in the lotus position—not that Grey had told him to sit like that, but what other position were you supposed to sit in when channeling magic from a shadow realm?

"Denizen?"

He opened one eye.

"Stop thinking so much."

"How can you tell I'm thinking?"

"You have a *this is stupid* frown on your face."

That's my normal expression, Denizen wanted to say. Instead, he tried to remember how it had felt the night of his birthday—the way the power had welled up in him, the irresistible heat of it.

It had felt like the birth of a sun in his chest, like a dragon of fire spreading its wings through him until the power had spilled from his eyes and mouth and hands, unable to be contained by such a fragile mortal body. He had felt transformed. A shiver went through Denizen at the memory.

And that's when it happened. A slow unfurling in his head. The power of the Tenebrae rose within him from some deep, dark place, winding its way up his spine. It felt at once powerful enough to crush his insides to powder yet gentle enough that he wasn't sure he felt it at all. If he concentrated . . . *yes*. There it was.

A heat.

A hunger.

A feeling that he could reach out and—

"Wait," Grey said. Denizen opened his eyes. His hands were trembling against his lap. He felt like he'd grasped a live current and he needed to do *something,* anything, with it or he would lose his grip and the power would burn him to ash. It cried out to be used. It wanted to be free.

"Denizen. *Focus.*"

Denizen did his best. The power didn't want to be controlled. It despised the idea. It wanted to eat the world up, use it as fuel, burn its way across the sky.

And Denizen wanted to let it. Seventy-eight Cants? He could do anything with this power! And yes, Jack had said something about paying a price, and he knew that there was a Cost, but surely *once* wouldn't hurt; there were so many things he wanted to do. He'd only have to give up a finger, maybe even a hand—

No. He pushed the inferno back down, doused it in cold reason. It retreated, slinking back to that dark place in his head. Had he really—*just a finger, just a hand?*

Denizen shivered.

"You see what I mean?" Grey reached over and patted Denizen's knee. "That's why there's a Cost. The power of the Tenebrae is as wild and dangerous as the creatures that inhabit it. It's a constant mental struggle for control.

"The Cants aid us in that battle, channeling the power in the direction we want it to go. That's a little bit down the line for you, though. Attempting a Cant you're not ready for can have dire consequences. Today we're just going to work on raising the power and holding it."

"How do you balance it?" Denizen said. "How do you know the right time to use it?"

"Experience, mostly," Grey said. "If you decide to stay with us, we'll start your physical training properly. Every one of us here is an expert at hand-to-hand and armed combat. Our prowess gives us the option not to use our power unless we really need to. Dropping a Helios Lance or an Apogee Circuit into a fight at the right moment ends it quick and dirty.

"Then there are the Epithets, the Higher Cants—only used in a moment of life or death. The Art of Apertura, the Starlight Caul, the Snare of Thoth . . . Remember the Tenebrous we met on the road?"

Denizen nodded.

"There wasn't time for subtlety, not out in the open. I needed to be quick, so I spoke Sunrise and paid the Cost. And, well . . ."

"What?"

Grey grinned. "I've never been much good at self-control."

"So . . . how long before I get to learn a Cant?" Denizen tried to keep the eagerness from his voice. The power coiled round his spine was eager too—it wanted out. It ached to be used, through the Cants or not.

"When you're ready," Grey said. "And before you ask, I decide when you're ready, not you."

They worked for hours. Denizen would let the power rise up through him and at Grey's nod grudgingly let it go. The process was surprisingly exhausting. He practiced calling on the Tenebrae when standing up. He practiced it when sitting down. He practiced it while jogging round the Room of Swords. He practiced it until the inside of his head felt cracked and charred.

Eventually, at six o'clock, Grey helped Denizen up. "That's enough for today."

Denizen wasn't sorry they'd finished. Those first twinges had evolved into a full-on headache, and he wanted nothing more than to push his face into a pillow, preferably one that had been left in a freezer for an hour. He did feel slightly cheated, though, and said so—six hours of work and he hadn't even *heard* a Cant.

"All right," Grey said, laughing. "Pay close attention. Listen to how it sounds. And *don't* go and attempt it yourself." He raised his gloved hand, the fingers spread, and Denizen saw a flicker of light pass behind Grey's eyes. He was drawing on his own power, just a trickle of it.

And he spoke.

It sounded like . . . no, *sounded* was the wrong word. What came from Grey's mouth weren't words. They were like nothing Denizen had ever heard before. He had studied French. He had seen German and Spanish on the page and could recognize Arabic if he saw it. When the Knights had talked about Cants or magic words, he had thought it was going to be some kind of secret language.

This wasn't language at all. It was more primal and elemental than that. It was the first taste of summer. It was the smell of grass cooking under sunlight.

Light spun into being above the palm of Grey's hand.

First a spark, weak and flickering. Then, fed by the alien syllables that slipped from Grey's lips, it swelled into a tiny captive star. The glow drove back the shadows, a whorl of amber that painted the blades on the walls a thousand shades of gold. Grey grinned at the shocked look on Denizen's face.

"Trust me," he said. "I never get used to it either." He turned his hand this way and that, the shadows lengthening and shortening. "The Cost for something like this is small. Barely noticeable. I could use it for years and hardly notice a difference. It's when you build upon it, combine the Cants to create new effects—"

He spoke again. This time the Cant was the vicious crackle of a wildfire—the light around his fingers sharpened, hardening into a gauntlet of seething flame so bright that Denizen had to look away. The flare of fire only lasted a moment before Grey let it die.

"That's when the Cost grows. You have to know when it's worth it."

They left the Room of Swords and made their way down to the kitchen of Seraphim Row. Candles glimmered from wall sconces. Seeing Seraphim Row with the *Intueor Lucidum* almost made Denizen miss the dark.

When he had first seen the house, the candles and

shifting shadows made it mysterious and full of secrets, exactly the kind of place you'd imagine housing an order of mystic warriors. Now Denizen could see every patch of peeling wallpaper, every exposed wire and tarnished fitting. Clots of wax crunched underfoot.

Seraphim Row had the air of an abandoned hotel—sagging, deflated, a place that should be full of people but was now depressingly empty. They'd already passed by half a dozen unused rooms. Denizen liked the bedroom he'd been assigned well enough, but he had the feeling there was nothing stopping him from picking another abandoned one, cleaning it, and using that.

Only a handful of Knights made this place their home, like bats in a derelict cathedral. *And me,* Denizen thought, glancing at his reflection as he passed a cracked mirror. That didn't make the place any more reassuring.

Nowhere was the emptiness of Seraphim Row more apparent than in the kitchen. The sprawling room could have fed a hundred Knights. Maybe it had once; there were a dozen long trestle tables stacked against one wall and a line of stoves along the other.

Denizen tried to imagine dozens of warriors here, resting between Breaches, sharing war stories or patching each other up after battle. Now only one table sat in the middle of the room, and all but two of the stoves were covered in dust.

Jack was already there when they arrived, stirring a pot of stew. This was the only place in Seraphim Row that could make him look small.

"Boys," he said, and raised a ladle to them in salute, "how was school?"

"All right," Denizen said, blushing slightly. He still hadn't gotten used to everyone's easy camaraderie.

They took seats at the table and soon were joined by Darcie and D'Aubigny. Jack ladled out bowls of thick stew. The Knights took turns cooking, and as soon as Denizen could be trusted with a spice rack, he would join them.

That had worried him slightly, until he realized that none of the others were great chefs either; instead, the rule seemed to be simple food in great quantities. Food was fuel, and each Knight's body was an engine. It had to be to keep up with their training.

If Denizen decided to take the oath and stay, he would be trained not only in the Cants but in all the disciplines of a Knight of the Borrowed Dark. Armed and unarmed combat. As many languages as he could master, including several that only existed in history books. And more—studies that seemed to have nothing to do with sword fights in dark alleys: chemistry, law, military science, and psychology. After all that, there was the study of the Tenebrae itself.

There was so much to learn. Before Denizen left

Crosscaper, he had been having trouble with algebra. Was that more difficult than sword-fighting?

He was lost in thought when Darcie nudged him. He turned to see her offering a tiny cupcake, its icing covered in so much glitter that you could have turned it upside down and used it as a disco ball.

"Your birthday," she said by way of explanation. "You didn't really get one. So I thought . . . I mean, it's small but—"

"It's lovely," Denizen said, and meant it. "I'd totally forgotten. This is really sweet of you." He blushed self-consciously. After three days of talking about total warfare, dread non-monsters, and the constant equation of bravery and iron, it was a relief to be surprised by something nice.

He examined the miniature cake. Every square centimeter was covered in glitter. "Em . . . how am I going to eat this?"

"Edible glitter," Darcie said with pride. "Happy birthday."

He laid it gently beside his bowl, grinning sheepishly. However, as dinner continued, it didn't take long for the conversation to turn back to darker things.

"The London cadre was on the phone," Grey said. "Three Breaches this week alone."

Jack let out a low whistle.

"Is that a lot?" Denizen asked.

Grey nodded. "They're run pretty ragged. More than usual, that is. Something has the Tenebrae stirred up."

"It is winter," D'Aubigny said grimly. "Things are always worse when the darkness is closer."

Grey poked at his stew with his spoon. "Last I spoke to the Malleus, she said she was going to stay with them for a few days, help them out. She took Abigail with her."

Denizen frowned. "Abigail?"

"Oh, you haven't met her yet," Grey said. "Abigail's great. She's training as well, but has a little bit of a . . . head start, I guess. You'll meet her when she gets back."

Denizen was suddenly aware of a slow fire crawling forth from that dark place in his mind. So there was another recruit. One that Vivian had taken on a personal errand. One with a *head start*.

He shoved the thought away. There was nothing wrong with someone having a head start. He'd only been told about the Tenebrae three days ago. It was only natural for other people to be more up to speed. *I mean, maybe if Vivian hadn't left me in an orphanage . . .*

"Darcie," he said quickly, before any more of his head caught fire, "are you still up for showing me the library this evening?"

Telling Denizen a week ago that he'd ever leave Crosscaper would have prompted a whole orchestra of frowns, but now that he'd spent a few days away, certain strange thoughts had crept into his head.

He missed Simon, of course—a moment rarely went by when he didn't imagine how his glacially calm friend would have dealt with all this. He missed his books as well, and when at breakfast Darcie had offered to give him a tour of her library, it had meant a lot.

"Ah," said Darcie, her eyes suddenly wide behind her dark glasses. "Well, that's . . . ah."

She darted a glance at Grey, who sighed.

"Denizen, for the moment at least, you won't be given access to the library."

"What? Why not?" Being kept out of a library wasn't exactly the height of cruelty, at least not by normal teenage standards, but Denizen had never claimed to be normal and that was *before* he'd found out there was fire in his bloodstream.

Anger flared again, and the feeling was so close to that of the Tenebrae coursing through him that he instinctively tamped it down. He let out a long breath.

"Your aunt just thinks that—well, you haven't chosen to stay yet. So showing you our histories might be a bit . . . premature." Grey flashed Denizen a sympathetic smile, one that Denizen didn't return.

"I see," he said stonily.

They ate in silence for a few more minutes before Denizen spoke again.

"So, my aunt?" he said suddenly. "Tell me some more about her."

Darcie cleared her throat, rising to take her plate to the sink. Jack was suddenly very interested in the contents of his bowl.

"Vivian?" Grey said. "Well. She's . . . uh . . ."

Jack frowned. "She's . . ."

It was D'Aubigny who finally got out a sentence. "She is a Malleus."

Hammer. Denizen considered the weight of the word, the heft of it in his head. "And a Malleus is a commander, right?"

"Each cadre is led by a Malleus," Grey said. He seemed a lot more comfortable now that the conversation had shifted away from Vivian specifically. "They are the most experienced of us, the Knights who have fought the longest and hardest. The hammers they carry are our most powerful weapons."

On his second day in Seraphim Row, after spending an evening staring at the door of his room, hoping that his aunt would come and talk to him, Denizen had gone to look at the portraits of the Mallei in the foyer.

Men and women with stern faces and old scars—each with the same iron hammer, each with the same pitiless look in their painted eyes.

Had Vivian sat for hers yet? *Maybe it's only after they die,* he thought, and then immediately felt ashamed.

"Your aunt has been a Knight for nearly two decades," D'Aubigny said. "She has a long and distinguished career."

There was something in the way she said it that made Denizen's eyebrows rise. "OK. But what's she like?"

"She has a long and distinguished ca—"

"Yes," Denizen said, "I get that. Thanks. But what's she *like*?" He struggled to keep his voice casual. "Off the clock. Out of the armor." The false cheer faded from his voice, but he couldn't keep the words from spilling out. "I mean, she takes this other Neophyte off with her, but she hasn't said one word to me since that first day, and as she brought me all this way, I thought she'd want to talk to me about my parents or even just . . . just talk to me . . . at all?" His voice faltered. "You know. Like at some point."

None of the Knights said anything. Grey looked away, but not before Denizen saw a hint of pity in his eyes.

It was a long walk back to his room.

12

Lux Precognitae

"Grey?"

Denizen knocked on the door again. He had been here a week and a half, and a sort of routine had developed. Usually, by this time, the door to the Room of Swords was already open and Grey was inside with a cup of coffee in his hands and a cup of tea gently cooling on the desk. This morning the door was closed.

Denizen had considered just opening it, but after the incident with D'Aubigny's throwing knife, he had developed a nervous habit of announcing himself before he opened doors or turned corners. Dangers of being a Knight aside, he would be mortified if he ended up a casualty because he put his head in the wrong door.

When he tried the handle, it was locked.

Denizen was about to leave—maybe wander up to Vivian's office to see if she or the mysterious Abigail had returned—when a polite cough made him turn. Darcie Wright stood there, her blue frock coat buttoned against the early-morning chill, her eyes as always hidden behind dark circles of glass. Delicately, she tucked a black curl behind one ear.

"It occurred to me that you haven't seen much of the city yet," she said. "So I asked Grey if I could steal you for the day." She smiled. "Shall we?"

DUBLIN SMELLED LIKE salt and smoke, and the Samuel Beckett Bridge rose like a harp for the fingers of a giant.

"I was thirteen," Darcie said, daintily nibbling at a chip. "But we're always thirteen. That's how it works."

Clouds chased each other across the sky, crashing against the horizon in steel-colored tides. Denizen and Darcie had bought chips and ambled down almost as far as the Docklands. The farther they walked, the more Dublin seemed to fade away—the crowds shrinking, the buildings becoming fewer, all retreating to gray sky and sea.

The cold still nipped at his fingers through the mittens he wore. Grey had offered him a pair of black leather gloves the day before, but Denizen felt a bit weird about wearing them. All the Knights carried a pair, the closest the Order had to a uniform.

Denizen imagined a warehouse somewhere—*one*

pair of standard-issue black gloves, please, so as not to freak out the general public.

Darcie flexed her gloved fingers in the cold.

"In a way, I had it easier than most. My grandfather was a Knight, so we were always . . . prepared, I suppose? The night of my birthday, Granddad took me out into the forest behind my house and we waited together. He knew what he was doing—talked me through the Dawn of my power so I didn't hurt myself or anyone else."

Denizen thought about his Dawn—the anger, the pain.

"Your granddad sounds nice," he said.

Darcie smiled. "He was. I used to hear the best bedtime stories—they're always better when you know the monsters are real. I remember Mum being so annoyed when she found out he was telling me about daring rooftop sword fights and dueling Tenebrous in dark caves. Called it brainwashing."

Her smile faded. "He died last summer."

"I'm sorry," Denizen said. It seemed a pathetically small thing to say.

"It's all right," Darcie said. "He died serving the Order. It's what he would have wanted."

There wasn't a hint of hesitation in her voice, as if she knew for certain that *was* what he had wanted. Denizen, who had never been certain about anything in his life, found that at once comforting and very strange.

Chips finished, they wandered through the city. After eleven years of living in the middle of nowhere, the hustle and bustle of so many people was almost overwhelming.

He would have been totally lost if not for Darcie. She talked constantly as they wandered—pointing out her favorite cafés, or interesting shops, or little bits of history about the buildings they passed. She seemed to know a small fact about every corner and alley, as if there was a shifting map of stories in her head.

They tagged along with a tour group walking through Trinity College, Darcie whispering a commentary on the guide's commentary until a sharp look made them dissolve into giggles and bolt.

Everywhere Denizen looked there was something new. Buskers serenaded them in Temple Bar. Clots of other teenagers dressed as Goths whooped and screamed outside Central Bank. Men painted like brass on Grafton Street nodded majestically at the people who threw them coins.

He bought a birthday card for Simon at a newsstand. So much had happened in the last few days, and he wished he could just sit down with his best friend and let it all spill out.

Thinking of Simon led to him telling Darcie about Crosscaper and his childhood. It was strange to describe the place to her now, to bring stories about Simon and the others to this place a country's width away.

He thought about the day he left—his plans to pry information out of this absentee aunt. They seemed ridiculous now. It had taken him five minutes to realize that if you wanted to pry anything out of Vivian Hardwick, you'd need a ten-man team and a diamond-tipped crowbar.

It wasn't long before the conversation turned to his parents, as he knew it would.

"Do you remember anything about them?" Darcie asked. "I'd understand if you don't want to talk—"

"It's OK," Denizen said, "and no, I don't remember a whole lot. There's just one memory, really. I remember her being small. Leaning down to pick me up." There was a lump in his throat. "She smelled like strawberries."

Darcie sighed. "I am so sorry, Denizen."

He shook his head furiously. "Please. Don't. I'm—I'm fine."

The sky had darkened, and their breath frosted the air in streamers of white and silver. Street lights glowed golden but gave the night no warmth.

They walked home in silence.

DENIZEN WAS IN his room after dinner, trying to think of what to put in his card to Simon, when Darcie knocked on his door, a bag in her hand.

She looked down at the card on the desk in front of him. "I'm not interrupting, am I?"

Denizen shook his head. "No. I wasn't writing anything anyway."

She smiled wryly. "Writer's block?"

He played with the top of his pen. "I just don't know what to say. Simon's my best friend. Not telling him all this stuff just feels . . . I don't know."

Darcie opened her mouth, but he waved his hand. "I know I can't tell him anything. Even if I could, he'd reckon I was mental. I don't even think he'd believe me if I told him face to face, let alone if I tried to scribble it into the corner of a birthday card."

That wasn't strictly true. Simon would believe whatever he said. That's what being a best friend meant. But it didn't matter. Denizen knew he couldn't say anything.

"What's up?" he said.

"I need your help with something," Darcie said. She seemed faintly embarrassed. "Do you mind?"

"Not at all," Denizen said. "What do you want me to do?"

They made their way through dim hallways, their path lit by flickering candles. It hadn't taken Denizen long to notice there was something peculiar about Seraphim Row—the building itself, not just the people who made it their home.

"Did you hear that?" Denizen said as they climbed a curving staircase. He stopped and stared down at the steps beneath his feet. "I thought I . . ."

He almost didn't want to say it. The line between *believable* and *unbelievable* had become porous, and every question he asked seemed to blur it further, but Denizen had been . . . hearing things.

He took another experimental step. *There it is again.* Darcie had stopped a few steps up, looking down at him.

He had been noticing it more and more recently. It wasn't enough that Seraphim Row *looked* like a haunted house; it seemingly had to go for the full effect. Sometimes Denizen would feel someone standing behind him, but every time he turned round there was no one there.

Sometimes floorboards would creak around him, even though nobody was walking on them. He'd hear footsteps from an empty corridor. Doors would slam when no one touched them. There were inexplicable patches of freezing air.

Now it felt as if someone was walking in his shadow, their footsteps almost but not quite mirroring his. Not an echo. A bad overlap. He said as much to Darcie.

"*Overlap* isn't a bad word for it, actually," Darcie said, adjusting her glasses. Her voice softened to what Denizen had already begun thinking of as her explanatory tone. "You've noticed the candles, of course. Has anyone explained why we light them?"

Denizen shrugged. "Grey said he'd miss colors."

Darcie smiled. "Of course he did, the poet, but there are other reasons. The wall between this world and the Tenebrae is never particularly stable." She thought for a moment. "Um. *Wall* is the wrong word. I'm not sure there is a right word. It's not . . . deep enough, or big enough; it just doesn't have the—"

She caught the look on Denizen's face and hastily cleared her throat. "Sorry. I get distracted. And there are dozens of books in my . . . in *the* library about what exactly causes a Breach, but we do know that in some places the worlds run close. That's why you get stories of haunted houses and castles and whatnot."

She waved a hand at Seraphim Row's walls.

"So many Knights here for so many centuries have frayed that barrier. Made things a little strained, like a dam worn thin by the passage of water. The candle-wards act as anchors or stones in a castle wall. They keep the Tenebrae out and reality in, protecting us from any Tenebrous that might try and attack us here."

"Right," Denizen said. "I thought the place was actually haunted or something."

"Oh, not at all," Darcie said brightly. "It's just in constant danger of falling into the dark end of the universe."

She frowned. "That's not better, is it?"

Denizen stepped very carefully round the candles for the rest of the climb. Eventually, they reached a narrow iron staircase, which led to a small windowless room. There were no candles here, but Denizen and Darcie both navigated the darkness easily.

It felt strange moving without any light. Denizen *knew* it was dark. He knew that before his thirteenth birthday he would have been blind and flailing. Now the darkness was just another detail of the room, as relevant as the number of floorboards or where the wallpaper was starting to peel.

Darcie set the bag down in the middle of the room.

"Do you know why we went into the city today?" Her voice sounded strange, and it took Denizen a moment to figure out why.

It was easy to forget sometimes that Grey, with his easy wit and constant smile, was a trained warrior. Jack was the same, even if he did look like he'd been built in a shipyard. You couldn't forget that with D'Aubigny—the violence ran closer to the surface with her. And as for his aunt . . . it was as if she'd forgotten to be anything other than a soldier.

But Darcie, with her prim accent, and her proper manners, and the shy way she smiled . . .

This was the first time Denizen had heard her speak like a Knight.

"No," he said. "I thought . . ." *I thought it was a gesture of friendship. We're the youngest people here. I thought you were being nice. I really hope you're not going to tell me that was work.*

Darcie knelt and opened the bag. It looked like a doctor's satchel, probably older than Denizen—thick black leather and a stained brass clasp. She spoke without looking up.

"Did Grey tell you what I do here?"

"He said you were their librarian?"

She smiled. "Yes. Librarian and record keeper. But that's not the most important work I do. We all have our gifts—our different ways of serving the Order. I serve by detecting Breaches before they happen. The other Knights are weapons, and I tell the weapons where to go."

Taking a deep breath, Darcie removed her dark glasses.

"Oh," said Denizen. "Oh. Of cour—"

The words escaped before he had a chance to swallow them, swiftly followed by a blush the temperature and shade of the surface of the sun. His cheeks burned.

"It does make sense," Darcie said as though she hadn't heard him, "when you think about it. There's a strange logic to the Cost."

She looked at him with iron eyes.

"They call us the *Lux Precognitae*. Loosely translated, it means 'Forewarning Light.'"

Darcie's pupils were the deepest black Denizen had ever seen, even in the colorless hues of the *Lucidum.* There were pale flecks amid the dark metal of her irises, as if silver had been mixed in through the iron.

"It is the rarest type of talent. Most cadres have to make do with other means of detecting Breaches." She turned her glasses over and over in her hands. "I can still see. Perfectly, actually. Better than when my eyes were normal, I think, though it's hard to be sure."

"Darcie?"

"Yes?"

"Why iron?" It had been bothering him since he arrived in Seraphim Row—since that first bloom of darkness in the middle of his palm.

Darcie smiled faintly. "That's a difficult question. Knights have written books on the subject. We're not all warriors, you know—somebody has to compile and record all the information that has been amassed over the years.

"Some of the Order's scholars think that it's scar tissue. The Cants, the Tenebrous—they don't fit in this universe. You've seen what it's like when something crosses over. The whole world rebels. Maybe the Cost is the world trying to repair itself—sealing off those that bring the power of the Tenebrae into this reality."

Denizen frowned. Like everything the Knights

believed about their gift, it was unproved knowledge, half guesswork and poetry.

"OK . . . but why iron? Why not something else?"

Darcie gave an elegant shrug. "I don't know. Jack says—and he's a blacksmith, so more superstitious than most—that maybe it's because the core of the world is iron. Iron is the most *here* thing there is."

Denizen ran a finger across the cool metal of his palm. "What do you need me to do?"

"I come up here every night—get Jack or Grey to sit with me—but I thought that you might like to . . ."

"Yes," Denizen said instantly. "I'm glad . . . glad you asked me."

Darcie sat on the floor and bid Denizen do the same.

Her bag opened with a click, and she pulled out a sheaf of paper and several pencils. The pencils were arranged in a neat line in front of her, and the pages went into Denizen's lap. Darcie balanced a drawing board across her lap, and Denizen passed her a page.

What Darcie whispered next was nothing like the raw avalanche of heat and sound that Grey had called Sunrise, nor the first feeble stutters of light that would be Denizen's first Cants. It was subtle, the barest stirrings of power.

Light glowed from behind her eyes, gleamed behind her teeth. The darkness shivered with it. Subtle didn't mean *weak,* Denizen realized, and the power Darcie was calling was in its own way as potent as anything that Grey or Vivian might use in battle.

Darcie closed her eyes and continued to whisper. Denizen could still see the light in her eyes, even with them closed. It shone through her eyelids like a backlit projector screen.

He felt a wind on his face. He flinched—*the door's closed; there are no windows*—and the feeling of unease grew when he realized that the wind was warm.

It's October. This wind wasn't blowing from outside but from somewhere else entirely. Sweat rose on his cheeks. He raised a hand to wipe it off.

"Stay still," Darcie said. Her eyes hadn't opened. Denizen froze—he was sure he hadn't made a sound. It was only then that he realized that, even though she had stopped speaking the Cant, he could still hear it. The room was too small for an echo; the Cant had simply stayed in the air after Darcie had fallen silent.

She exhaled raggedly. "Well," she said, "that was the easy part."

The words still bounced round the room. It made Denizen's skin crawl. He could *feel* the Tenebrae boil up through the room, like the walls were falling away and they were surrounded by a vast emptiness, as if they no longer sat in Seraphim Row at all.

Denizen was almost afraid to blink. The wind grew and grew until his face burned with it. The Cant was all around—a thousand voices all whispering, shivering from everywhere at once. The air shook with them, building and building and building—

"Now," whispered Darcie. "Now."

Silence fell, the lack of noise suddenly deafening. Darcie raised her face to the ceiling, light pulsing from beneath long lashes, and lifted a pencil. Slowly, eyes still closed, she began to draw.

IT TOOK THREE hours.

The pencil tip darted this way and that, pulling shapes from the whiteness of the paper—arcs and curves that made no sense until the pencil slashed again and Denizen suddenly saw how they were connected, how they had always been connected, only needing Darcie's skill to bring them out.

She went through eight sheets. When the white space on one was filled, Denizen would hand her another.

Eventually, she sat back, the light behind her eyes fading away. Darcie set down the pencil—she'd gone through two—and waved at Denizen to help her up.

It took him two tries to get to his feet—his knees were aching after hours of sitting on the bare floorboards. Joints popped as Darcie stretched, perspiration shining on her face. Carefully, she set her glasses back on her nose.

"Thank you," she said awkwardly. "I hope it wasn't too boring—I just like having company. What I do can be . . . intense. It unnerves some people. Even Knights sometimes. So thank you. It was nice to hang out today before—"

Impulsively, Denizen wrapped her in a hug.

"Oh," she said in a muffled voice, "brilliant."

They broke apart and Denizen handed her the bag. "So what now?" he said.

"Now we go and get Grey and the others," she said, her smile faltering. "I found something."

13

Night Vision

Up until then, Denizen had never realized how much the Knights were coddling him.

They'd never lied to him about the dangers of serving the Order, but whenever they'd spoken about their duty, there'd been a sort of theater about it as well.

Jack talked about being a Knight like a craftsman discussing a job—difficult but necessary. D'Aubigny did the same, in her own terrifying way. *Pest control.*

Grey was the worst offender, grinning as he peppered their lessons with stories of daring rescues and wild adventures.

He wasn't smiling now.

The black of Grey's shoulder holster stood out starkly against the crisp white of his shirt. His sword hung at his waist. D'Aubigny sat cross-legged on the kitchen table, running a whetstone up her katana's murderous curve. The slow rasp sounded like a snake clearing its throat.

"It's local," Darcie said. "We were lucky." She sat on the carpet, paper surrounding her like the petals of a flower. Each sheet was covered in dozens of pictures, crammed so close they bled together. Some appeared more often than others. Denizen saw a hurried sketch that might have been an aerial view of fields, all tightly packed squares and rectangles, fences and roads a tangle of shaded lines.

There were more drawings of what might have been the same landscape, but depicted as if Darcie stood within it—looking up at squat houses on hillsides, the blunt sweep of a hedge—and beside those a woman's eye so detailed that Denizen could almost see a reflection in the pupil's depths.

The scene that appeared most often, the lines drawn blackest and most urgent, was a crossroads, one road forking to become three around a massive outcrop of stone. There Darcie's pencil had nearly gone through the page.

"How do you know it's local?" Denizen asked.

"The art of the *Lux Precognitae* isn't a precise one," Grey said, frowning down at the sheets. "Images and impressions present themselves, but it's like trying to read a reflection in a rippling pond. Sometimes we catch a break and Darcie picks up something solid—a street sign, a landmark—but if we're unlucky, the process can take hours. Thank God we have her."

Darcie looked away, but not before Denizen saw her blush. "Yes. Well. We were very lucky. I should have caught it before now, but it's only an hour away, so you should be in time.

"I should have caught it before now," she repeated, almost to herself.

Denizen hovered awkwardly by the table. He was feeling the special kind of uselessness that comes from standing in a room full of busy people. The amount of edged weaponry moving around didn't help. Even as he had the thought, Jack tossed a bent-bladed knife to Grey, almost giving Denizen his first shave.

"That will hamper your mobility," D'Aubigny said as Grey slid on a long black coat. It hung to his calves, hiding the scabbard on his belt. She wore a light T-shirt and combat trousers, tattoos writhing as she worked a strap through the sheath of her sword.

"It's called discretion," he said good-naturedly, "and I'd rather have my mobility hampered than look like a one-man invasion force."

D'Aubigny, who was now weighing a sickle in one hand and a long dagger in the other, frowned and put both down.

"It'd take more than a coat to stop her looking like

an invasion force," Jack said affectionately, and then grinned when D'Aubigny gave him a look.

"Em . . . ," Denizen began, stepping forward. No one looked up. "Is there anything I can do?"

Darcie was poring over the pictures she had drawn, Grey comparing them to an Ordnance Survey map in his hands. D'Aubigny and Jack were lost in quiet conversation.

Denizen felt a new frown coming on. No. 24—the Frown of Being Spare. He couldn't decide whether it was worse than being in the way or not. The Knights were working as if they'd done this a hundred times before—which, of course, they had. It wasn't their fault he was feeling utterly useless.

"Hold this," D'Aubigny said, dropping a satchel into his hands and slinging her blade over her shoulder. As one, the Knights made for the door and Denizen followed, carrying the satchel.

Jack's voice was grim. "Darcie, anything else you can tell them before they go?"

"I'm afraid not," she said. "Normally, I see *something*. The only times I don't are when the Tenebrous coming through are weak, barely anything at all. Maybe that's why I didn't feel it before now—"

Grey didn't seem to hear the worry in her voice, already turning toward the great wooden doors that led out to the street.

"Hear that?" he said. "Barely a thing at all. And we have time to get there, don't we?"

Darcie nodded reluctantly.

"Then let's not panic," he said. "It's local, it's weak, and it's a nice night for a sword fight. I have a good feeling about this."

"Can I come?"

Slowly, very slowly, everyone turned to stare at Denizen. He blushed.

"I mean . . . can I come? With you? If you think . . . em . . . em . . ."

Denizen was used to expressions saying volumes. He had twenty-four frowns. The Knights didn't say a word, but what they were thinking was perfectly clear: *Are you insane?*

And as his question died in the wake of their shock, he suddenly couldn't help agreeing with them. *Am I insane?* He had just volunteered. *Volunteered.* He had asked to go into battle against a ravening beast from a realm of shadow nightmares. Maybe it was several ravening beasts. He had been too busy *volunteering* to ask.

And why? It wasn't excitement. He hadn't suddenly remembered a childhood spent learning kung fu. It was because—and he hated himself for thinking this—maybe his aunt was waiting for him to impress her. He had been born with the potential to be a Knight, but perhaps that wasn't enough. Maybe he had to show her that he was brave enough to be one as well.

"That," D'Aubigny said, "is a terrible idea."

"It's not a safari," Jack said.

"Hmmm," Grey said, "I don't know."

"Don't know what?" Darcie said incredulously. "Grey, tell me you're not considering this."

"It wouldn't be the kid's first Breach," Grey said, flashing Denizen an encouraging smile. "And he didn't let the side down that time. If he wants to see if he's up for the job, show him the job. Besides, you brought Abigail on that Breach last week—"

"Yes," Jack said, "but Abigail's—" He suddenly caught Denizen's eye and coughed. "That was different."

"Different?" Denizen said, anger creeping into his voice before he managed to smooth it away. If he annoyed them, he'd never be allowed to come along. Logical arguments were the answer. That was what worked with teachers. Being *reasonable.*

"Darcie said it's a small one," he said, a note of pleading in his tone.

"Well, I'm not—" Darcie began.

"He will have to do it sooner or later," D'Aubigny said thoughtfully.

"If he chooses to stay," Jack said. "And he hasn't. Not yet."

That made Denizen blush harder. These people had spent their whole lives being Knights. They'd prepared for battle without blinking an eye, and here he was, talking about *choosing*. Walking away and leaving them to it. No wonder his aunt wasn't giving him the time of day.

"I'll stay at the back," he said. "I promise."

"At the back?" Darcie said incredulously. "It's not *chess*. And I don't fancy finding out what the Malleus thinks of us bringing her nephew back to her in a body bag. Or several body bags. He's young. He's untrained."

Denizen was surprised at the venom in her voice, but then he realized how difficult it must be, sitting here in Seraphim Row and sending other people into danger. She had been waiting for Grey on the steps the night Denizen arrived. How many other nights had she sat there, not knowing if her comrades would be coming home?

Grey frowned at Denizen. "Are you sure you want to do this?"

The panic in his stomach had vanished, replaced by an electric sort of excitement. Was this how it felt to go into battle?

He let out a deep breath. "Yeah. I am."

"If he so much as catches a cold, the Malleus will melt you both down and use you as scrap," Jack said. "Corinne?"

D'Aubigny shrugged. "I will bring him back."

They stared at each other for a long moment. Denizen looked away.

Grey pulled the knife Jack had given him out from under his coat and held the hilt to Denizen. It was old—the handle yellowed bone wrapped in leather, the sheath ancient wood lacquered black.

"You won't need this," he said, "but keep it on hand." His eyes met Denizen's. "Now what are you doing?"

"I am staying at the back," Denizen said dutifully.

"That you are. And if one of us says 'Run,' you *run*. I mean it."

He let his stare linger a moment longer and then winked. Denizen couldn't help smiling, even as Darcie shot them both a disapproving look. She came down the stairs toward Grey and handed him the sheets of paper.

"Good luck, Grey."

He grinned like a little boy. "Ha. Yes. Thank you, dear."

He gave the sheets one more look before shoving them into a pocket and reaching for the door. The night beyond was still, curls of tree-choked light trying and failing to push back the dark. The night's chill eagerly swept inward, and Denizen's breath smoked in the air.

D'Aubigny joined him to stand before the darkness. Grey glanced at her, then back at Fuller Jack standing on the stairs. Maybe other cadres gave rousing speeches before battles. Maybe they swore oaths and rattled their blades at the sky. Denizen didn't know. Grey just sighed. "One more time, then?"

It had the ring of a familiar phrase, an inside joke. Jack nodded at him. "Sure. If not us . . ."

D'Aubigny's smile was faint. "Who else?"

She and Grey vanished into the black. Denizen took a deep breath and stepped after them.

14

Pieces

THEY DROVE IN silence.

Denizen sat awkwardly in the backseat with two swords across his lap as the Interceptor traded amber-lit streets for country roads.

Grey drove, his fingers tapping out a restless tattoo on the wheel. His hair had been scraped back from his face, leaving his cheekbones stark and bare, scar lines of silver on white. D'Aubigny sat beside him, a knee against the dashboard, staring out into the dark. Street lights spun occasional light across them, like the dappling of a tiger through undergrowth.

"Is it far?" Denizen asked.

Grey shook his head. "We should be close. We're lucky it's within driving distance and we have a head start."

"Oh yeah, obviously," Denizen said, and then smiled

awkwardly. "I would have thought you guys could just . . . I don't know . . . teleport there."

"We can," D'Aubigny replied.

"But we don't," Grey said.

"Ah," Denizen said. "Right." He waited for more of an explanation, but neither D'Aubigny nor Grey seemed prepared to offer one.

Was this one more secret that Vivian had ordered them to keep? Apparently, she had decided he was some kind of security risk.

Denizen despised the idea of someone else deciding he wasn't fit to know something. If he was going to make the life-changing—the phrase *life-shortening* presented itself, but he shoved it down—decision to be a Knight, then shouldn't he be in possession of all the information?

Besides, who was she to judge him? She didn't know the first thing about him.

Even if he didn't choose to become a Knight, the damage was done. He *knew* that the Order existed. He was in on the big secret. He'd have a constant reminder of it in his palm for the rest of his life. What was the harm in letting him learn a bit more?

A disturbing thought crossed Denizen's mind. Maybe there were things that she didn't want him to see.

A sign swept by them in a blur of reflected green, artificial against the frozen, tree-haunted dark.

"Nearly there," Grey said.

Had Grey not announced their arrival, Denizen might have missed the village altogether. Little more than two streets lined with small, squat houses, it seemed barely big enough to deserve a name. Maybe that was why the name was emblazoned everywhere Denizen looked.

The Rathláth florist tried desperately to compete with the extravagant waterfalls of plastic flowers hanging from the baskets outside the Rathláth Inn. One house had a banner stretched across it, thanking "our boys in gray" for their "hard work in the Championship," which seemed to Denizen very carefully worded to avoid the words *won* or *lost*. Another simply had *Rathláth* mowed into its lawn, as though there was nothing more to be said. The whole scene had the glassy, unmoving perfection of a postcard.

The Interceptor growled to a halt, the only car on a deserted street. Somewhere in the distance was the screech of tires, the briefest flash of headlights over the hedges. Someone seemed to be in a great hurry to be elsewhere.

Denizen felt it too—a sudden pinch behind his eyes, a queasiness in his stomach as if he had smelled something rotten. No, not rotten. *Alien*. Something his body didn't know how to accept.

There was a strange, headachey pressure to the air.

The Knights donned their weapons with chill efficiency and began walking up the street. Grey had hidden his beneath his long coat, but D'Aubigny brazenly carried her blade in its scabbard. The feeling worsened—like fingertips on the skin, pressing hard, just the other side of pain. The quaintness of Rathláth became something forced and strange, like a familiar smile with too many teeth.

Grey and D'Aubigny stalked down the street, their eyes closed as if listening for a sound only they could hear. After a moment, Denizen followed.

He glanced at the houses as they passed. Doors were locked. Window shutters were closed and blinds pulled down. A church rose on the dark end of the street before them, its spire wounding the sky.

Denizen didn't need to ask where everybody was. The sick taste of a Breach was in the air, seeping into everything. At least Denizen knew what the feeling was and where it came from. How much worse would it be if you didn't? How many families were at home hugging each other, feeling fear they couldn't explain? How many children were having bad dreams?

Wind rasped along his skin like a tongue. Somewhere a dog wailed, long and high and afraid.

"It's this way," D'Aubigny said, pointing ahead to where the street lights had petered out. "Maybe . . ." She turned her head this way and that, her hand held up before her. It might have looked silly if it were anyone else. "A kilometer or so. We should hurry."

Her pale features creased in a frown. "It shouldn't . . ."

"What?" Denizen asked.

Grey was grimacing in the exact same way. "Darcie said it was a weak Breach. It shouldn't feel this"—he rubbed his temples—"violent. This intense."

Denizen's fingers ached round the hilt of the knife.

They walked out into the night, leaving the village behind until it was nothing more than an isolated glow, the sky above sick with clouds. In the silvered shades of the *Intueor Lucidum,* each curling branch and blade of grass in the hedgerows was sketched perfectly as if by the killing hand of frost.

When they found a crossroads—marked by a great outcrop of stone, like someone had flung a crude ax down to split the road in two—Grey didn't need to tell Denizen that they had reached the site of the imminent Breach. It was exactly what Darcie had drawn back in Seraphim Row.

Grey was checking his phone, sword bare in his other hand. "Fourteen minutes. Ish."

"What do we do until then?" Denizen asked. Grey shrugged.

The next quarter of an hour was the longest of Denizen's life. He'd read once that the worst part of war wasn't the fighting, but the waiting around for it to start. He now understood what that meant—a strange feeling of helplessness as each second ticked away.

He wanted to talk, ease the tension, but at the same time he didn't want to disturb the others—not when they would be doing the real work. What Grey had said kept running through his mind. *It shouldn't feel this . . . intense.*

What was coming?

D'Aubigny had begun running through blade exercises where the road split, the point of her sword slicing through the air like an oar through water. Grey just stared into space as if he'd been switched off. It was like all his jokes and charm were a mask that could be folded away at any moment.

The more time Denizen spent with the Knights, the more he noticed that their experience as soldiers had stained them—a haunted look around the eyes, a tremor in the jaw. It was like they could never fully relax, even in the safety of Seraphim Row, their eyes following every shadow, every movement in the dark. They all had it to some degree, though the hollowness seemed to pass from Fuller Jack and D'Aubigny when they were together. He'd even seen it in Darcie tonight as she sent her friends into danger.

Grey had it worst of all. The man was scarred and not just physically. There was something beaten and raw about him, an exposed weakness that only came out when he didn't think anyone was looking or when he spoke about his past.

People did that—buried their weakness and fear behind high walls. Denizen had seen it a lot in Crosscaper. If he was being honest, he saw it in the mirror.

And then Grey caught Denizen looking at him. "Feel that?" he said. "Not long now."

Denizen shivered. Those invisible fingers against his skin had sharpened to needling claws. He was finding it hard to breathe, willing the Breach to happen just to stop this weight on the world. Tenebraic power twitched in his chest. He fought the urge to fill himself with its light.

"Steady," Grey said, glancing at him. "I know it's hard."

The clouds above seemed to shift—colors bleeding into each other as if the world were a television with the settings distorted. Nauseated, Denizen dropped his gaze from the sky and saw a discarded doll by the side of the road.

The randomness of it fascinated him. Had someone thrown it from a car? Did it belong to one of the houses on the hill? It hugged the rigid grass as if unhappy to be forgotten.

Denizen stared at its frozen smile. It was just a faded little thing in a handmade dress. He reached out to it.

Just a little thing.

The moment stretched. His hand seemed to move in slow motion.

Just a—

The pressure broke.

He never saw the first Tenebrous die, just the throwing blade that killed it. The shard of steel seemed to grace D'Aubigny's hand for the briefest of moments before slicing the night apart.

A second Tenebrous bounded from the undergrowth, roaring like a chainsaw blade on bone. A third pulled itself out of raw darkness, flanks heaving with murderous intent.

Well, that answers the "how many ravening beasts" question, Denizen thought numbly.

They looked like cats, in the same way the very first Tenebrous he had seen looked like an angel. Their bodies were gravel and dirt, studded with other rubbish that had been swept up as well: half a pizza box rose at an angle from one's heaving flank; another's mouth was a mass of nails and steel shavings. Puddles of black ink formed their eyes, their limbs too long and thin, their heads so heavy their whole bodies staggered under the weight.

Not-cats, Denizen thought. Something real made ugly and fake.

"I hate cats," D'Aubigny said coolly. "Come on and die."

The not-cats cocked their misshapen heads, speaking in a single rasping voice.

Pick-Up-the-Pieces.

And a fourth not-cat hit D'Aubigny from behind.

She rolled, whipping her blade in a return strike that took off its front leg and split its skull into a shower of dust. The other two took advantage of the distraction to lunge at Grey, and he barely beat them back—a slash across the snout scattering steel shavings, beating a howl from maddened jaws.

The Knights whirled, keeping Denizen behind them, their eyes wide with fire. Etchings on D'Aubigny's and Grey's blades began to glow, the spoken steel feeding on the power underneath their skin.

The not-cats paced back and forth just out of reach of the light of their blades. Dirt shivered as if molded by invisible hands, and the two feline shapes that D'Aubigny had slain began to pull themselves back together, limbs and flanks rebuilding themselves from the dust. Their mouths opened wide to snarl.

Grey was back to back with D'Aubigny, blade in a guard position. "Darcie said this wasn't a—"

"Darcie was *wrong,*" D'Aubigny hissed, and slid a blade into her free hand.

The not-cats howled.

Pick-Up-the-Pieces. Pick-Up-the-Pieces. The Tenebrous's voice sounded like a blender full of nails and motor oil.

Pick-Up-the-Pieces hunts in the name of the King. The not-cats bared their teeth in mouths of dirt. ***Where is it?***

"Do you have any idea what it's talking about?" Grey said out of the side of his mouth. D'Aubigny shook her head.

Thieving fools, the voice snarled. ***Tempting the wrath of That-Which-Is-Endless. The shadows will boil and drown you. The King will come in darkness. Snap your lives. End you all.***

The not-cats shook with rage, dust drizzling from their flanks. Grey's head darted this way and that, trying to keep them all in view.

The Tenebrous's voice rose to a howl.

You will give it back!

They leapt.

The world was suddenly full of bodies fighting for their lives, sand and rubbish and howling mouths, and in the middle of it all Grey and D'Aubigny—blades and eyes blazing with light.

The not-cats feinted and lunged, trying to separate the Knights, pull them off balance so others could drag them down. That, more than anything, frightened Denizen. The beast was using strategy. One mind in four bodies, and it was *clever,* nothing like the dumb creature that had attacked Denizen on his birthday. Worse, its ploy was working. Blood already darkened D'Aubigny's upper arm, and Grey's face was slick with sweat.

Denizen's hand was sweaty on the hilt of his

borrowed knife. He wanted to do something, he *did,* but it would have been suicide. The Knights were locked in such an intricate dance of blades—a half-second by half-second battle for life and death—that Denizen throwing himself in there would likely kill all three of them.

How did one even jump into a fight like that? It was easy for someone like Jack—the man was half ocean liner. If Denizen charged in, he'd bounce off.

There was a growl from behind him.

Denizen turned without thinking to see a wind howl down the road in a storm of dirt that was cat-shaped before it hit the ground. He had a long, awful moment to watch its pounce—the coil and release of its muscles, mud avalanching from its flanks, the crooked slant of its spine. This one's left eye was a brass coin swept up in the wake of the wind; its right, a mad swirl of black.

Denizen lifted his knife in a shaking hand. *Beginner's luck. That's a thing, right?*

The beast gathered itself to leap and met a white-gold bolt coming the other way. Denizen flinched back as the Tenebrous came apart in a shower of cinders and grit.

Grey had already turned back to the fight, light still leaking from one hand.

"Run," he panted. "Back to the car."

"But—"

"It's us they want," he said. "Go. *Now.*"

Denizen ran.

It's an order, he told himself, *and I promised I'd obey.* His stomach was sick with relief. And shame.

Trees whipped by him, their gaunt frames like closing fingers, the shadows between them knots of sinister black. The pressure seemed to be fading, the effects of the Breach drawing back like the world was slowly repairing itself.

Feet echoing on the pavement, Denizen ran back the way he'd come—silently grateful that, for all the twists and loops in the country road, it was still basically a straight line. The idea of being lost in a maze of byroads with the night full of Tenebrous did not appeal to him at all.

Somewhere behind him, a not-cat let out a furious, agonized scream.

They'll be all right. They're warriors. This is what they do.

It didn't sound very convincing, even in the privacy of his mind.

I'd be in the way.

The lights of the village appeared ahead, a false dawn beckoning hope.

Now they don't have to worry about me—

There was a woman standing in the middle of the street.

The Breach still infected the street lights, curbing their luminescence to firefly glimmers trapped in glass. Her shadow arched across the road, huge and gaunt and close enough to touch.

"Hello," Denizen said awkwardly. It was all he could think of to say.

White lips curved in a smile.

15

Run

"Hello," Denizen repeated, feeling a little silly. "Are you . . ."

He trailed off as he took in the woman's blank smile, the way she stood with one shoulder higher than the other, her whole body stooped as if held up by the pinch of a thumb and forefinger. She didn't seem to understand what he had said.

". . . all right?"

The woman didn't respond, hands digging in the pockets of her white overcoat. Eventually, she pulled out a loose cigarette and jammed it in the fold of her smirk. It hung there, unlit.

Horror curled its way through Denizen's gut. *Was this what Breaches did to normal people?*

The woman looked like she wasn't quite there, as if something essential had been taken from her. Her hair was a ragged white cascade framing thin cheekbones and colorless lips. There was something familiar about her, but he couldn't put his finger on it, and familiarity was supposed to be reassuring, wasn't it?

The woman took a staggering step forward, cigarette bobbing in the air.

He couldn't just leave her. She was the first person he'd seen—he should help her, get her somewhere safe. It wasn't exactly fighting a Tenebrous, but it was the right thing to do.

"Miss? Miss, why don't you come with me? I know some people who might be able to help you."

It was only then he realized he was still holding the bent-bladed knife Grey had given him. Cursing inwardly, he fumbled it back into its sheath.

"Miss?"

The woman raised her head in a series of slow jerks, and Denizen suddenly realized he'd made a huge mistake.

It was her eyes. They were bright, and pale, and normal—or at least a fiend's guess at what normal should be. Grey's words from the park suddenly came back to him.

They look . . . wrong, even the really old ones that try to pass as human. It's the little things. The face. The eyes.

She hadn't done a terrible job, at least as far as Denizen could see. All the bits were there. Irises, eyelids, whites—any doll maker would be proud. It's not like there was a way to fake the things that actually made an eye *human,* like love or pity or hope.

The cigarette fell away as the woman's jaw clacked open, baring a hollow filled with a mass of delicate clockwork—a tunnel of cogs and gears and spindle wheels, all wet and shining with a Tenebrous's oily black.

Her howl made the ground vibrate and far-off windows shatter. The echoes took a very long time to die away.

"Oh," said Denizen in a small voice, "right."

Denizen Hardwick might not have been a warrior like D'Aubigny or a commander of Knights like his aunt, but no one could accuse him of being stupid.

He didn't turn round and run back the way he came—it was doubtful the Order gave medals to Neophytes who brought reinforcements to the *other* side—but instead bolted to the left, flinging himself between two expertly coiffed bushes and onto the lawn beyond.

He didn't look back. He didn't dare.

Ahead was a sprawling estate, row upon row of identical redbrick houses with identical peaked roofs, like a flock of cardinals bedded down for the night. Each road was adorned with a neat little sign—Rathláth Terrace becoming Rathláth Way, Avenue to Park to Green—in a halfhearted attempt to provide individuality, but there were no cars and no lights in the windows. The whole estate had the feel of a cloning facility during a power outage.

Denizen didn't care. The houses could have been on fire, for all he noticed—he just ran. No thought. No planning. No destination in mind except *away from here.*

Away from her.

The woman in white wailed again somewhere behind and Denizen ran as if all of Hell was following him.

Maybe it was. What else had eyes like that?

Turning a corner, Denizen nearly fell, cursing through gritted teeth. The woman's footsteps rang out behind him—arrhythmic, as if she never possessed quite the same number of legs between one step and the next.

Each house had its backyard separated from the street by a wall of red brick, set with a wooden door. The doors were probably locked, but maybe he could scale the wall, lose the Tenebrous woman in the honeycomb maze of back gardens. It was a long shot, but it was that or try to outpace her, and he had a feeling that clockwork beat flesh every time. He just needed to hang on until Grey and D'Aubigny came looking for him.

Hope lit a fire in his stomach. Two of the scariest people he had ever met and *they were on his side.* Of course they would rescue him. There was probably some Cant that located wayward, exhausted Neophytes. They'd find him and save him and he was *not* being delusional, and crazy clockwork people would be swatted like flies.

Behind him, the woman howled.

Howl all you want, he thought breathlessly. *See how you stand against two full Knights of the Borrowed Dark.*

He flung himself against the wall, heaving himself up and over with muscles fueled by equal parts hope and terror. The garden beyond, streaky and distorted through red flashes of exhaustion, might not be a sanctuary, but it was a start.

Denizen allowed himself a tight, vicious smile—which promptly vanished when he dropped from the wall and landed on someone's head.

Together, physics, awkwardness, and unexpected heads in gardens conspired to give Denizen's landing all the grace of a wheelbarrow full of rocks. He rolled once, banging his head on something so hard a whole galaxy erupted behind his eyes, and ended up facing back the way he'd come.

Thoughts returned slowly. There was . . . something. Something he was supposed to be doing. A distant part of him was screaming *run run run,* but his brain seemed to have shorted out from sheer embarrassment.

And there was a little girl staring at him.

She was blond, cherubic, wearing an oversized

T-shirt and a pair of pajama bottoms. A doll lay at her feet, probably dropped when Denizen had landed on her. Maybe she had left it outside earlier and was now breaking curfew to retrieve it. Maybe four-year-old girls took their dolls on late-night walks. Denizen didn't know.

He stared at her.

She stared at him.

And then, with the deliberate slowness all little children exhibit when they're not quite sure if they're hurt or not, she threw back her head and started crying.

"No, no, no, no, no," Denizen said, scrambling to his feet. Memories were crashing back, his embarrassment replaced by a nuclear desire to be elsewhere. "There, there. Come on, we have to go. We have to go now."

Running was a sport that suited Denizen. It was the *only* sport that suited Denizen. He was small and wiry, and eleven years of eating at Crosscaper meant he was fairly underweight. Now his hard-won lead was being eaten up by a squalling kid who'd probably just wandered out to find a lost toy.

Screw it. He grabbed the child by the waist and ran.

It took him a whole three steps to completely regret that decision. Children obviously didn't understand when they were being rescued, and the little girl squirmed out of his grasp, screaming at a pitch to break glass. He tried awkwardly to pick her up again, but the child must have been part eel. She wriggled away and began to run back the way they'd come—

—and the woman in white appeared on the top of the wall, limbs kinked in arachnid grace.

The little girl froze. *Well, that shut her up,* Denizen thought, before terror overrode his natural sarcasm and he froze too.

A slow, ugly smile spread across the woman's face. She dropped to the ground—utterly alien in the domestic normality of the backyard, like a scorpion in a lunch box. Her eyes raked Denizen up and down before darting over to the little girl.

Denizen swallowed, and that little noise made the woman's eyes flick to him again. His heart nearly gave out. *Why isn't she attacking?*

Then he understood. *She can't decide.*

They talked about it in nature documentaries all the time, even the cringingly eighties VHS ones Denizen had been raised on in Crosscaper. All predators—whether they be wolves, sharks, or clockwork women in rumpled coats—were drawn to the weakest prey. It wasn't even a thought process; it was hardwired into their biology.

Nature was so *practical* sometimes. It made so much more sense to avoid the healthy and strong and zero in on a more vulnerable target. The wounded. The old. The young. To a ravening predator, a crying toddler might as well be covered in ketchup.

That, more than anything, was what held the woman back. She was thinking with her stomach. Denizen could have run for it and the woman would have been too fixated on the four-year-old to care.

But Denizen wasn't going to run.

The thought came from nowhere. It wasn't a decision, not really. The word *decision* implied he had considered doing something else.

Denizen wasn't leaving the girl behind. It wasn't because he was brave, because he wasn't. He didn't mind admitting it. There hadn't been a single moment tonight when he hadn't been scared. It wasn't even because he wanted somehow to impress his aunt. He had left that notion behind several streets ago.

He was thinking about the little girl's parents. If he ran, the little girl would disappear. She'd never be seen again; he doubted this thing, with its woman's skin and sick white smile, even left bones behind. Long after the police searches and missing-person reports had been abandoned, her parents would always wonder where their daughter had gone.

That, he realized with a start, was why the Knights did what they did.

A war with no chance of victory. Families left behind for a life of blades and fire, a few short years ending in violent death or the slow swallow of iron. And every Knight swore an oath to see it through because if they didn't, someday, somewhere, there would be a Tenebrous and a child—and nobody in between.

The woman-thing grinned, clockwork gleaming in the pit of her mouth. The little girl had stopped crying and just stared, tears staining her cheeks.

"Em," said a quiet voice. "Excuse me."

The Cants were deadly to the untutored. That was what Grey kept saying. They were only to be used in the direst of circumstances. It had taken Denizen a whole week just to master *touching* the power of the Tenebrae, and so far he hadn't even been allowed to attempt the magical equivalent of a nightlight.

Fortunately, he'd seen a real Knight at work.

Denizen let the power in. It didn't need to be asked twice, crackling off his ribs, spitting sparks up and down his throat. *Eager. Really, really eager.* It was funny, Denizen thought. All the Cants were called such fancy things—the Atraxes Girth, Charonstaff, the Scintilla Scythe—but the more powerful the Cant, the simpler its name.

The alien syllables rose in his head just as he'd heard Grey speak them—circling like ravens, buoyed up by the fire searing his throat.

Denizen didn't draw his knife. There was no point. He lunged forward, pushing the girl aside so he stood between her and the Tenebrous. The clockwork woman's fingers curled into claws—

They weren't words. That wasn't what the Cants were. They were light cresting the human tongue. They were fire bent to the hand and tamed.

Sunrise in sound.

The air blazed. A newborn star woke between Denizen's fingers to paint the surrounding buildings in black and white, the whole world made a negative of itself.

It *shrieked,* or maybe that was Denizen. Power wailed from him to toss the woman in white backward like a twist of paper caught in a breeze.

She might have screamed. It might have been the snarl of burning air. The wave of gold slapped her *through* the red brick of the wall to cross the street almost lazily before impacting like a comet into a pile of rubbish bags, which promptly ignited as well. The flames sounded like applause.

The light between his fingers ebbed and died. The night suddenly felt very dark without it.

Denizen took a deep breath. His throat felt scorched, as if he'd unwittingly sucked some smoke into his lungs. He swallowed to clear it, but that just made it worse. That was when he noticed the four-year-old staring at him, her mouth open. The air still sizzled. The tears on her cheeks had dried.

"Em . . . ," he began, but she had bolted inside, dragging the porch door open with a whine of metal and glass.

Denizen watched her go, frowning. It escaped him at the moment exactly what number frown it was.

"You're welcome," he whispered hoarsely, more for his own benefit than hers, and then flinched when a light upstairs flicked on. He should get away before the kid woke her parents. Explaining all of this to his aunt would be difficult enough.

Loping out onto the street, Denizen eyed the smoldering rubbish bags across the road with a mixture of trepidation and pride.

He'd done that. With *magic*. Just his luck there hadn't been anyone proper around to see it—

Something in the burning rubbish stirred.

Denizen took a step backward.

A raw shape lifted itself from the flames on limbs gaunt-muscled with clockwork. The flesh disguise had been seared away—the Tenebrous ticking itself upright by degrees, joints as stiff as scissor blades. A tatter of black plastic hung from its mouth like a tongue, coiling and crinkling and burning away.

"I'm sorry," Denizen said, mouth running off a script his brain hadn't quite caught up with. "Did you not hear me the first time?"

It stared at him a moment longer, then fled.

Denizen waited until the burning shape had disappeared into the darkness. Then he began walking slowly down the road.

He was suddenly very tired. He knew he should be getting away from here as fast as he could, but the events of the last few minutes were starting to catch up with him. Some of them were absolutely cringeworthy.

Did you not hear me the first time? He had said that. He'd actually said that. *Good grief.* It was only a week into his career as a magician Knight and already he was starting the one-liners. At this rate, he'd be buying bandannas before the fortnight was out.

Denizen sniffed. "Did all right, though," he said to no one. A thought struck him. "Unless there's some rule about doing magic in front of normal people." *Hmm.*

He staggered forward another few steps. *Best not find out.*

Strange, Denizen thought idly, once he'd turned the corner and left the burning rubbish behind. Blinking seemed to take longer than usual. *Grey told me there were consequences to using a Higher Cant.*

But Denizen felt fine. Some blinks just . . . took longer, didn't they? He tried again, and it was *ages* before his eyes reopened. He'd heard a song too—in the darkness just before his eyes opened. He knew that song. Someone had sung it to him a long time ago. Why couldn't he remember who?

I'll ask my mam, he thought before his eyes closed for good.

16

Where the Monsters Are

Day 13

Crosscaper had darkened.

Through broken windows and keyholes, through the hollow gape of shattered doors, came wind and cold and bitter rain. Frost gave the walls a miserable sheen, hardened the carpets to crunch underfoot.

Lights still existed—a single glowing exit sign, feeble lamps in the infirmary, a fluorescent tube in the canteen stubbornly refusing to die—but they were the last. Darkness had slid into the orphanage like a hand into a glove, filling it, warping it, giving its soul a different shape.

Simon no longer knew what day it was or even if it was day at all. Sunlight didn't enter the windows anymore, and he didn't dare peek out to see for himself. It didn't matter anyway—it was always night in

Crosscaper, and Simon had far more to worry about than the passage of time.

The boy was crying again.

Simon froze perfectly still, every sense straining. He had been halfway to the kitchen when the haunting sound reached his ears—thin and wavery, like an echo from somewhere very far away.

He picked up his pace anyway. The boy's crying might have sounded like it was coming from far away, but that was no guarantee of safety. The first thing Simon had learned about Crosscaper's occupiers was that there was a horrifying inconsistency to the trio—in the sounds they made, in how their voices echoed or carried—as if they didn't quite fit with the world, as if they horrified reality itself.

It was a reaction Simon understood perfectly.

His stockinged feet were silent on the peeling linoleum of Crosscaper's kitchen. He hadn't been in the kitchen much before the strangers came, but hunger had driven him from his hiding place on the second night and he had become intimately familiar with the place—its cupboards, the maze of stainless-steel counters, the massive pantry with its tantalizing boxes of cereal that were too noisy to attempt eating.

Like any other hunted animal, Simon was living on the raw edge of his senses. Every noise that reached his ears was noted and assessed for danger. He only stepped out into the corridors when it was absolutely necessary, such as nerve-racking foraging excursions or the—painfully—occasional bathroom trips.

He'd never understood how loud peeing was before. Though obviously there was no good time for him to be brutally murdered by pale strangers with ticking joints, he always found himself praying, *Not now. Not while I pee.*

He peered into the pantry, looking for something he could take back to his hiding place that might last a few days. There was no point bringing anything that needed to be cooked or—

Something colorful caught his eye.

There were three of them—bright blue-and-white boxes, laid neatly side by side. Simon's eyes had long adjusted to the darkness that had invaded Crosscaper, and so it was with a minimum of effort that he read the printed labels on their lids.

GRACE COFFEY—10/19

SIMON HAYES—10/26

PATRICK MCCAFFREY—11/30

He'd completely forgotten about his birthday. The realization made him straighten suddenly, though no emotion accompanied it. What was a birthday in this maze of darkness and prowling monsters?

Simon had become far more focused on things like staying alive and less on the idea of parties and cards.

Maybe Denizen will be back.

No. Denizen was better off far away from here.

The boy's sobbing drifted through the air as Simon gently lifted a stale loaf of bread from its shelf. He had been careful not to take too much, just in case one of the trio came down here and noticed. But from what he could see, they hadn't so much as touched a grain of rice.

What did they eat? *Did* they eat? Simon clutched the bread to his chest and left the kitchen behind. *Just one more strangeness.*

Spending one's days hiding in a cupboard, trying to soundlessly chew bread, gave a person a lot of time to think. Questions had bloomed like mushrooms in the dark, fed on scraps of knowledge he had learned, and as always, they came down to three.

What are they?

Because they weren't people. Simon knew that much, if nothing else.

Why am I awake?

He checked on the other students sometimes, though listening to them tremble and being unable to help them was just about the most heartbreaking thing in the world.

It was an argument he came back to again and again. Was he better off because he somehow had been spared a moaning, twitching sleep? Was it better to be unconscious, trapped and submerged, or awake to wander this nightmare? Maybe Simon was asleep. Maybe this was the dream, and they all wandered the corridors alone.

And the tentative question, the crucial one, a question he couldn't come close to answering . . .

Why are they here?

There was evidence of their passage everywhere. Windows had been put out, pane by pane, thorough and deliberate. Doors had been kicked in, lights smashed. Huge encyclopedias had been taken from teachers' offices and pressed flat on the floor so the spines had split, pages drifting loose over the floor.

That had upset him.

It was obvious how they were spending their days, but it wasn't obvious *why*. There was no point or pattern to the destruction, at least none that Simon could see. Occasionally, he heard laughter, usually followed by the sounds of something new being broken. It was as if they were *amusing* themselves, just as the woman had been when idly chewing lightbulbs.

Destruction for destruction's sake.

The boy's sobbing grew louder, and Simon immediately felt bad, even as he carefully peered round the corner to make sure his path was clear. It was silly to be worrying about ruined books and lightbulbs, not when . . .

When the other two became bored, they hurt the boy. They got bored easily and they got bored often, and on those nights the sobs turned into screams.

It was such a *lonely* sound, full of pain and fear, an eternity of it. Had the boy been human, Simon might have gone to help. As it stood, he had no idea what the etiquette was when you were dealing with a boy-shaped hole in the air. Besides, he hadn't heard the other two for a full day and night now and the boy had made no effort to escape, though of course neither had Simon. He was too scared of what might happen if he were caught.

Perhaps the boy was the same.

But there had been something else in those sobs the last couple of nights. It had sounded like remorse.

He was just slipping through the door of the English classroom when he heard it—rising over the wind and the rain, a sound he hadn't heard for weeks, something reassuringly human and *outside*—

An engine.

A car or a van, growling to itself, crunching gravel under its wheels. Simon darted to the window, kneeling with his nose pressed to the sill, desperate to see someone, *anyone,* outside this waking dream of dark corridors and bitter cold.

The paranoid, trapped-animal part of him whispered that it could be nothing, or even the visitors returned, but as his eyes adjusted to the glare of the headlights he saw that it might be his salvation after all.

Students in Crosscaper lived in a jar. An enclosed ecosystem, as their biology teacher liked to say. You knew every teacher. Or sort of—you didn't know their first names, but you knew their Monday ties, or their entire range of facial expressions, and the one time they almost swore. And you knew what they drove. Mr. Gilligan, the science teacher. He had been on holiday. Simon had no idea where, because all Mr. Gilligan had said was "away from ye lot." Mr. Gilligan liked to think he had a sense of humor.

And now he stood—tall and floppy-haired—staring up at the school in which he worked and lived, with no idea that he was going to save everyone's lives.

Suddenly the hope guttered in Simon's chest. What if he came into the orphanage and was struck low by the same sleep? What if the . . . the *three* found him?

Simon didn't think. He just moved—bounding to his feet and slipping out of the door as quickly and quietly as he could. If he could only get down a floor, somehow reach Mr. Gilligan's line of sight, wave or something—he wouldn't dare shout.

Somewhere distant, the boy had stopped weeping.

Simon didn't dare stop to check at each window he passed. He prayed instead that Mr. Gilligan had hesitated, was still in the courtyard, looking for his keys or just asking himself why the front door was open. *Let him look up at the windows. Let him see me and stop—*

Down a flight of stairs, swinging on a banister and wincing at the creak.

A door half opened, enough for a pair of skinny shoulders to squeeze through.

When Simon finally reached a second-floor window, Mr. Gilligan was still standing in front of his car and staring down at his phone, shoulders hunched against the rain.

Simon's fingers trembled on the clasps, but opening it would be too loud. Instead, he waved his arms, fed all the nascent panic in his limbs into great sweeps, his mouth open and silently shouting—

See me.

Please see me.

Mr. Gilligan looked up, their eyes meeting for one long moment, and then his car exploded.

It looked exactly like explosions were supposed to—a sooty chrysanthemum of flame that scalded the rain as it fell. Mr. Gilligan tumbled forward to land in the dirt, a limp shape with one arm outstretched. The glow of his phone held for a moment, then blinked off as if it had never been.

Disbelief kept Simon standing. His ears rang. His night vision was shot; the air stank of burning, the courtyard a shifting morass of shapes and smoke.

And the man in the waistcoat laughed with joy.

Look what we made you do!

The voice oozed through the air, seeping slow and gleeful. Like the crying of the boy, it seemed everywhere at once, filling the orphanage to the brim. It felt as if he were whispering the words meant for Simon, and Simon alone.

He's not, Simon told himself, already backing away from the window, *or you'd already be . . .*

The place needs work, admittedly, but here we are with time on our hands. . . .

There was a long silence, as though the man was having a conversation with someone Simon couldn't see or hear.

I wouldn't fight it, little Knight. Worming into the heads of mortals is a talent of ours. Of course, the process isn't perfect, flesh being what it is. There have been so many. . . . Well, tools often break in the hand.

There was amusement in the man's voice.

But is not every failure a chance to grow?

Simon could see him now, that jolly stance, that cruel curve of chubby lips.

We have failed, in our time. We have tasted fire. A touch of anger now. ***Who would have thought the boy– No matter. We will have him in time.***

A shriek rang out, and Simon flinched. The sound was so pained, so desperate, and the worst thing was it didn't reach his ears through the strange echoes of the intruders.

It was a person. They had someone, and they were hurting him.

The Clockwork Three have need of you, little Knight.

They had a name. The monsters had a name, and it fit them the way a scab fits a wound. *The Clockwork Three.*

We need you to build us a cage.

17

Extinction-Level Event

Moments. Little scraps of moments and Denizen a piece of them, drifting.

Hands gathering him up off the pavement, a spot of blood falling from his nose.

"Don't."

He didn't know who was speaking.

"Don't be dead."

There was blood on his hands too. Where had all of it come from?

Denizen had a vague sense of motion—of coiled power somewhere close by, the roaring of a great beast—but at least it was warm. He would have liked to stay there, feeling the vibration of the leather on his face, but suddenly hands were dragging him again out into the cold.

There was an arm under his shoulders. His feet scraped along the floor.

"Home now, Denizen. You're home. Come on. Don't fall asleep. You have to—"

And then there were blankets over him. A pillow against his back. Denizen blinked. Someone was staring down at him, cold and imperious, eyes as gray as his.

"Are you *insane*?"

Denizen could barely keep his head up. A handkerchief dabbed at his nose roughly—coming away red—and slowly his thoughts reassembled, memories stitching themselves together with each scrape of the cloth.

The village. The Higher Cant. The woman in white burned to clockwork.

Denizen groaned. He felt like someone had packed every bit of him in cotton wool and then beaten him with a hammer. Feeling returned in a rush of pins and needles, and part of him almost missed the disconnected numbness because now all his body wanted to do was torture him with all the pain he had been missing.

His hair hurt. How can hair *hurt*?

And through all the muzziness, Denizen knew the truth: this was only a prelude. The pain he was feeling now was just the extended trailer. Any moment now, he'd be getting the feature-length presentation.

His aunt was shouting at someone. He could vaguely hear it through the cotton wool filling his brain. *Glad I'm not them,* Denizen thought.

"Denizen."

Oh. Right.

"What in the name of black terror *possessed* you?"

Vivian Hardwick stood above him, her voice thrumming with fury. Her scarred lips twisted, and he had the distinct feeling that if the desk hadn't been too far away, she would have thumped it with a fist.

At least she's not wearing the armor. I don't think I could handle the armor.

"You could have been killed. *Worse* than killed," she snarled, jamming both hands in the pockets of her trousers as if to take her mind off the lack of desk-thumping. The way Denizen felt, he might have offered his head as a substitute.

"Worse than dead?" he said in a faint voice. "Is that—"

Vivian's eyes narrowed. People probably didn't interrupt her rants very often, but Denizen was too out of it to care.

"Is that *what?*" she snapped.

"Is that not just a thing people say?" He was actively rooting for some cranial trauma now. Maybe even decapitation. The headache had cut through the cotton wool, and Denizen was certain his only hope of getting through the next few minutes was for his head to be as far away from his body as possible.

"Like when they say *a fate worse than death.* Is that not just a thing people say when they want to be dramatic? What's worse than death?"

D'Aubigny, sitting cross-legged on the desk, gave Denizen a look made sharper by the crust of dried blood over one eye. The cut on her arm had reopened somewhere along the way and a sheet of red covered her from biceps to wrist.

Jack stood beside his wife as if he never intended to leave her side again, massive knuckles flexing and unflexing.

A girl Denizen had never seen before was rummaging through a first-aid kit, her dark hair tied back so she could work. She looked up and flashed Denizen a smile so bright it hurt his brain.

Who are— He shook his head, and then immediately regretted it. There were far too many things going on at once. With an effort, he turned his gaze back on Vivian. She looked furious.

Well, there's a constant.

"Anyone who attempts one of the Higher Cants without the proper training is lucky if they only suffer the way you did," Vivian said, her voice lowering the room temperature by twenty degrees.

"A Cant pulls power *through* a Knight like water

through a pipe. Trying to use a Cant you're not prepared for has deadly consequences."

"Consequences?" repeated Denizen.

Still rummaging through the bag, the girl spoke without looking up. "Have you ever seen a burst pipe?"

"I'm sorry," Denizen said, with as much viciousness as he could muster, "*who* are you?"

"You could have burned out your mind," Vivian said, ignoring his outburst, "and lived the rest of your days as a useless husk. Or you could have drawn in too much power to control and ended up incinerating yourself and half the street. Or you could have channeled so much power that it created a whole new Breach. Innocents could have *died*."

"Oh," Denizen said faintly. "Worse than death. Right."

The cotton-wool feeling was starting to fade, but he still felt hollow, scooped out and empty.

At least Vivian had stopped scrubbing his face—his skin raw and tingly where the cloth had scraped it. Maybe if he could survive the rest of her rant, then they'd leave his room and he could just sink under the duvet for a while.

He didn't need long. A couple of centuries, perhaps. A moderately sized ice age.

The girl—something sparked in Denizen's head, but the rest of him was too fried to make sense of it—was laying out medical supplies in a neat row on the desk. Her movements were sure and practiced. She barely looked at each package before setting it down.

Jack was dipping a sponge in a bowl of hot water and gently washing the blood from D'Aubigny's face. Her eyes were closed, her lips set in a firm line. She didn't wince, even when the sponge passed over the cut and Jack had to apply pressure to wash out the dirt.

A vague memory surfaced of that staggering run back to the car.

Don't be dead. D'Aubigny's voice soft in his ear, warmer than he had ever heard it before. *Don't be dead.*

"Thank you," he said, blushing. "D'Aubigny. You saved me."

"You saved yourself," she said, eyes still closed. "I just brought you home."

She didn't seem at all perturbed by how close they had all come to death, even with her arm laid open to the bone. Maybe after all the battles she'd seen, this qualified as a win. *Makes sense,* he thought, *in a horrible way.* At least they had all made it home—

"Wait," Denizen said, sitting bolt upright in bed, despite the pain. "Where's Grey?"

That made D'Aubigny open her eyes. The girl glanced at Vivian. Jack's sponge paused, and then continued wiping the blood from D'Aubigny's arm.

"Grey?" Denizen asked again, panic a hot little knife in his chest. "Where is he?"

D'Aubigny spoke. "The beast was clever—it separated, sending two of its forms away from us. We had to split up, stop them before they could find innocent prey. I did so—with difficulty—and was about to look for Grey when I felt you unleash the Higher Cant. In a way, it is almost fortunate. I do not know how I would have found you otherwise."

Vivian shot her a disgusted look, as if to say *do not encourage him,* but D'Aubigny didn't seem to notice. There was something like . . . respect in the warrior's voice.

It was scant comfort.

"And you didn't *wait?*" The pain in Denizen's head was nothing compared to the sick dread in his stomach.

Grey had to be OK. Of all the Knights, it was Grey who had taken on Denizen's training. It was Grey who'd brought him here, who talked to him like he was an adult, not a nuisance or something underfoot. He *had* to be OK.

"I needed to get you home," D'Aubigny said coolly. "You were bleeding from your eyes and your nose. I could not leave you there to search for a comrade I know and trust to make it home by himself. Grey is a Knight. He will come back. Or—"

"Or?" Denizen snapped breathlessly. He didn't want

to hear the word *or*. There wasn't an *or* in this situation. He had nothing against the word normally, but right now *or* had absolutely no place in the world.

D'Aubigny let out a sigh but left the sentence unfinished. "There is something else," she said instead. "Malleus, we fought Pick-Up-the-Pieces tonight."

Vivian's eyebrows rose. "Pick-Up-the-Pieces? What brought that devil here?"

"It wasn't brought; it was sent," D'Aubigny said. "By the Endless King."

That title cast a chill through the room, not something mystical or magical, but in the faces of those who heard it.

Jack dropped his sponge back into its bowl of hot water. The whoever-girl fumbled a set of bandages with a nervous jerk. Vivian's lips thinned to blade edges. Even D'Aubigny looked uncomfortable.

The Endless King. Denizen shivered involuntarily.

"No," said Jack. "It can't be. Corinne, you're—"

"I know what I heard, *mon petit géant*," she replied. "*Pick-Up-the-Pieces hunts in the name of the King*. That is what the beast said." She turned toward the open door. "Darcie?"

Denizen's heart broke when he saw her.

Darcie seemed to have shrunk, lost in her coat, her arms folded across her chest. She didn't look at Denizen. She didn't look at any of them.

"I . . ." Her voice was so small. "I should have . . ."

"Darcie," Vivian said, and there was no pity in her voice, only cold command. "This was not your fault. It takes a very experienced *Lux* to catch a thing as wily as Pick-Up-the-Pieces."

A single tear ran down the night-sky curve of Darcie's cheek.

"Pick-Up-the-Pieces," she began, "is one of the Endless King's most loyal servants, a Pursuivant of the Forever Court." Her voice steadied a little as she spoke. "And it said that something had been taken from the King?"

"And that we are to blame," D'Aubigny finished.

"The Order?" Vivian asked.

D'Aubigny nodded. "This wasn't an accident. Pick-Up-the-Pieces is old and canny enough to have slipped into this realm without us ever knowing. It wanted us to see it. And I am quite sure that it let us live so we could deliver the message ourselves."

"What message?" the girl asked.

"The Endless King is angry," D'Aubigny said, "and he is coming."

Vivian let out a long breath, her gray eyes creased in worry. "I need to contact the other cadres. If we can find out what was taken, maybe we can get it back. We need the entire Order on this, maybe even our counterparts abroad."

"I have a few contacts in PenumbraCorp," said D'Aubigny, "and Gedeon and I have fought together more than once."

"PenumbraCorp?" Denizen asked.

Jack's face was grim. "Knights abroad have different ways of doing things. In the States, they've gone corporate. Farther east, it's the Thousand Choirs. In Russia, it's just one man, Gedeon, the *zhelyeza vaieen*. If the King really is coming, we'll need them all."

"Is it that bad?" Denizen said hollowly.

"Yes," Vivian said simply. "It would be the end of the world as we understand it. An extinction-level event."

Oh. Denizen should have known. Anything that made Malleus Vivian Hardwick's face switch, however briefly, from her default expression of barely contained anger was obviously the apocalypse.

"What is he, the Endless King?"

"The ruler of the Tenebrous," Darcie said, and now the sadness in her voice had been replaced by fear. "Or their god. A thing that does not lend itself to description. Some say he *is* the Tenebrae, and all the Tenebrous his stray and hungry thoughts, bleeding over into our terrified world."

"I'd love to find out who does actually say that," Jack said gruffly, "and punch them in the face for being overly dramatic. Are our jobs not hard enough?"

"What about the—" Denizen began.

"What about the Order?" the girl interrupted.

Denizen shot her a look he immediately regretted, facial muscles protesting the sudden movement. "That's what—" He took a breath. What was *wrong* with him? "Could we not stop him?"

The Knights exchanged glances.

"It's possible," Vivian said eventually. "If every Knight was rallied, our allies contacted, every favor we owe called in . . . At the very least we would make a fight of it. But it won't come to that. It can't. There would be too much death—on both sides. I don't think the King wants that any more than we do."

His aunt ran gloved fingers through her short-cropped hair. "This was a warning." She seemed to be testing out each word before she said it. "There is a strange kind of honor to the Endless King. He is warning us. He is giving us time."

"I'll begin immediately—" Darcie began, but Jack cut her off.

"In the morning," he said. "Right now you need some sleep."

Darcie didn't argue. She threw Denizen one last look before disappearing through the door.

"This was not her fault," Vivian said. "I will not have her blaming herself." Her voice softened. "I will speak to her."

She looked around at Denizen and the others. "We

will discuss this more tomorrow. I'll brief you all on what needs to be done. For now, is there anything else?"

"I want to stay," Denizen said abruptly.

They all turned to look at him.

"There was a little girl. I was . . ." He looked down at his blankets. "I was looking for somewhere to hide, and I led a monster right to her. I could have run. I could have left her. But I . . ."

No one would ever know what happened to her but me.

He raised his chin. "I want to be a Knight. I want to train. I want to fight."

"That sounds like an excellent idea." Grey was standing in the doorway, holding a bag of ice to his forehead. "Because I'm about ready to retire."

"Grey!" Denizen exclaimed, and then winced as pain jolted through his skull. "You're all right."

"Not in the slightest," he said with a lopsided smile, handing his coat and sword to the mystery girl.

"Graham McCarron," D'Aubigny said, and relief warred with annoyance on her bloodied face. "You rogue. How did you get back here?"

"Rathláth has an excellent taxi service," Grey said airily, before looking a little sheepish. "To which I owe quite a lot of money, actually, but I managed to convince them I'd been mugged, so I'll worry about that tomorrow."

He raised an eyebrow at Denizen. "What happened to you?"

Jack grinned. "Well, our newest recruit here"—at this Grey gave Denizen an exaggerated bow—"decided to greet Pick-Up-the-Pieces with an Epithet. The one he learned from you, apparently."

Grey let out a low whistle. "Sunrise?"

Denizen nodded, embarrassed. "I had to—"

Grey waved a hand. "I'd say you did. That's . . . I'm impressed."

"Have you both quite finished congratulating yourselves for being reckless?" Vivian didn't look the least bit impressed. Her expression could have been cut from a storm cloud.

Grey shot Denizen a wry look. "I'm not even here and you get me in trouble. Although I would have loved to see the look on the damned cat's face when you—"

"It wasn't Pick-Up-the-Pieces," Denizen said.

Vivian frowned. "What?"

"It wasn't Pick-Up-the-Pieces," Denizen repeated. "At least I don't think it was. I ran when you told me to. The thing that chased me didn't look like a not-cat—"

"Not-cat," Grey said. "I like it."

"It looked like a woman. I thought she'd been affected by the Breach and I tried to help her, but then I saw her eyes. She was dressed all in white, and she *screamed,* and her mouth was full of—"

"Clockwork," Vivian whispered. "Her mouth was full of clockwork."

"Em . . . yeah," Denizen said. "How did you know?"

The Malleus turned on her heel and strode out of the room. Had Grey not moved swiftly, she might just have walked through him. The sounds of her footsteps echoed down the corridor for a long time before Denizen spoke.

"What was that all about?"

Jack shrugged, his face twisted in confusion. Even D'Aubigny looked surprised.

Grey wore no expression at all.

18

Iron Inside

Denizen couldn't sleep.

He was definitely tired enough; he had been wrecked after his walk round Dublin with Darcie earlier, and that seemed like a hundred years ago. The soles of his feet were on fire. Under the covers, his bones felt like they'd been replaced with jam.

It wasn't the pain in his head keeping him awake, though it certainly wasn't helping. Grey had given him two fat headache tablets and left some more on the desk. They hadn't done much, and the sight of them had disappointed Denizen somehow. He'd been expecting an enchanted salve or bubbling potion, not something you bought over the counter for a couple of euros.

The only real cure was rest, apparently. If the Higher Cant was going to kill him or burn him out, it would have done so outright. Denizen was just going to feel like D'Aubigny's punching bag for a few days.

He rolled onto his side and coughed, his thin body shaking under the blankets. The Epithet had *hurt* on the way out. It felt like he'd gargled a hedgehog.

But it wasn't that keeping him awake either.

Never had he been so grateful for a Knight's ability to see in darkness, to have every bit of the room visible to him. It did a lot to convince him that there weren't horrors lurking in the shadows. The problem was he knew that there were.

How many times had he almost died tonight? There was Pick-Up-the-Pieces, which he was happy to count as one, not one per set of fangs. There was the woman Tenebrous in her white coat, and of course his near-suicide by magic.

Three. Three near-death experiences. Was that a lot? How did they ever get anything *done*?

Denizen shivered as he remembered the woman's blank eyes. Of the two Tenebrous, he knew which one had frightened him more. Monsters that looked like monsters he could deal with. Monsters that looked like people were something else entirely.

And then there was the Endless King. Even *thinking* the name made his guts crawl. The biggest, scariest Tenebrous of them all, a being so powerful that it would take the entire Order of the Borrowed Dark to stand against him.

What had been taken from him? And who had taken it? There couldn't be that long a list of people brave or stupid enough to rob the Endless King.

Denizen's palm itched. *Speaking of brave or stupid . . .* He held his hand up in front of his face. Until tonight, the Cost in the center of his palm had been no larger than a penny. Now it spread over half his palm in a jagged petal of dark iron. Grey had said that screwing up a Cant—as he had, quite loudly and impressively—made the Cost far worse. He was lucky he hadn't lost his whole hand to it.

He closed his fist. Denizen didn't regret paying it, and not just because it had saved his own life. Somewhere there was a girl curled up in her parents' lap—*hopefully after getting the scolding of her life for being out of bed at night*—because of him. That felt good. Really good, despite Vivian giving out. He'd say as much to her tomorrow when—

Denizen's eyes widened in surprise. Vivian said she was going to brief them tomorrow—all of them—but Denizen was the only one who'd seen the woman in white. She'd have to talk to him. And maybe, when he answered all her questions, he'd get a chance to ask a couple back.

He grinned in the darkness and fell asleep.

* * *

Sunlight sneaked in through the curtains.

Denizen laid down his broom and sighed. The floor of his tiny attic room had been swept. His clothes had been neatly folded and stowed away in his wardrobe, and the window was propped open to let in some air.

He had even wet a towel and scrubbed at the windowsill, dislodging the spiders' graveyard that had accumulated there. It wasn't that the room had been particularly messy before—he would've needed to own more stuff than that—but now it gleamed.

Denizen reached out and adjusted the slant of the broom against the wall, then *hmm*ed and adjusted it again.

There. Better.

He had thought about moving the desk into the middle of the room to present a sort of professional office atmosphere, but after five minutes of spine-creaking effort, Denizen decided the desk and his back muscles were fine where they were. His aunt would probably stand anyway. Pace, maybe. She seemed the pacing type.

He glanced at the clock. Grey and D'Aubigny first, obviously. They'd relate everything they'd seen in Rathláth. Darcie, as well—there would have to be some information in the library about what the Endless King might have lost. The Knights were early risers. She'd be up to him soon enough—

A knock at the door. Denizen took a deep breath. "Come in," he called.

The door opened and Denizen's shoulders slumped. Grey stood there, a bandage round his temple and a stack of books under his arm.

"Hey, kid," he said. "Can I come in?"

Denizen sat heavily on the bed, not looking at Grey. "Sure," he said tonelessly, "whatever."

Grey laid the books on the edge of the desk and sighed. "Not who you were expecting?"

Denizen didn't respond.

"We need to go over what happened last night," Grey said. "What the Tenebrous looked like, anything it said—we need to know if it was another Pursuivant of the Court or something else entirely. Let's start with what happened after I told you to run—"

"Where's my aunt?"

Grey frowned. "She's gone to speak to the Order. We need every bit of help we can get to figure out what the Endless King wants before he comes looking for it himself. She'll be back in a few days, I expect."

A few days?

"Have I done something?" Denizen blurted.

"What do you mean?"

"Have I *done* something?" Denizen's fingers clenched into fists, pressing down on the iron in his palm as if trying to take solace in the cold hardness of it. "Something to make her avoid me? When I came here, I thought I was going to get some answers from her, especially after finding out that I had a connection to the Tenebrae." *Just like her.* "But she won't talk to me at all. I thought she'd tell me about my parents. I don't know their names. I don't know if they were Knights. I don't even know how they *died.*" He gritted his teeth. "Why is she being like this?"

"Honestly?" Grey said. "I don't know why she's not talking to you about your parents. But this can't be easy for her either. Vivian's not just your aunt—she's a soldier. That doesn't leave a lot of room for emotional connections."

"What do you mean?"

Grey ran a hand through his long hair. "You don't rise to the position of Malleus by setting fire to coffee cups; you do it by proving yourself to be of a different metal than anyone else.

"Those hammers aren't just a symbol of office—they're the most powerful weapons the Order has, forged long ago by ancient, forgotten means. There are some Tenebrous so powerful that only a Malleus's hammer can defeat them. They're incredibly valuable. And your aunt earned the right to carry one."

"How?" Denizen asked. "What did she do?"

Grey shrugged. "How long have you got? Belgrade and Redpenny. Whitby and Dunshaughlin, Rawhead

Rex and the Tearsipper Girls. I could tell you stories that'd make your toes curl.

"Your aunt has thrown herself into some of the worst Breaches I've ever read about, let alone seen first-hand, and she's walked right back out again. I couldn't tell you how many lives she's saved. She could be leading the Order right now, not just running a cadre. And to be honest, sometimes I think she'd actually be happier if she was working on her own."

"Then why doesn't she?" It was hard to keep the sullenness from his voice. Vivian might have been a hero of the Order, but it didn't excuse her from being a human.

"Because the Order doesn't let Knights run around with priceless hammers and no backup," Grey said. "It's not easy trying to keep up with her, I can tell you that."

His smile disappeared. "Look. Your aunt has been doing this for a long time. She's nearly died countless times. You have no idea what that does to a person. The injuries, the friends lost . . . You have to be iron. Inside and out."

"Well, you seem all right," Denizen said bitterly.

Grey stared at him, the silence sudden and uncomfortable. The moment dragged, giving Denizen what felt like an eternity to note the premature lines at the corners of the Knight's mouth, the bright, fractured coldness of his eyes. Old scars gleamed in the sunlight, the new ones shadows beneath gauze.

"Do I?" Grey whispered.

Denizen flushed and looked away.

"You don't know what it's like," Grey said shortly, "so cut her some slack."

"Sorry," Denizen said finally. "I didn't—"

"Don't worry about it." The Knight forced a smile, popping his knuckles against his jaw. "So, let's run through last night."

It didn't take long. Denizen described what he had seen, Grey asking occasional questions. There wasn't a lot to tell. The woman Tenebrous hadn't exactly been forthcoming with information, and everything after using the Higher Cant was a blur.

"Good," Grey said when they had finished. "Now, here's your second contribution to the war effort." He held up one of the books he'd brought with him.

"Oh?" Denizen said, a smile creeping unbidden to his face. It surprised him that even with everything going on, a new book still made his ears prick up. "What about what Vivian said?"

"We're going to need every set of eyes on this," Grey said as Denizen stared down at the titles in his hands. *The Endless King and the Forever Court* by Gregor Tredly, *Sworn to the Endless* by Palatinus the Bold, and *Lords of Lower Shadow* by Eilish McPhilips.

Grey tapped each book in turn. "We need to know who or what the Endless King might send next. Who knows, there might be a clue toward what—"

"The woman," Denizen said suddenly. "The woman Tenebrous from last night."

"What about her?"

"Vivian recognized her description." Denizen didn't know why it hadn't occurred to him before. "Did you not see how she reacted last night? She stormed out without saying a word."

"Have you met your aunt?" Grey said drily. "The woman doesn't do teamwork well. And maybe your description reminded her of something. She's a Malleus. Her knowledge of the Tenebrae is—"

"It was more than that," Denizen insisted. "She didn't just recognize the description—she *knew* that Tenebrous. And it made her angry. Really angry."

"Maybe they encountered each other before," Grey said. "I'm sure she'll tell us about it when she gets back." He glanced at the clock on the wall. "Lunch is in an hour." A sly smile crept onto his face. "And wear something nice."

"What?" There were a lot of lessons that Denizen expected to get as a Knight, but fashion advice wasn't one of them. "Why?"

Grey grinned like a fox. "So I can properly introduce you to Abigail Falx."

19

ABIGAIL FALX

ABIGAIL FALX SPOKE four languages and had left footprints on three continents before her twelfth birthday.

"Australia's amazing," she said brightly, passing Denizen the salt at lunch. "Have you been?"

"Em," Denizen replied. "No."

Abigail Falx had trained with knives since she was eight years old—on her mother's orders—and favored a 200-gram knife over distances of less than five meters.

"Heavier ones are more stable, but I just haven't the wrist strength to do them justice," she said at dinner, fanning out blades for D'Aubigny to examine. "Denizen, do you throw?"

"Em," Denizen said, busying himself with taking plates from the cupboard. "No."

It was apparently no surprise that Vivian had been taking Abigail out on certain missions, or that she knew her way round the inside of a first-aid kit. Abigail Falx's family had been Knights for generations. There had been no mysterious notes and absentee aunts for her. Abigail had been raised to be a Knight. In fact, the more she talked, the more Denizen suspected that her entire life had been leading up to her thirteenth birthday.

When Jack and the others discussed the threat of the Endless King, Abigail didn't have to interrupt constantly to have things explained. She took notes instead, or asked the kind of incisive questions that showed she really knew what she was talking about.

The one time Denizen did venture an opinion—that his aunt had recognized the Tenebrous woman from Rathláth—it was only Abigail who'd answered him.

"Oh, I'm not surprised the Malleus recognized the Tenebrous," she said, smiling brightly. "Not with her career!"

Denizen had spent the rest of dinner thinking quite seriously about setting Abigail on fire.

He wasn't the only person around the table feeling uncharitable. As soon as her plate was empty, D'Aubigny left without a word. Grey was his usual chatty self, but Denizen could see that it was mostly for Abigail's benefit; whenever she was distracted, all the good cheer drained from his face and a dark, faraway look filled his eyes. Even Jack didn't seem in the best form.

Darcie hadn't come down for meals today at all.

"All right, hero," Grey said, when everyone was done. "You're on washing-up."

"I thought I was recovering," Denizen said hopefully. Jack snorted.

"Well, don't use a Higher Cant to do them," Grey responded lightly, already on his way out.

Denizen sighed and began collecting plates, stacking them by the side of the sink in preparation for washing. He pointedly didn't look at Abigail, even when she picked up a cloth and began drying the plates that he had washed.

They worked in silence, Denizen staring fixedly at each plate in turn. Work was good. Work kept you busy. Washing plates gave you the chance to turn your back on a person without being rude, and if she did ask him something, he could turn the water up and pretend he hadn't heard her.

If only there weren't just five plates.

Denizen suddenly began to dread the end of the stack. Why couldn't this have been a dinner party? Nothing major—the entire Order, perhaps. A nice fortress of plates between him and Abigail.

The last plate came too quickly, hot water splashing over his hands. *Nothing good lasts forever.* It went to Abigail to dry, Denizen glancing pleadingly back at the empty counter for something else to do. At least last night there had been the end of the world to talk about.

When finally he turned round, Abigail was staring at him.

"So," she said, "everyone's in a bit of a mood and I've only caught snippets. What exactly happened?" She smiled brightly. "Hero."

Bright was a word that came easily when describing Abigail Falx. Her eyes were the bright blue of birthday wrapping paper or a child's drawing of the sky. Her hair was black, sleek, and shining, framing her face like stray curls of night.

Denizen had heard the whole story at lunchtime. Her mother was from Iran, her father American, both Knights currently stationed in . . . Sumatra. No, Jakarta. A place from an odd end of the map with some sharp consonants in it. Denizen wasn't sure.

"What?" said Denizen. "Oh, it was . . . I don't know . . . We kind of . . ."

She had an odd way of staring—not rude exactly, but penetrating, as if everything you were saying was the most crucial thing that had ever been said. It put a lot of pressure on a person, a stare like that. The only consolation was that it was the way she looked at everything. It was the way she'd looked at the sandwiches they'd had for lunch.

She cocked her head. "Yes?"

He found himself fighting the urge to take a step

backward. *You're being ridiculous,* a voice in his head whispered. *You've faced Tenebrous. Shrieking horrors from unlit skies. Why are you being weird now?*

Because she's standing really close. I'd be just as nervous if it was a Tenebrous. It's the proximity. Nothing else. She's in my personal space.

"Em . . ." He blushed.

The story came out, slowly at first, and with a lot more stumbling than when he had told Grey. She'd already heard the main parts—Pick-Up-the-Pieces, the Endless King and what he'd lost—but Denizen started from the beginning, cringing inwardly at certain parts.

Volunteering to go with D'Aubigny and Grey had seemed like the right thing to do at the time. He'd felt brave, like he was taking the initiative, finally *doing* something instead of just waiting for his aunt to give him the time of day. Looking back, it felt like the actions of a naive child.

"—and then D'Aubigny found me and brought me back here. My aunt wasn't . . . Well, you saw her."

Abigail stared at him for a long moment. "That," she said, "was brilliant."

Denizen blinked. "What?"

"Really, really brilliant," Abigail said with no trace of sarcasm. "You've only been here a short time and you insist on accompanying the Knights into battle. And it wasn't that you used the Epithet—*Sunrise,* by the way, *wow*—by accident or anything. You laid life and sanity on the line to save a little girl."

"Well, that's not what . . ." Denizen thought about it. "Well, it is what *happened,* I suppose, but that's not—" Frown No. 2—Slow Realization. "Huh. Sorry. It just sounds different when you say it."

"Different?"

"Good," Denizen said. "It sounds good."

Abigail flashed him a bright white smile.

IN BANDAGES AND bruises, the Knights hunted for answers. There was no such thing as recovery time when the threat of the Endless King loomed on the horizon like a great guillotine waiting to fall. The Order was on high alert. Pursuivants were slinking through the shadows, and Denizen flung himself back into his training with renewed determination.

Meals were spent poring over books in silence, searching for any mention of the dread master of the Tenebrous. Jack sharpened blades. D'Aubigny broke a punching bag and another had to be ordered. Grey was a dark shadow in the corridors, pacing ceaselessly from one end of Seraphim Row to the other, a bleak smile playing across his lips.

The tension rose as the nights grew colder still.

Tempers were short. Even the strange phenomena that haunted Seraphim Row had become distant and muted.

Things were different now. The war was coming to them.

"Real swords?"

The back garden of Seraphim Row was a belligerent tangle of trees and bushes, stiff and prickly, hungry to grab at skin and sleeve. Denizen had no idea how far it stretched back beyond the circle cleared for training and the squat bulk of Jack's forge. He found himself wondering if even the razor-sharp sword in Abigail's hand would be able to part those black-green snarls.

She rolled her wrist, rapier blade slicing the air with a dry *whop*, stepping lightly between the flowerpots Grey had laid out to test her footwork. Despite the cold, she wore a light hoodie and a pair of tracksuit bottoms, breath fogging in the air before her.

Just looking at her made Denizen pull his woolly hat down lower. The old coat he had brought with him from Crosscaper was doing an admirable job keeping the weather out, but still the cold snaked round him, seeking entry through gaps and seams. He pulled it a little closer about himself as Grey lifted his own sword.

"Real swords," Grey responded.

Grey's vest left his arms bare, muscles shifting

beneath a net of scars. He had a tattoo on one shoulder blade—a bird, Denizen thought, wings sharp as blades, orange and red and gold. Bandages still marred one arm and the side of his face.

"Shouldn't we use practice swords?" Abigail asked. Against the bleached hues of the winter garden she stood out like the first flower of spring, twirling gently on the balls of her feet, her blade a shining ribbon of steel. "I mean, not that I—"

"You need to get used to the weight," Grey said. His customary smile was nowhere to be seen, as if it had been stolen away by the cold. "And you're not going to hit me."

He lunged.

Denizen watched them spar with wide eyes. He'd often wanted to learn martial arts, which was probably a natural thing for all children, especially the smaller ones. Unfortunately, rural Ireland was a little short on dojos, and while books like *The Lord of the Rings* and *The Magician* had plenty of battles, they tended to be more about dramatic moments and less about numbered diagrams on where to put your feet. Luckily, it seemed like he'd found a very good teacher.

All the emotion had faded from Grey's face, just as it had when he waited for Pick-Up-the-Pieces. It was as if he'd been emptied and something else had taken his place—instinct, perhaps, or training so ingrained it had become instinct. There were no hesitations, no moments where he seemed to be deciding on a strategy—just move after move after move.

In fairness to Abigail, she was also pretty impressive. Distressingly impressive, actually, considering Denizen—against the advice of his own brain—was already thinking about how good *he* might have been with Abigail's head start.

Starting from scratch, learning an entire new world, wasn't easy, and it was especially difficult watching Abigail move like she had been born with a sword in her hand. *That was obviously why Vivian gave her the time of day,* he thought a little bitterly. *She's good enough to keep up.*

It was some consolation that, no matter how good she was, she still had some way to go. Abigail's strikes were perfectly balanced, perfectly executed, and perfectly incapable of coming anywhere near Graham McCarron.

"Denizen?"

Denizen's heart was in his mouth just watching them. Abigail didn't hold back, and no matter how she stepped or twisted, no matter to what trajectory she fed her blade, Grey's sword was always there to stop it.

It took Denizen a moment to realize that his name had come from somewhere within that maelstrom of flashing swords.

"What?"

Grey backhanded Abigail's blade so hard she nearly lost her grip.

"How many cadres of Knights are there currently active in Europe?"

Denizen's brow furrowed. *I know this.* "There's . . ."

"Seventy-eight," Abigail called out. "Same as the number of Cants. Symbolic. Though there are—"

"—roving cadres," Denizen interrupted, shooting Abigail an annoyed look. She was too busy backpedaling as Grey suddenly went on the offensive, chopping his blade down in short, hard strokes. "The—"

"—Peregrines," Abigail said breathlessly. "Started in 1457 in response to—"

"Next question!" Denizen said, and it took quite a lot of control not to snap.

Grey spun on a heel. "All right. The leader of the Order is called the . . ."

"Palatine," Abigail and Denizen said together.

"Plural of Malleus."

"Mallei." Denizen was first on that, but mostly because Grey had taken advantage of Abigail's distraction to knock her off balance, staggering left to scatter the flowerpots. She spun, chest heaving, and gave them both that bright, fascinated stare.

"What?" Denizen said.

She flicked her hair out of her eyes. "Isn't this *fun*?"

* * *

At least reading was quiet. Mostly.

"I've decided we should study together."

Denizen had opened his door to find Abigail barely visible behind precariously balanced books. She had placed her forehead against the stack to keep them from falling backward and kept weaving and sidestepping to prevent them from toppling sideways, and Denizen had nervously begun to copy her, so the overall effect—and the sight of books in peril—was making him slightly nauseated.

They eventually maneuvered the tower of volumes onto Denizen's desk, and Abigail sank cross-legged to the floor, rummaging in a plastic bag.

"Do you mind?"

"No," Denizen said, trying to keep his voice neutral. And it was true—he didn't. Abigail was perfectly nice. It was just that when she was there, he was . . . *aware* she was there. It made it hard to concentrate.

"OK," she said, holding up two brightly colored bags. "I have chocolate. And some things covered in chocolate. And . . ." She looked down. "This is actually completely all chocolate."

She threw one of the bags to Denizen. It hit him in the face.

"Thank you," he said, and buried his sore nose in a book.

* * *

They read for hours, the silence occasionally broken—mostly by Abigail. She talked a *lot,* and Denizen wasn't even sure she knew she was doing it. Part of him envied her being so easily comfortable with someone she had just met. He was trying, though. Occasionally, an interesting piece of knowledge would pop up in his book and he'd share it with her. That was sort of talking, wasn't it?

"Look at this," Denizen said. "'Beware the Nation of Wasps, for obvious reasons.' How is that helpful?"

Abigail shrugged. Untold centuries of literature spread across a dozen countries had provided some wildly differing approaches to describing the Tenebrous. The author Denizen was reading now had obviously assumed that other people knew as much about the Tenebrous as he did. Many sentences started with "As you know"—a phrase Denizen hated because most of the time he *didn't* know. You couldn't just go around assuming people *knew* things, or why write books at all?

In a way, the Tenebrae reminded him of the books he had read about the Middle Ages. Not just the names—which were somewhere between poetry and black humor—but the constantly shifting alliances and power struggles. The Tenebrous seemed to fight each other as much as they did the Order. Feuds between Warmfellow and the Widows of Victory, the love affair between Chirugeon and the Ahklut, were all made so much more confusing by the fact that the Knights only ever heard about them secondhand.

"So . . . em . . ."

Denizen glanced up to see Abigail staring fixedly at the wall. She was chewing her lip, possibly because it was so chocolate-stained.

"What?" he asked.

"My dad got hurt."

She didn't look at Denizen when she said it, just stared at the wall, pretty features blank and set.

"A clash with one of the Pursuivants. They don't know which yet. Mum's fine. Dad . . . got hurt. His leg."

"Abigail, I'm really sorry—"

"No," she said. "No. It's fine. People get hurt. It happens. He's not going to lose it or anything. So that's something."

Denizen realized with a chill that, yes, that was something. They were in a world where keeping your leg was a positive outcome.

Abigail took a long breath. "Thanks for being around tonight."

All he could do was nod.

The girl shook her head as if letting the thought fall away.

"I can't read anymore," she said, and closed her

book with a snap. "Sorry. I'm just not much of a book person."

Denizen couldn't help himself. He gave her the kind of look he'd normally reserve for someone who made puppies into jam. "I know. You mentioned it."

She stuck her tongue out at him, and he laughed. Then Abigail stood up and stretched. "I might give my parents a quick call."

"Oh," he said. "Cool." That had been another source of awkwardness between him and Abigail, though he felt awful thinking about it now. She'd shown him pictures of her family—a woman in a hijab whose smile was the image of Abigail's, a man who looked like he could arm-wrestle Jack, and a tousle-haired little boy.

Denizen had been happy for her—she obviously loved them and they her; it practically glowed from the photo—but he couldn't help looking at it and wondering about his own parents.

"Did they mind you coming here?" he asked suddenly. "To Dublin, I mean. It's a long way."

"I wanted to work under the best," Abigail said, "and right now that's your aunt. My parents have great respect for Malleus Hardwick."

She paused. "Were . . . were your parents Knights?"

Denizen had been wondering how much she knew about his background. None of the Knights seemed to be gossips, but word would get around, and Abigail seemed the curious type.

"I don't—" Denizen forced the words out. She'd hear about it sooner or later. He supposed it was better coming from him. "I don't know. I don't know anything about my parents, actually."

It hadn't been for lack of trying. Long evenings had been spent searching the sprawl of Seraphim Row, hoping for a photo, a newspaper clipping, some indication that his parents might have stayed under the same roof he did now. He had found plenty of references to Hardwicks—the annals of the Order were full of them. Vivian's pride wasn't misplaced—the history of the Order *was* the history of the Hardwick family. It was just frustrating that there was a wealth of knowledge about Hardwicks from centuries past, yet a distance of eleven years was insurmountable.

He wasn't sure exactly what reaction he expected from Abigail. Pity, maybe. Shock. Instead, she just frowned.

"Well, why don't you check the Book of Rust?"

"What's that?"

"It's our . . . well. It's our graveyard. Our memoriam. A list of all the Knights who have died in a particular garrison. If your parents were Knights and served here, then they'd be in the Book."

Denizen stared at her. "OK," he said finally. "Now I can forgive you for not being a book person."

The library was the largest room in the house, and every available surface had been commandeered by books. At some point, all the great wooden shelves lining the walls had been filled and the books had broken free to march across the floor in great stacks.

Tables had been dragged up from the kitchen, their surfaces covered in notes and drawings, books laid at their edges to anchor them against one of Seraphim Row's phantom breezes. There were no candles, no open flames to tempt the ancient paper.

I could live here, Denizen thought, moments before he realized that someone already did.

A cot had been made up in the corner—surrounded by books, of course—and as he and Abigail stepped into the middle of the room, a dark shape sat up and fumbled for her glasses.

"Sorry," Denizen said. "Did we wake you?"

Darcie slid her glasses onto her nose, scrubbing at her eyes with a palm.

"Yes," she said. There was a thickness to her voice, as if she'd been crying. "Do you need something?"

It suddenly occurred to Denizen how irregularly he'd seen Darcie since Rathláth. There was a stack of dirty plates by the bed—she must have been taking her meals here. Her hair hung loose down her back in a thicket of curls.

"Yes, actually," Denizen said, flushing a little. "Abigail said that we—well, the Order—"

"We?" Darcie said sourly. "That was quick."

"What do you mean?"

"There are other options, you know," she said, as if she hadn't heard him. "I don't know why you're in such a hurry to sign up for this, not when there are so many other things you could do. Yes, fine, you'd have to wear gloves, but there's certainly less chance of—" She took a deep breath. "Less chance of—"

"Darcie, what are you talking about?"

"You could *leave*," Darcie snapped. "Your aunt wouldn't force you to stay. She'd want you to have your own life. You could leave and not have to do this, and I wouldn't have to worry about you as well. But here you come, and look how excited you are. A new recruit. *Great*. Just one more person I have to worry about accidentally killing if my information is wrong."

"I can't imagine what it must be like," Abigail said, and Darcie's head snapped round.

Abigail spoke slowly, as if stepping once more through the precise dance of a sword fight. "I've wanted to say it before. Parents in the Order hope for a *Lux*. It's an honor, obviously, but what they're really thinking is that their kid will be safe at home while other Knights fight and . . ."

Darcie didn't respond.

"And I've always thought it must be far worse," Abigail continued. "Because you see it, but you can't be there. You can't be there for the people you send. And they make you start so *young*."

"We're needed," Darcie said softly. "Maybe you understand better than you think." She closed her eyes. "These fatal family traditions." Sitting back on the cot, Darcie picked up a book and began absently flicking through it. "What do you want?"

"The Book of Rust."

Darcie might have been upset, but she was still a genius, and before Denizen had even finished speaking, she was shaking her head.

"Denizen, I understand that you want to find out what—"

"No," Denizen said as calmly as he could, "you don't, Darcie. I could sit here for years waiting for my aunt to come down and talk to me. She probably thinks I'm just going to give up, but I'm not. There's a reason why she's avoiding me, and I want to know what it is."

Candlelight reflected off Darcie's glasses. "Are you sure you want to know?"

"I don't understand," Denizen said. "Why wouldn't I?"

"How do you think a Knight's life ends?" Darcie asked. Her voice was bitter. "I can tell you. When Fuller Jack or Grey is killed in battle, I'll be the one to write down what happened. The Tenebrous that did it. Where their body fell. Better than that, I'll be the one who sent them there. Do you really want to know the name of the monster that might have killed your parents? And when you do find out, what then? Revenge?" Darcie slammed the book shut. "A fine reason to be a Knight."

"I still have to know," Denizen said quietly. "She might be your Malleus, but to me she's just a woman who won't tell me why I spent eleven years in an orphanage."

Without taking her eyes from him, Darcie pulled a book from her coat pocket—a slim volume in black leather, embossed with the hand-and-hammers. A motto was engraved on the front in silver:

LINGUAE CENTUM

SUNT ORAQUE CENTUM

FERREA VOX

"A hundred tongues, a hundred mouths, one iron voice," Darcie said. "The motto of the Order."

She held the book out to him. "I've already looked. Sorry. I've sat enough times with this book in my hand, waiting for Grey or D'Aubigny to come back. It was June, right? Eleven years ago?"

Denizen nodded, afraid to look.

"Eleven years ago," Darcie began, "every single Knight in Seraphim Row was killed. All of them. In three weeks. The Book doesn't say why. And it *should.* That's the point of having it in the first place."

Her lips twisted grimly. "All I know is that they died. Adebayo Sall. Christopher Wilde. Lisa O'Reilly. And the last on June twentieth, Malleus John Carsing."

"That's the day before I was left in Crosscaper," Denizen said in shock. "And Vivian?"

"No mention of her," Darcie said, "obviously. And there's something else."

"My parents?" The book was suddenly very heavy in his hands.

Darcie shook her head. "They're not there."

Shock plunged Denizen's spine into ice. "What do you mean they're not there? I don't understand."

"Open it," Darcie said. "Page one hundred and thirty-six."

He thumbed open the Book of Rust. Pages and pages, neat black writing in a dozen different hands, dead Knight after dead Knight until . . .

Page 136 had been neatly ripped out.

20

Very Nearly the End of the World

The next few days were a blur.

Book after book passed under Denizen's eyes, but they might as well have been in Latin. There was no room in his head for anything but what he had learned from Darcie and the Book of Rust.

Eleven years ago, the Knights of Seraphim Row had been wiped out one by one—all but his aunt, the famous and respected Vivian Hardwick. Eleven years ago, Denizen had been left in Crosscaper Orphanage with nothing more than a birth certificate and a silly name. Denizen had been asked to accept the existence of a lot of strange things in the last few weeks, but he drew the line at coincidences.

The two events had to be connected. But how?

If that weren't bad enough, reports streamed in daily of more clashes with Pursuivants of the Court.

Aberraxes, the Bloody Mice, Bittersweet . . . So far, no Knight had died, but it was clear the Endless King was running out of patience.

He wasn't the only one. Denizen and Abigail were studying old texts in his room when there was a sharp rap at the door.

It was D'Aubigny. "Follow me," she said, and strode off down the corridor.

The other Knights were waiting for them in the foyer. Grey stood at the bottom of the great marble staircase, his arms folded.

"Grey," Denizen said, and flashed him a smile. "I thought we were going to meet earlier today. For some training?"

Grey just gave a distracted shrug before turning back to his argument with Jack.

"What's going on?" Abigail said.

"I'm trying to tell Jack and D'Aubigny that they're making a mistake," Grey said. "They're talking about going to Os Reges Point."

"What's that?" Denizen said, still a little stung by Grey's dismissal.

"I've never heard of it either," Abigail said with a frown.

"There are ways one can contact the King," Jack said.

"Risky, terrible ways of grabbing the attention of

a thing you don't want paying attention to you," Grey interrupted.

Jack shot him a look before continuing. "It's not risky. The Emissary at Os Reges Point is a Tenebrous sworn to . . . to pass messages. To answer Knights truthfully. Sometimes the answers aren't much good, but if it does work, then it'd be a lot quicker than sifting through a thousand years of books."

"That's what the Order wants us to do," Grey said.

"We do not know what the Order wants us to do," D'Aubigny countered. "The Malleus has still not returned. We are searching through our histories because it is a way of avoiding doing anything at all. I am not going to sit in a library, waiting for the sky to go dark."

"D'Aubigny's right," Jack said. "We need to *do* something."

"And what if something goes wrong?" Grey snapped. "The Emissary is incredibly powerful. What if he decides the best way to recover what's been lost is to rifle through your mind and see if there are any clues in there?"

Abigail had gone pale. "He could do that?"

Grey nodded. "There's no telling what some of the ancient Tenebrous are capable of. That's why it's risky. The Emissary might decide that the Order is responsible for the theft and keep you as a hostage. Or as a snack. Either would be bad."

"Os Reges Point is sworn ground," D'Aubigny said. "A place where Tenebrous and Knight can speak without fear or danger. The *only* place. The Emissary is bound by that, as are we. It might be the safest place on the planet when the Endless King comes." She turned to Abigail and Denizen. "So get your coats."

"Oh, great," Grey said, throwing up his hands. "Let's make this a school trip, then, shall we? The last one went *so* well."

"We are supposed to be teaching them," D'Aubigny said coolly, but Grey had already stalked away.

"What's wrong with him?" Denizen asked. It wasn't like Grey to be so cautious. He'd been the only one supporting Denizen when he had wanted to join the Knights against the Breach. And if Os Reges Point was neutral ground like D'Aubigny said . . .

"We're all on edge," Jack said. "The lad hasn't been the same since Rathláth. He needs time in bed to recover, not"—he waved his hand—"all this. And I have my own reservations. Os Reges Point can be . . . intense."

"I want to go," Abigail said hurriedly. Denizen nodded in agreement.

"Then dress as warmly as you can," D'Aubigny said. "We have a long journey ahead."

* * *

DENIZEN'S ENTHUSIASM AT traveling to the mysterious Os Reges Point lasted about twenty minutes.

Had he known that the trip would involve taking a cross-country bus with a stone-faced Frenchwoman, he might have reconsidered, or at least packed more than one book. And he *definitely* would have thought twice had it occurred to him that it would mean spending a great deal of time with Abigail as well.

I need to learn to stop volunteering for things.

"Have you heard anything from the orphanage?"

Denizen looked up from his book. He had read the same page eight times, but if he moved on to the next one, then eventually the book would be over and he wouldn't have anything to look at anymore.

Abigail had draped herself over a seat with feline grace, absently batting at the strap of her bag in the overhead shelf. She had been doing that for the last two hours, and he assumed she was going to continue doing it until the heat-death of the universe.

No one on the bus seemed to find it half as annoying, though the only person sitting near them was D'Aubigny, and she was wearing headphones so large that they deserved their own bus ticket.

"No," he said finally, rearranging himself on the uncomfortable bus seat and starting the page for the ninth time. "Not a word."

There might have been some kind of burgeoning

friendship between Denizen and Abigail—especially after she had offered the information about the Book of Rust—but with the revelations about the dead cadre, and the swiftly approaching death sentence from the King, Denizen's nerves were so wound up he thought he might snap.

Besides, Denizen didn't just go around *making* friends; there was . . . a process. Like Jack making a sword. Like his friendship with Simon. A long process, but one that eventually produced something stronger than steel. And like forging a sword, there were any number of places along the way where someone could screw it up.

So far, Abigail had committed the mortal sins of:

- sitting beside him (though that had ended after a rest stop, when Denizen had pointedly moved to a different seat, arranging his coat and bag into a makeshift Fortress of Solitude);
- talking (while Denizen was trying to pretend he was the only person on the bus);
- and (worst of all) asking about Simon.

It was the last one that was the kicker.

It's his birthday today—October 26. In all the talk of Os Reges Point, Denizen had completely forgotten. It would be the first of Simon's birthdays that Denizen had ever missed, though obviously that would be more of an achievement if they hadn't always slept a meter apart.

He even had a good reason—it was very nearly the end of the world, after all—but that didn't make him feel better either. It was one short step from prioritizing things like the apocalypse over his friend to forgetting him entirely, and it didn't help being reminded of him by a complete stranger.

Denizen wasn't stupid; he knew he was being petty. Abigail was just making an effort, that was all.

Of course she is, a cruel part of Denizen whispered. *It isn't like she's feeling lonely, or wondering why there's a great big mystery surrounding her parents and aunt. That must free up all sorts of energy.*

Stop it, countered his more reasonable side. *You're acting like a kid, and you know it.*

Hearing the words in Simon's voice just made things harder.

The bus was only the start of their journey. Five hours and a whole country bisected, only to be dumped unceremoniously at the side of the road, a good ten kilometers from anything that resembled civilization.

Wind shrieked its loneliness after the departing bus. On three sides, barren hills shambled away to the horizon, and on the fourth there was only ocean—a great steel blade slicing the land away. From the gravel under their shoes to the stark emptiness of the sky, the landscape was as bleak and unforgiving as the surface of the moon.

Staring at it almost made Denizen homesick.

They made their way along a thin path that wound down the cliffs. There was a beach there, just a strip of rocks and sand, an old wooden pier jutting halfheartedly out into the cove. The cliffs rose on either side like the jaws of a great beast, draping tongues of shadow across them as they descended.

A boat bobbed by the pier. Denizen hadn't noticed it at first, too concerned with metaphors for being swallowed, but D'Aubigny *hoosh*ed her duffel bag up on her shoulder and nimbly jumped on deck.

"Is this . . ." He frowned. "Is this your boat?"

D'Aubigny shook her head. "A local man hires it to us when we need it. We pay him enough never to ask why."

It was the first time she'd spoken since leaving Dublin. Abigail and Denizen exchanged glances and followed.

The boat was a blunt little . . . something. Cruiser, maybe? Denizen knew that there were *boats* and there were *ships,* but Crosscaper's library had been light on nautical adventures about anything more modern than a longship. It looked sturdy enough, though, and well maintained. There was even a little cabin toward the . . . front bit.

The prow. I think.

Someone had painted the words *The Cormorant* on the side in flowing black script.

D'Aubigny evidently didn't share his unfamiliarity with boats. She was checking dials and controls as if she'd been born on the high seas, reaching across to tap the three fuel drums that had been laid out neatly on the deck to make sure they were full.

"Is Os Reges Point far?" Abigail asked, watching D'Aubigny's preparations with interest.

"It will be night when we get there, making good speed," the Frenchwoman replied. "Make yourselves comfortable."

As he watched Abigail join D'Aubigny at the wheel, already asking questions, Denizen could feel his heart begin to sink through black waters of dread. Five hours with Abigail on a bus was one thing. A whole day crossing the ocean on a cramped island of wood and metal was something else entirely.

The engine purred to life under D'Aubigny's hands, and slowly *The Cormorant* began to move.

21

Needlework Sky

In the end, the trip turned out to be a lot less awkward than Denizen was expecting.

"Water?" Abigail said an hour after they'd left the shore.

"Sure."

"Water?" This came six hours after they'd left the shore, annoyingly right as Denizen began to feel rather thirsty.

"Sure. Thanks."

Four hours more and the horizon ignited in sunset.

"Wat—"

"Yes. Sorry. Thank you."

"No problem."

The land had fallen away, replaced by a rolling carpet of leaden waves that rose and fell and rose again, eternal and endless. Only the white scar of *The Cormorant*'s passage broke the monotonous heave of the sea, and even that faded in time. Night fell, and the stars came out. Not a shy unveiling, but in sweeping grandeur, unbowed by city lights or cloud.

They *blazed,* fierce as furnaces, an army of soldiers aflame.

Denizen found himself glancing over at Abigail more and more as the day dragged on. There had been many times over the last few weeks when he had looked up from a meal or a book and seen her staring at him with those bright blue eyes. He'd always looked away, embarrassed, unable to work out the emotions in that stare. Abigail Falx looked at everything with interest; maybe he was just one more puzzle, one more fact to be learned.

Now she wasn't looking at him at all.

Had she picked up on how uncomfortable she made him? *I should say something.* She was perched on the rail of *The Cormorant,* graceful as a dancer, eyes fixed on the ocean ahead. She'd been that way for an hour or more, nightshade hair dancing in the breeze as the day died around them.

Denizen bit his lip, awkwardly crossing the deck toward her. He'd been delighted to find that he actually possessed sea legs, and didn't spend half the journey vomiting over the side, but each step was still taken gingerly, still hesitant, even as the deck rose and fell to egg him on.

"Abigail, I—"

And then he saw what she was staring at, and all the words went out of his head.

Five great spears of slick black stone rose out of the sea. At their base, the ocean dashed itself to spume and spray, trying and failing to bring them down. They marched like soldiers of ever-increasing height, the fifth and final one a massive pinnacle that must have been more than half a kilometer tall, its staggering bulk bullying the horizon aside.

Beyond them, the ocean went on forever, rising in iron-gray swells, then falling to lines of foam. The air was crisp and clear, the night sky filled with stars, but clouds had massed on the horizon in a vast continent of gray and white and black. Lightning stung its depths.

Denizen's jaw dropped. It actually dropped. He had always thought that phrase was a cliché. It wasn't. He'd just never been to Os Reges Point before.

He turned in a slow circle. There was no mainland, not in any direction. Standing here, he could believe that Os Reges Point was all there was—the whole world reduced to sea and sky and storm.

"Os Reges Point," D'Aubigny murmured over the

growl of the engine. It was the first unnecessary thing he'd ever heard her say.

It took them another hour to reach the base of the smallest spire, which still must have been a hundred meters of wind-scarred rock. At its base was a pier, just a crude tongue of rock carved by some long-dead mariner.

D'Aubigny tied up *The Cormorant,* while Denizen resisted the urge to check her knots. What would happen to them if the boat sank or they ran out of fuel? Would they be stranded here in this unforgiving place?

Climbing up on the rail, feeling the cold but somehow reassuringly modern metal beneath his fingers, Denizen hesitated. The slick black stone of the pier was just above his head. He suddenly had no desire whatsoever to touch it. There was a crawling feeling in his stomach.

The Tenebrae—this whole Point quivered with it.

"What is this place?" Abigail asked, arms wrapped round herself.

There was a vertical tunnel, like a chimney, cut into the back of the stone spire, rising up through its core. A ladder of iron was set into it and it was this that D'Aubigny approached, her bag slung over her back.

"There are certain places where the skin of the world is thin, where this universe and the Tenebrae run close together," D'Aubigny said. "Os Reges is the closest. Here we are separated by a mere breath."

Denizen heaved himself up onto the pier, trying to ignore the queasiness in his stomach.

"You both feel it, don't you?"

They nodded. D'Aubigny's face was grim.

"It will get worse as we climb."

FIRST, THE LADDER—A creaking, rusting structure that rose through the core of the first spire like the spinal column of a long-dead serpent.

That wasn't so bad actually—shielded from the wind, unable to see how far up you were, just a hand-over-hand climb to the top.

A hundred-meter straight climb was still more than he had ever done before. Denizen found himself counting rungs to distract himself from the burning in his muscles before he finally clambered, exhausted, onto the summit of the first spire.

Each finger of rock was connected by a thin rope bridge, held in place by long iron stakes. Denizen eyed the first one with suspicion. The stakes seemed sturdy enough. The actual bridge looked older than Europe. Its boards were splintered, the ropes frayed. One good gust of wind, one heavy footstep . . .

Denizen and Abigail stared at it apprehensively.

D'Aubigny kicked at one of the stakes with a boot.

"It is fine," she said. "This bridge has outlasted empires. It is perfectly safe."

That's not reassuring, Denizen thought. You couldn't just say that it had outlasted things. Everything outlasts everything else until the moment it doesn't.

D'Aubigny stepped onto the bridge. It dipped under her weight—Denizen's heart skipping a beat—but it held. The Knight crossed the gap in five long strides, one hand held to the flat black cap she wore, the other out for balance. She may as well have been walking on concrete.

"Em," said Denizen. He looked at Abigail, and then at the gap. "After you?"

Abigail just stared at him. Denizen sighed and followed D'Aubigny.

Step by faltering step, he extended himself out over the void. Every breath he took made the bridge sway a little, but that was all right because the wind was the breath of the entire world and it was making the bridge sway a *lot.*

Denizen tried looking at the boards beneath his feet, but that meant looking at the ocean below. And if he looked up, then he couldn't see his foot coming down on a *moving surface* above a *hundred-meter drop*—

His foot landed on cold and solid stone. It took all of Denizen's control not to kiss it.

Abigail made her way slowly across after him. It

was almost worse watching someone else do it, but at the same time he couldn't take his eyes from her.

"That," she said, stepping off the bridge and letting out a long breath, "was unpleasant."

Denizen flashed her a relieved grin, but Abigail had already turned away.

Each spire they crossed brought them higher and higher. The wind grew as they climbed, and Denizen suddenly became very glad that he had worn extra layers, even when the exertion of climbing made his armpits itchy and wet.

Eventually, all that remained was the final peak—a huge spur of granite, rising into the sky like the pocked fin of some vast sea creature. It dwarfed the other spires to such a degree that the bridge from the fourth spear only reached its midsection, leading to a staircase that wound round the peak.

Each step of the staircase was narrow, roughly hacked out of the stone. Denizen was very glad it hadn't rained; one slip on wet rock and it would take a long time for him to hit the ocean below. Even so, it was a fraught climb—the wind plucking at his hair, each step barely visible, even with the *Lucidum* lending everything a silver glow.

Finally, the staircase ended and Denizen walked out on to the summit of Os Reges Point.

"It's beautiful," Abigail said, and she was right. The view was dizzying.

The ocean heaved beneath them, a whole world of white and gray. The stars felt close enough to touch. Denizen kept catching himself ducking in case he caught his head on them.

His sense of the Tenebrae was stronger here, but it didn't feel like a Breach. It somehow felt stronger yet more natural. A Breach was like a knife wound or a needle pressing through fabric, distorting everything around it. Here it was as if the two worlds existed in the same place—overlapping, coexisting.

The Tenebrae woke in his stomach, full of tingling warmth. He drew on it gently, let it flood into his limbs, feeling prickles between his fingers. Abigail was doing the same—light too golden to be reflected starlight gleamed behind her eyes.

"Control yourselves," D'Aubigny said. "Let your power go."

Grudgingly, Denizen did so. It came so easily here, a furnace in his spine that made him want to reach out and . . . *no*. He shoved the power away, embarrassed.

"How do you do it?"

Abigail was staring at him, light still roiling fitfully behind her eyes. Her hands were balled into fists.

"What?"

She took one last deep breath and finally the light died away. "You're good at tamping it down," she said. "I noticed. Sorry."

"No," Denizen said. "Thanks. I guess I just . . . you know. Burned once." He waggled his fingers at her and then blushed.

"OK," she said. "Mental note. Get burned." She thought for a moment. "And survive, obviously."

D'Aubigny had already made her way to the center of Os Reges Point, staring at something on the ground. An ancient suit of armor lay at her feet. It was huge—at least four meters tall, its empty helm yawning at the sky. Rough iron gauntlets clawed at nothing with rust-furred fingers, the massive shoulders as wide as Denizen was tall.

The longer he looked at it, the more the suit of armor unnerved him; there was something subtly wrong about its dimensions. The fingers were too long, possessing too many joints. The helm bulged outward at strange angles. It didn't seem to have been forged for a human face.

The armor had collapsed where the wearer had been felled in battle, the body within long rotted away. It didn't take any imagination to guess who had done it and with what.

The hammer of a Malleus had been buried in the center of the chest plate, buckling the metal inward as though struck by a comet. The weapon looked like a grandfather to the one Denizen had seen his aunt carry—the head of dark stone, the haft of gleaming black wood. It pinned the armor to the ground.

D'Aubigny removed her gloves, stretching fingers of iron. "Stand back."

She took a deep breath, power suddenly radiating from her eyes. Light bled from between her teeth, her hands spasming open. The air shivered and pulsed. D'Aubigny's lips moved, and the Tenebrae moved with them, thrumming along Denizen's skin like the patter of rain.

Abigail let out a shocked exclamation. She could feel it too.

"What—"

Her words were swept away by D'Aubigny's crackling intonations. She didn't seem in the least bit distracted or perturbed, and Denizen wondered just how long it took before you became used to feeling another world breathe along your skin.

"Denizen," Abigail whispered beside him. "The stars are changing."

She was right. They burned with alien fire, brighter than he had ever seen stars glow before, and as he stared up at them, they began to *move,* wheeling round the sky like birds circling or sparks from a campfire spun and eddied by the wind.

Denizen couldn't tell if the earth moved or the sky, but he knew instinctively that where they were had *shifted*. Lightning streaked down in the distance to paint the sea a hellish white. Somewhere, the storm was breaking, screaming its fury down, but here at the very center of things, the wind had died and all was calm.

As if the world was waiting for something.

The air sizzled with the taste of the Tenebrae. The armor trembled with it. Power bled from the sky, funneling downward in an invisible stream, and with the creak of iron, the hammer bucked to the side as something shifted beneath it.

The fingers of the gauntlets twitched, flakes of rust drifting free. Denizen and Abigail flinched as first one shoulder rose, then the other. The pressure in the air hummed.

The Emissary of the Endless King rose to its feet, darkness boiling within the hollows of its armor. The helm stared blindly down at them.

Where is my sword?

Its voice sounded like a tidal wave. Hoarse and dragging, each word pulled up from somewhere deep in the darkness—things washed up on shore to die. Every breath whistled hollowly through the gaps in its armor, rust bleeding from its neck as its helm creaked from side to side.

Denizen stared up at it. The Emissary's shoulders nearly blocked out the sky.

Where is my sword? it said again, voice splitting the air.

"You set it aside," D'Aubigny said, her head bowed. The words had the feel of a ritual.

Where is my sword? Its gauntlets curled into fists. Darkness drooled from its joints. There was a fetter, thick as Denizen's neck, closed around its massive ankle. A chain fell away from it to sink into the rock of the Point itself.

"You set it aside," D'Aubigny said again. "You put it away." The Emissary's head lifted to the sky as if listening to something only it could hear.

I did, it intoned. ***I chose peace. I chose to sleep. To wait to be called. I chose to speak for That-Which-Is-Endless, the Father of Shadow, the King of the Tenebrae.***

"You did," D'Aubigny said, "and the Order is grateful."

The Emissary drank great snuffling breaths through its helm. The stars above slowed in their movements, glittering pin-sharp in the blackness of the sky.

D'Aubigny folded her arms. Not a trace of fear showed in her pale features, as if questioning a towering suit of armor impaled by a hammer was something she did every day.

Iron inside.

Ask your question, the Tenebrous said.

"What was stolen?" D'Aubigny said. "What has the Endless King lost? The Order is not your enemy in this. We will help you find it if we can."

The Emissary was still for a long time, the only sound the crashing of distant waves and the lonely cry of the wind.

I will consult, it said, its voice a drowning. ***I will consult.***

The armor went still—darkness slinking into the crevices of the suit, shoulders slumping, arms swinging slack by its sides. The haft of the hammer dipped.

Whatever mind had inhabited the body was gone. Denizen could almost believe that the Emissary was just a statue, some long-ago monument to a forgotten war, a silent guardian of an ancient peace.

D'Aubigny sank to the ground, pulling off her cap to rub her forehead. Summoning the Emissary had seemed to exhaust her.

"Are you all right?" Abigail said in a concerned voice.

The Knight nodded. "Now we wait."

They left her sitting there, staring up at the Emissary's prone form.

Denizen went to stand at the edge of the summit. Distant lightning stabbed at the sea or climbed between great towers of cloud.

How long had this deserted little speck of stone been here? He tried to imagine what it must have been like for sailors back when they drew dragons on the maps to fill in the blank spaces. What must they have thought when Os Reges Point loomed over the horizon—five fingers of stark black stone against a needlework sky?

"Denizen."

He turned. The wind had caught Abigail's hair, lifting it in a froth of glistening black until he couldn't tell where it ended and the sky began. In the unlight of the *Lucidum,* her eyes were sparks, raw nebulae, shining brighter than all else.

"I'm not going to apologize," she said, her eyes fixing him like crossbow bolts.

It took Denizen a minute to find his words. "Apologize?"

"Yes. I'm not going to."

He shook his head. "I'm not— I mean, I don't want you to. What are you not apologizing for?"

She took a step closer, her arms folded across her chest. Denizen was suddenly very aware of the long, long drop behind them.

"You tell me. Either you're the grumpiest thirteen-year-old in the world—which I'm not discounting—or I've done something to offend you."

"No, no," Denizen said, lifting his hands in protestation, "you haven't—"

"I know I haven't," she interrupted. "We've only

known each other ten minutes. So I have to assume that you're annoyed at me for something else."

It was a mistake, Denizen was realizing, to have assumed there was anything naive in Abigail's wide-eyed appreciation of the world. The stare she gave Denizen wasn't quite of Vivian's intensity, but it was close. He felt bits of himself peeling away beneath it.

"Is it that I had a head start with my training?" Abigail asked, and this time her voice was gentler. "Or because I wanted to work with your aunt? Or, I don't know, you're just annoyed at the world in general—"

"Yes," Denizen said.

A frown flitted across her features. "Yes? Wait—which one?"

"All of them," Denizen said, giving her a halfhearted smile. "Sorry. It's not your fault. I *know* it's not your fault. I just . . . a few weeks ago, I was at home. My biggest worry was homework . . . or, I don't know, having to do sports. Now it's the end of the world.

"And you're . . . better at this. I'm scrambling to catch up, and you've known about this all along. I arrive and I hear loads about you, and then I meet you and you're *brilliant,* properly brilliant, and my aunt has actually *talked* to you. She probably wishes you were her niece rather than me being her nephew. You were *meant* for this. I'm just—I don't know. Tagging along. Getting in the way."

Abigail nodded. "Do you know what I got for my tenth birthday?"

Denizen shook his head.

"A crossbow. And I loved it—I did, it was the one I wanted—but there was a part of me that was hoping I'd get a phone. Or . . . I don't know. What do ten-year-old girls get as presents?"

Denizen shrugged.

"My brother's three years old," Abigail said. "And apart from him, I've never lived around anybody but adults. They tried to keep some of the worst of it away from me, but when you're moving five times a year and all your parents' friends have battleaxes, the truth comes out pretty quickly.

"So I learned. I'm a crack shot. I can stitch a decent set of sutures. And I'm pretty sure that this is the longest conversation I've ever had with someone my own age."

"Really?"

She thought for a moment. "Well, in English, anyway." She crossed her arms. "Point is, I've spent my whole life with a bunch of people who are quite preoccupied with other things. So I learned them. I mean, you know all these guys so well already. . . ."

Denizen blinked in surprise. "What?"

"They totally dote on you," Abigail said, grinning. "Jack is planning to teach you smithing. Says it'll cure your skinniness, put some muscle on you. Grey talks about you like you're brothers. And you saw how upset Darcie was at the thought of putting you in danger."

Denizen frowned. "What she said . . . about not having to be a Knight. Do you ever think about that?"

"Sometimes."

"Do you . . . Do you enjoy it? The training?"

"I do," she said. "I always have. But part of that is because"—she looked down at her feet—"when the time comes, I want to be good enough. Fast enough. As fast as I need to be. And I was never going to be anything else, you know? I'm a Falx."

Denizen sighed. "I was going to be a teacher."

They stood silently for a little while, both deep in thought. Which was worse—a whole new world coming out of nowhere to derail your future, or never having a choice of future in the first place?

Eventually, Denizen reached out and touched her on the arm. He doubted she could feel it through her coat. He could barely feel it through his gloves. But it was there. A peace offering. A little moment of connection.

"You're very direct," he said, and then gave her a quick grin.

"Raised by Knights," she said. "You pick it up with the throwing knives."

As they spoke, the Emissary suddenly twitched,

darkness boiling out from a thousand rents in the armor to lift the head and set the shoulders, life suddenly returning to the body like a puppet's strings pulled taut. The haft of the hammer quivered in its chest.

Its voice was a roar. Denizen could feel it vibrate in his bones.

TAKEN.

Even D'Aubigny took a step backward. The thing's massive fists rose to smash the petite Frenchwoman to paste. Denizen and Abigail froze.

What do we do?

He could see D'Aubigny gather herself, utterly fearless, eyes narrowed, hand lifting to—but not gripping—the sword on her back.

"You chose *peace,* creature," D'Aubigny snapped, and the fists paused in the air, shaking with barely contained rage. Particles of rust floated down.

Woman and Tenebrous faced each other, D'Aubigny's jaw outthrust as though she meant to hold the giant with her willpower alone. Eventually, it lowered its fists.

"What has been taken, Emissary?" D'Aubigny said.

His heart. The Endless King has had His heart carved out. It is lost. It is stolen. He will burn this world looking for it.

D'Aubigny scowled. "What does that mean, *his heart?*"

A piece of Him. His mercy. The King rages in the dark. His

hunters come from every shadow. If they do not find what was lost . . . war, Iron-hand. War unending, between our kind and yours. The Pursuivants walk the worlds. If it is not found, we will eat your cities and take your night. Make you fear the dark again.

Denizen could swear there was eagerness in the Emissary's voice.

I will find my sword.

"That will not happen," D'Aubigny snarled. She didn't seem in the least bit afraid, as if she spoke to animated suits of armor threatening an apocalypse all the time. Her hand still hovered near her sword.

"War serves no one. And we will not go quietly, wretch. The Order will unite. We will stand against the King with light and fire. A war will serve *no one*."

Then find what was taken, the ancient Tenebrous growled. ***And soon.***

With that, the Emissary of the Endless King fell silent. The helm bowed as the spirit animating it departed. Piece by piece, the armor fell to the earth.

Denizen shivered involuntarily as the tension seeped from the air, the sharpness of the stars fading until they were simply dots of white light again. The wind began to rise, bringing with it the smell of salt rather than the electric taste of the Tenebrae.

"What did he mean?" Denizen asked. "The Endless King's mercy?"

"I do not know," D'Aubigny said. "We need to get home and speak to the others. I do not like being here any longer than I have to." Her face was grim. "The Endless King crossed over once before. I have no desire to spend any more time with the body he left behind."

"What do you mean?" Denizen said.

"Os Reges Point. This is where the King crossed over before. Made a body, as all Tenebrous do, and left it here as a warning."

"Where is it?" Abigail asked.

D'Aubigny gestured down to the massive fingers of rock beneath them. "You're standing on it."

22

PANIC

DAY—

THE STORM HAD gotten in.

Nowhere was safe. Wind howled through Crosscaper's corridors, tearing sheets from beds, hammering on doors, and shaking windows in their frames. Frost climbed the walls in ugly traceries of silver and white, ready to stick to skin, to freeze tears, to blister unwary hands with cold.

Simon had memories of other storms—vicious tempests held back by a thin sheet of glass, a blanket round his shoulders and the silent company of a friend—but they were long gone. He barely remembered what they were like. Maybe they had never existed at all.

This wasn't anything like nature. Nature was pure and unthinking. This was a *sly* storm, a hurting storm. It carried flecks of broken glass; it hunted and it hated and it hungered.

The Clockwork Three were bored.

Hide. Hide, scrabble, hide. Simon had lost track of just how many times he had moved in the last few hours. Nowhere was safe anymore, not even for a night. The strangers *prowled* now—sweeping through rooms, looking for anything fragile left to destroy.

The cold wooden floor scraped his chest as he slithered under a bed. He didn't know what dormitory he was in, or if it was a dormitory at all; the world had become unknown rooms and hard corners, them and him and the distance between—

A howl sounded from somewhere in the orphanage, followed by the crashing of something heavy pushed down the stairs.

That was the woman—or what had been the woman. He'd known all along they were nightmares, and the clicking-clacking thing that now left half-human footprints down the corridors was just the beast revealed.

The others could be anywhere.

He hadn't slept in so long. He hadn't eaten. He hadn't done anything other than run and hide and run again—

It's my birthday today.

The thought came out of nowhere, and Simon pushed trembling fingers into his mouth to stifle a hysterical laugh, every muscle clenched so the slightest vibration didn't carry through the floorboards.

He was thirteen. Had been for hours now, probably. He honestly had no idea.

As soon as it had come, the realization was dismissed. There was a sort of crazed practicality to Simon now. All nonessential systems had been shut down. All that mattered was keeping one step ahead of them—or rather a step behind, as the only places he trusted to harbor him were those that the Three had exhausted the night before.

As always, the room was a mess. They had passed through this dorm twice at least. Simon could tell because the obvious things were destroyed, and the Three had taken to tearing clothes and ripping at light fixtures instead. The only things that weren't disturbed were the children in their beds, though they still moaned and twitched as if eternally in nightmares.

Why them? Another question he no longer had the energy to contemplate. *Why leave them alone?*

The man's voice purred through his memories, and Simon bit down harder to stop shaking.

We can grow fat here.

More crashes sounded, echoing from elsewhere. With the sick sort of expertise bestowed by an eternity in the dark, Simon knew that meant they had found something new to ruin. Something they'd neglected, something they hadn't seen—

And then the storm said his name.

Deeeeeaaaarrrr Siiiiiimmmoooonnnnnn.

Simon banged his head on the bottom of the bed. He let out a hoarse wheeze of pain and immediately flinched at how loud it was in the sudden silence.

The man in the waistcoat. He'd said Simon's name. How did he—

Panic. Panic, panic, panic. Every single little piece of fear he'd been trying to suppress since the night the strangers came washed over Simon in a freezing black wave. He nearly drowned in it.

I hope this reaches you by your biiiiirthdaaaaaay.

He had to get out. He had to leave. He had to run. All his barely kept control vanished, and he scrambled to his feet, a sick, churning terror in his chest. It was hard to swallow. Sweat leapt from his temples as he whirled. *Where do I go? Where do—*

THEEEEERRRRRE'S SOOO MUUUUUCH IIII WAAAAANT TO TELLLLLL YOOOOOU.

Simon ran.

A blast of painful cold as he darted through the corridor. The gale was constant now, a shrieking pressure that might have been as much inside his head as outside—it was hard to tell—it was so hard to *think*.

They'd found him. Had they found him? He'd dreamt of the moment since that first night, that first bolt of lightning: the doors of his cupboard ripped open, a hand closing on his ankle as he slept—

His bare feet pounded on the floorboards; after so long being silent, it all seemed horrifyingly loud, but he had to get away from here, he had to run. He braced himself for the sight of them coming round the corner—

Nothing.

Simon forced himself to slow, skidding to a halt and turning back the way he'd come. The voice had stopped.

Breathe. Breathe. Breathe.

They hadn't . . . they hadn't found him. They were just amusing themselves. The man in the waistcoat had unearthed something, a letter perhaps. He'd just been . . . reading aloud.

That was all. Simon had moved without caution, flung himself out into the open, nearly thrown away his life because *panic* had gotten in. Just for a moment. This was what happened when—

Hsssss.

It was the woman in white, though neither of those titles was truly accurate anymore. Someone somewhere had subjected her to great heat and violence, and now she was little more than fabric over clockwork. Simon watched with wide, terrified eyes as threads of skin started to pull their way across her face, the damage repairing itself slowly, cloaking her once more in meat.

She stood at the far end of the corridor, staring up

at the boards of the ceiling as if wondering how best to pull them down. All she had to do was look down.

Please don't. Please don't. It's my birthday.

Sudden pain at his temples. A tingle in his palms. He'd been so very careful. So very careful up until now.

Just let me not be seen.

The woman turned to look at him. A slow grin tore her face apart.

23

Singular Intent

Seraphim Row had never seemed so dark.

They had assembled in the kitchen, all clustering in a corner as if hoping to somehow ward off the gaping emptiness of the room. Darcie and Denizen hunched over one of the tables, staring down at untouched cups. At some point, Darcie had laid her hand over his—nothing romantic, but for comfort.

D'Aubigny's arms were wrapped round Jack, her head resting on his massive chest. Her katana still hung from her back, the hilt close to her hand as though she expected to be attacked right here in the kitchen. Maybe she did.

"What are we going to do?" Grey said. It was the first time Denizen had seen him since they'd returned from Os Reges Point two days ago.

Grey's face was stricken with pain, gloved fingers

trembling against his temple. He must have been hurt worse in Rathláth than Denizen had thought. He looked like he hadn't slept in days.

"I've contacted the Palatine," Jack said. "Cadres are searching their records for any reference to the Endless King's mercy, but it could take days. Weeks. And the first reports are coming in—it's no longer just clashes in alleyways now. The war is starting. The Order is mobilizing. There's been word from PenumbraCorp in the States, from the Russian and the Thousand Choirs. They're ready when we are."

"Does that mean we have a chance?"

"It's not about that, Denizen," Jack said. "We can't afford for this war to be dragged into the light."

Denizen's tea cooled between his fingers. How would people deal with the knowledge that the Tenebrae existed? Lately, the world seemed constantly in danger of falling into war anyway.

If the Tenebrous started pouring from every shadow, there would be global panic—armies trying to fight an enemy that could come from nowhere and everywhere all at once. And if people found out about the Knights . . . Denizen was too much of a skeptic to think that the governments of the world would welcome a secret order of sorcerer Knights, even if they were trying to help. At best, they'd be jealous and mistrustful, and at worst . . .

His stomach went cold as he imagined doctors and scientists prodding him, carving out samples of the iron in his palm. *Don't we have enough to worry about already?*

That said, there was a tiny part of him that was thrilled at the thought. A tiny, *insane* part, but a part nonetheless. If he became a Knight, then his life would be hidden in the shadows; he'd be fighting battles no one would ever know about. But if the war came out into the open and the King was defeated . . .

The Order of the Borrowed Dark, saviors of the world.

Listen to me, he thought. *I don't even know how to use a sword. The last time I tried to face a Tenebrous, I nearly blew myself up. Go off to war with the Order? They wouldn't even let me hold their coats.*

D'Aubigny was now pacing like a collared cat. The hawkish focus normally present in Abigail's eyes had been replaced by a pinched look of apprehension. In how many garrisons across the world was this scene being repeated? Wounded, worried Knights preparing for a battle that might consume the world.

"Where's my aunt?" Denizen said. He couldn't stop a thread of bitterness from curling round the words. "Shouldn't she be here? Isn't this an emergency?"

"I don't know," Grey said. "She said she was going to Berlin to reinforce a cadre."

Jack shook his head. "There isn't a Berlin cadre anymore. They were attacked two days ago. No survivors."

"Wait," Denizen said. "Then my aunt—"

"She wasn't there," Jack said. He seemed reluctant to say the words. "All the bodies were checked. She was supposed to reinforce them, but she never did."

"Then where was she?" Denizen asked.

"I don't know," Grey said. "She hasn't been answering her phone." They all shook their heads.

"And none of you find that weird?" Denizen said angrily. "The fact that we're about to go to war and she's nowhere to be found?"

Is this what happened eleven years ago? Did she get her whole cadre killed because she wasn't there when things got rough? The cruelty of the thought shocked him.

"Denizen, your aunt is a war hero," Jack said. "Whatever she's doing, I'm sure she has a good reason for—"

"A good reason for what?"

They all turned to see Vivian standing in the doorway in a long black coat, hammer held loosely in her hand.

If the strain of the last few days had taken its toll on the other Knights, Vivian seemed grimmest of all; a bruise had stained one cheek and there were dark hollows under her eyes. She looked like she hadn't slept in days, as if it were sheer force of will keeping her upright.

Denizen's eyes were drawn to the weapon in her hand. It suited her. Like the hammer, there was no art to Vivian, nothing but hard edges, the singular intent of a warrior.

Her eyes glittered.

"Malleus," Grey said. "We need to talk. The Endless King—his . . . mercy has been stolen. We don't know what that means, but we have to find it before the King crosses over."

"I know where it is," Vivian said.

"Where?" D'Aubigny asked, stepping away from Jack. "Where is it? We need to contact the other Knights. We need to—"

"We're not going to the other Knights." Vivian's words were cold. "Your orders are to stand down. Inform the other Knights to stand down as well."

"Stand *down*?" D'Aubigny said in a low and dangerous voice. "The Endless King thinks we have taken something from him. We are in terrible danger."

"No, we're not," Vivian said. "Not after tonight."

"Malleus, how can you know that?" Jack asked.

"Because I know who took it from him!" Vivian snapped. "You're to stay here. All of you. That's an order." Without waiting for a response, she strode off into the flickering darkness. They stared after her.

"What was *that*?" Denizen asked.

"Go to bed," Jack said. "Both of you."

Denizen and Abigail began to protest until D'Aubigny silenced them with a sharp look.

"Now," she hissed.

They went upstairs in numb silence.

"Do you want to talk?" Abigail asked.

Denizen just shook his head.

DENIZEN HAD BARELY been in his room ten minutes before there was a knock at the door.

It was Grey. He stuck his head round the door. "Can we talk?"

The first thing Denizen noticed was that Grey looked awful. His fingers clenched and unclenched rhythmically, as if missing the hilt of his sword. The bandages on the side of his head had started to come loose.

The second thing Denizen noticed was that Grey was dressed to travel.

"You're going after her," Denizen said. It wasn't a question. He'd thought about nothing else since D'Aubigny had dismissed them. A thousand different plans had darted through his head, and if any of them had been possible, he'd have been after Vivian like a shot.

"*We're* going after her," Grey said. "You know Crosscaper, right? The layout of the place?"

Denizen nodded in confusion. That was an understatement. But why—

"You think she's going to Crosscaper?"

Grey pulled a crumpled envelope from his pocket. "This was on Vivian's desk."

SIMON HAYES
CROSSCAPER ORPHANAGE

Every molecule of Denizen froze. He'd posted Simon's birthday card a week ago. He'd never received a response.

"No, no, no, no . . ."

It took a moment for Denizen to realize that he was the one speaking. The power of the Tenebrae woke in his stomach, curling through him like a serpent, making the pads of his fingers itch. Crosscaper. His friends. The people he'd grown up with.

Simon.

"Denizen."

He suddenly ached to unleash the power straining within him, panic twisting through the rage. They were supposed to be safe. That had been the *point.* The only thing that had kept him going the last few weeks was the knowledge that, though he missed Simon terribly, their separation was keeping him safe.

"Denizen."

He shook himself, suddenly seeing in the mirror that his eyes were glowing in the darkness of the room.

Something fell from the envelope into his hand, and he stared down at the jagged shape. It was a cog—a little brass piece of clockwork, bright against the dark iron of his palm.

Clockwork. Like the white woman.

"They're in Crosscaper," Denizen said numbly. "It's a message."

Grey glanced back down the corridor. "It's a trap. They're luring her right to them, and I'm not leaving your aunt to face them alone."

"How will we get there?" Denizen asked, already shrugging on his coat. "Is there another car—"

Grey whipped a hand through the air. The Cant he spoke was far too complex for Denizen to follow—a surge of dizziness, the taste of rain, a gale sucking at your throat. No sooner had it drifted from Grey's lips than the shadow cast by Denizen's open door seemed to *invert*—falling into itself with a sound like ripping silk.

Denizen's stomach lurched. It was like he was back at the cliffs behind Crosscaper, staring out over the drop, vertigo swaying his heels. There was a chill breeze on his face.

"The Art of Apertura," Grey said. "A method of slinking through shadows. Dangerous. Very dangerous. Even Vivian only uses it sparingly. But you saw her tonight. If we don't hurry, we'll never catch up with her."

Denizen nodded slowly. Suddenly he thought of Abigail. "Should we—"

Grey jerked his head toward the shadow on the wall. "No time. Go."

For a second, Denizen felt like Grey was playing some ludicrous joke on him, that Denizen would walk forward and bang his face on the stone wall. His stomach still churned, though, as if he were suspended over some great height.

Like a Breach, he thought. *Like the first stirrings of a Breach.*

"Do I just . . . step into it?"

Grey was drumming his fingers on the side of his cheek, his words forced out through gritted teeth. "Yes. Just—" The veil of shadow pulsed behind him. "Step in. The Cost will show you the way. And whatever you do, don't open your eyes. Understand?"

No, Denizen thought. *Not at all, actually.* "What—"

"Now or never, kid," Grey said. There was a bright sheen of sweat on his forehead. "Are you a Hardwick or not?"

Denizen's eyes narrowed. He took a deep breath and stepped into darkness.

24

Dark Water

Denizen fell through a sunless sea.

His limbs drifted in the murk, slow as dreaming, something like a heartbeat pounding sluggishly nearby. His eyes were screwed shut. His chest burned with the need to breathe, but somehow he knew that opening his mouth would be a mistake. There was still a core of warmth in him, and inhaling the dark water of this place would put it out.

He had no idea how long he fell. Years seemed to pass. He knew without opening his eyes that there was no light beyond them—no, more than that, there had never been light. Light had never existed; water was all there was to the world, deep and black and cold.

There was a pain in the palm of his hand.

Soon he forgot the feel of sunlight. He forgot

whether he was falling or rising, forgot what his name had been before the water had surrounded him.

Calm stole over him. His arms slowed. His heartbeat slowed with it.

Centuries, drifting in the dark.

And then—

The water shivered. He didn't open his eyes to see what might have caused it. What would be the point? There had never been anything to see and no light to see it with.

And then—

Again. A disturbance in the sea, the water displaced as if something huge had passed him by. He twisted his head for the first time in a thousand years.

Nothing. It was hard to think. It was like the water had seeped into him, made him heavy and slow.

The shape circled again, a vastness that shook the world, dragging him along in the backwash of its current. His hand *ached* like it had been punctured by a needle of frozen steel.

Denizen—*That's my name, my name is Denizen*—shook his head to clear the numbing cold. Thoughts began to return.

Memories. Awareness. Fear.

Something circled him and he couldn't see it. The prey part of his brain urged him to open his eyes, to kick, to flee, to get as far away from this unseen predator as he could. And there was something else too—a new heat coiled round his spine.

Denizen began to swim.

His movements were slow at first, hatefully slow. It wasn't a needle through his hand; it was a hook—and he had to strain against it with every stroke. Up or down, forward or back—he didn't care. Anything was better than waiting here like dangling bait.

The unseen predator circled faster, as if his panic excited it.

The Cost will show you what to do.

The frozen ache in the center of his hand was iron, the iron of his world. *The most here thing there is.* He stopped fighting its pull, sweeping his arm through the chill until he felt it, a tug so strong Denizen nearly cried out.

He clawed his way toward it. *Where else am I going to go?*

The thing circling him grew restless, its unseen limbs writhing, tearing the water apart in its wake. There were more now. He could feel them—drawn by his struggles and the hammering of his heart—but he didn't care.

The harder he swam, the stronger the pull became. Denizen began to fall toward it, as if the whole sea were emptying out through that single burning point. Just as he reached it, an eddy spun him, and his eyes opened with shock, and Denizen Hardwick saw what had been circling him, their huge and terrible shapes. . . .

He opened his mouth to scream—

—and fell out onto wet earth.

He coughed and spluttered. Air reached his lungs, and that first breath was the sweetest thing he'd ever tasted. For a long moment, all Denizen could do was let his chest rise and fall, reacquainting himself with how utterly *magic* breathing was. How had he never noticed that before? All this air around and he had taken it completely for granted. He rolled onto his back and stared up at the sky.

At the *sky*.

They were no longer in Seraphim Row. The sky above was a tumble of diamonds across velvet—stars, shining so bright they made Denizen squint. They were beautiful. No, more than that.

They were familiar.

"Are you all right?"

After so long in silence and dark water, it took a moment for Denizen to understand the words.

"Denizen?"

There was a man standing over him, a concerned look on his face. *Grey*. Denizen shook his head to clear it, oily black water beading the ground beneath him.

He started as each of the droplets came apart in a thin streamer of black smoke, as did the water soaking his coat and jeans. It boiled away as if it couldn't stand the touch of the real world. The sensation made his skin tighten uncomfortably, but in moments he was completely dry, the smoke hanging in the air for a second before it too faded.

Grey knelt beside him. "First time is always a bit rough."

"Was . . . was that the Tenebrae?" Denizen said a little shakily. *Don't open your eyes.* A Knight could see in the darkness, but just because you *could* didn't mean you *should.* What he had seen . . . what he had *almost* seen . . . the barest glimpse of it. . . . He shivered so hard his teeth clacked painfully.

Grey's nod was sympathetic. "We can dart through its shallows as a sort of . . . shortcut." He took a ragged breath. "Just need to watch out for the sharks."

The iron of his palm still shivered with a phantom ache. Denizen never thought he'd be grateful for it.

"Come on," said Grey.

Denizen got to his feet and just . . . stared.

Everything was as he remembered—the beach gleaming silver in the moonlight, the vast bulk of the mountain behind, Moyteoge Point curving down into the bay like the curled tail of a prehistoric beast.

Mountains marched off into the distance, their shapes as familiar to him as the angles of his face. Even the air smelled the same.

But Crosscaper itself . . .

The Aperture had left them where the orphanage driveway met the road, a hundred or so meters from the gates. All Denizen could think of as he and Grey approached was that someone must have come in when Denizen was gone and dismantled it—taken it apart, stone by stone, and replaced it with bricks a little smaller, materials a little shabbier.

The place loomed in his memory, a vast labyrinth containing every fragment of his childhood. Now Denizen couldn't believe it was so small.

"Come on," Grey called. Denizen hurried after him.

Vivian Hardwick knelt in front of the open gates, her hammer planted squarely in front of her in the ground. Beyond her Denizen could see the torn-open, charred remains of a car, metal twisted apart like the petals of a flower. And beyond that—

A body. Denizen lunged, but Vivian's hand caught him square in the chest.

"No," he snarled, squirming. "Who—"

"Stop," she said, and pushed him back toward Grey. "He's alive. Just sleeping."

"What—"

"That's what they do," she said, rising to her feet.

"Like spiders wrapping their prey in silk so they can . . . so they can feed."

The look Vivian gave them then would have given the Endless King pause.

"What are you doing here?" Her eyes gleamed far too brightly in the moonlight—she was holding her power, a lot of it. Plumes of breath smoked between her teeth, heated by the inferno within.

Denizen threw the piece of clockwork at her. Vivian looked so surprised she actually took a step backward.

"What is *wrong* with you?" He didn't know whether it was nearly a month of utter frustration at the way he'd been treated or the liquid fire in his chest, but, terrifying warrior or not, Denizen was absolutely sick of the great Malleus Vivian Hardwick. "Why won't you tell us what's going on?"

"Grey," Vivian snapped, "get him out of here—"

"No!" Denizen countered. "You need to tell me what's going on. What happened eleven years ago? Your whole cadre died, all of them, and the next day I'm dumped in Crosscaper. What *happened*?"

He was shouting now. He couldn't help it. He knew he should stop talking—if anything, he was completely ruining their chance of sneaking up on anybody—but he couldn't help himself. Everything he'd been dying to say to his aunt spilled out, and he couldn't have closed his mouth even if he'd wanted to.

"They killed your friends and they killed my parents, didn't they? *Didn't they?* Just tell me. Tell me the truth!"

Vivian stared at him. "Denizen." Her voice trailed away. He blinked away hot tears, turning away from her. "I never planned to . . ."

"Never planned to what?" Denizen said, a lump in his throat.

"I never planned to let it go this far. . . ."

She stepped past Grey, reached out a hand—

—and was suddenly flung forward into Denizen's arms by the loudest sound he'd ever heard. Her eyes, shocked and wide, found Denizen's just for a moment before closing, her weight bearing him to the ground.

Grey lowered the pistol, a look of despair on his face.

"Well," he said hollowly, "you know what they say about plans."

25

MERCY

"YOU HAVE TO understand," Grey said, staring down at Vivian's body in its spreading pool of blood. "This is a mercy."

The shot still echoed against the walls of Crosscaper, chasing itself round the bay before finally escaping into the sky. Denizen had never heard a sound like it before—the unnatural, violent loudness of it. The noise was the sound barrier breaking. Had he read that somewhere? Denizen couldn't remember. He'd never had occasion to think of it before. He'd never . . .

"You . . ."

Panic squeezed Denizen's throat. His hands began to shake.

"You shot her."

The stupidest statement ever uttered. The most idiotic arrangement of words in the universe.

Grey's eyes were wild. "So I did."

His hand was trembling as badly as Denizen's. The gun swayed left, then right. Denizen couldn't take his eyes off it. More than any other weapon he'd seen in Seraphim Row, including actual *magic* weapons, the gun had a power to it—like gravity, its muzzle a black hole exerting irresistible force.

Why did Grey even carry a gun? Did guns work on Tenebrous? Or was it just for Denizen's relatives?

Focus. The thought had an edge of hysteria. *Oh God. Focus.*

Grey was looking past him at Crosscaper, a sort of dreamy recognition on his face. "I grew up in a place like this," he said.

"Grey," Denizen said. Each word had to be dragged up from somewhere deep. "What . . . what are you doing?"

"They call it thralldom," Grey said, and there was the most awful look of despair on his face.

"They took me in that village. *Did* things to me, and then made me forget. I didn't know what was wrong. I'd hear a clock and I'd flinch. I'd dream of buttons, bright buttons on a waistcoat. Pale fingers. The smell of cigarettes. The sobbing. God, the sobbing of the Boy."

The gun shook in his hand. "But now it's all been coming back to me. What they are. What they want me to do."

"What are you talking about?" Denizen asked. Grey's

left eyelid was twitching. He'd looked like hell the last few weeks, but now he appeared positively unhinged.

"They're called the Clockwork Three," Grey whispered. "I can tell you now. Their control . . . it comes and goes." He grimaced. "They have a poisonous kind of *inconsistency*. I hear . . . I hear ticking. It vibrates along my bones. It makes me . . . It makes me do things and I don't remember them. Not unless they want me to. Not unless they want me to hurt."

He scrubbed a hand through his long hair. The action was so unconsciously Grey that it made Denizen sick.

This couldn't be his friend—this wretched, stammering thing that had just gunned down the only family Denizen had left. He'd been told that the older Tenebrous were capable of anything, but seeing it in front of him made his stomach rebel.

"The Man in the Waistcoat. The Woman in White. The Opening Boy. The Boy is every child they've ever hurt. They keep him just to . . . just to make him watch."

With horror, Denizen realized Grey was crying.

"They want a war. They want He-Who-Is-Endless to come. A little more misery in the world. The King wins, the Order wins—it doesn't matter. They just want to pick the bones. They wanted me to bring you here. Both of you. The last two Hardwicks."

"But why?" Denizen said, suddenly hating the

pleading tone that had crept into his voice. "Why us? What do we have to do with starting a war?"

"Symmetry," Grey said miserably. "They were going to take you from Vivian, just like they stole from the Endless King. Your wrong birthday saved your life—they thought you were normal, useless to the Order."

He swallowed thickly. "Now they know different. But they want you anyway, if it helps. All their plans and schemes, and they still can't help following their stomachs. Seeking vengeance. Chasing whatever shiny thing is in front of them."

Grey's jaw twisted with sudden rage. *"Animals."*

He leaned over and picked up Vivian's hammer. The sight of him touching it made Denizen irrationally angry. *How dare he?*

Power suddenly woke in his heart, sending tendrils of heat through his veins. Grey had shot his aunt in the back. In the *back*. That's not how Vivian Hardwick should die. She should fall in battle. *Yield not to evil.*

Not like this. Not betrayed by someone who was supposed to be her comrade. The power of the Tenebrae coiled in him, ready to strike.

"Don't," Grey said tiredly. "You know you don't have a chance against me. Don't make me hurt you any more than I have to."

He stared down at Vivian's body.

"This is a mercy, Denizen. Their process isn't . . .

perfect. I can fight it, find ways round the things they make me do. They made me leave the envelope where Vivian could find it. I was just supposed to keep you both here until they return. They give me orders, but there are loopholes. Wiggle room. I can take them literally. They never said not to . . . They never . . .

"This is better for her. I know what they were going to do to her. At least this was quick. A last service to my Malleus."

He believed it too. Denizen could see that. There was a sort of raw hope in his face as if he expected . . . understanding? Forgiveness?

Denizen's hands curled into fists. "If you can fight their control, why are you doing this? Fight *harder*. Isn't that what a Knight's supposed to do? *A hundred mouths, a hundred tongues, one iron voice?* Grey, *fight*. You just have to—"

"Don't quote the motto of the Order back to me," Grey snapped. "I've been fighting by those words for thirteen years. I know what they mean.

"But iron rusts," he whispered in a wretched voice. "Enough casualties on both sides and a war will happen whether the King has his mercy or not. But that's not enough for the Clockwork Three anymore. They're not used to being in this world for so long. They're fraying, getting distracted. And they *hate* Vivian.

"She hurt them, you see. Eleven years ago, she hurt

them worse than anyone's ever hurt them before. They can't get her out of their heads."

A glove fluttered to the ground.

"And I can't get them out of mine."

Grey's hand had turned to clockwork. The iron skin had split—toothed ridges forcing their way up through the flat of his palm, jagged hollows filled with minute cogs and casters. The fingernails had fallen away, dislodged by rising pins and components Denizen had no name for.

Denizen had almost become used to seeing the effects of the Cost, but this was something else entirely—a shaping unnatural and wrong, like a Breach in the shape of a claw.

A ragged strip of skin wound through the gears like a ribbon caught in the bowels of a machine, and as Denizen watched in horror, Grey tore it free.

With a rattling hiss, the gears began to turn.

"Horrible, isn't it?" Grey said, and he was almost his old self again. "But it won't be for much longer." His voice hardened. "And do you know what the funny thing is? Vivian's just as bad as they are.

"They sent her that card to provoke her, like children picking a fight out of boredom. She could have brought reinforcements, other cadres—hell, with her reputation, she could have brought half the Order . . . but she didn't. She wanted them all for herself."

The wind was starting to rise.

"Why are you telling me this?" Denizen said. He knew the answer even before he asked. There was generally only one reason people in this situation became chatty. They didn't expect the information to go any further.

Sure enough, the gun rose to point right between Denizen's eyes. Grey's hand shook, but at this range there was no chance he'd miss.

Denizen took a deep breath. He'd have to be quick. If Grey got the slightest inkling that Denizen was going to draw on his power, the Knight wouldn't hesitate. Could he get out the Sunrise Cant before Grey killed him? Maybe even attempting it would do Grey's job for him.

Strangely, Denizen didn't feel afraid. Maybe you did get used to life-or-death situations. This was . . . what? Five now? He'd lost count. He'd actually lost count.

The cold breath of the wind carried a tear down his cheek.

Mam. Dad. I'll see you soon.

Denizen Hardwick reached for his power—

—and the gun went off.

The sound was so loud that Denizen staggered backward. His concentration frayed and the power slipped from his grasp, scalding his mind as it went.

His first thought—*I've been shot*—pushed everything

else out of his head. It was only when no pain followed that he realized what had happened.

Smoke rose from the mouth of the gun. Grey had jerked it aside at the last second, the bullet disappearing to ricochet against the orphanage's walls. The Knight's eyes were wild, his teeth gritted, sweat pouring down his face.

"Run," he said. "Please."

And suddenly Denizen understood. Grey had been told to keep them both here; as horrible as it sounded, shooting Vivian technically wasn't disobeying an order. But to let Denizen leave went directly against an order by the Three. It was hurting him. Hurting him terribly. As Denizen watched, a trickle of blood escaped Grey's nose to paint his trembling lips bright red. The clockwork of his hand whined as it ground against itself.

"Go," he snarled.

"They'll kill you," Denizen said. "They'll kill you for this."

Grey flashed him a mad smile. "One can only hope."

Denizen ran.

THE STARS WERE knife wounds in the sky.

Even without the *Lucidum,* it would have been bright enough to see the thumbnail scrape of Keem Bay and the distant crashing waves. The road was a thin scar of black against the mountainside, and Denizen ran until he felt his heart would stop.

Where he was running to escaped him at the moment. He wasn't really running *to* anything. Right now his life was mostly about running *from*.

His heels pounded against stone. He didn't dare look back at Crosscaper, and not just because he was running down a steep hillside road and one slip would do what Grey had planned but with a lot less noise.

Was that why the Three had chosen Crosscaper for their nefarious schemes? None of that difficult body disposal nonsense, not when you could just push the body off the side of a mountain.

Denizen slowed as a thought struck him. Why *had* they chosen Crosscaper? He stopped, finally looking back at the dark shape of the orphanage. He should be running. That was the priority right now, not trying to figure out the motives of those creatures.

And yet . . .

Frown No. 1—I Don't Understand. His least favorite.

Why had the Clockwork Three come to Crosscaper? They'd been here before, according to Grey, but why come back? They wanted misery—loved it, fed on it—and so Crosscaper must have been quite attractive. But why bring Vivian and Denizen somewhere where there'd be a hundred witnesses and general panic?

They must have made the orphanage their own, felt safe enough here to use it as a place of ambush. Fear for Simon and the others made his throat clench, but there was something else too. In fact, the more Denizen thought about it . . .

Crosscaper was the perfect place to hide something you didn't want anyone to find.

The mercy of the King.

Denizen had to get inside. If he could find out what it was, somehow return it to the King or get it back to Seraphim Row . . . Of course, to do that he'd have to get by Grey—a powerful and dangerous Knight, even before the Three had unhinged him—and search an entire orphanage before the Clockwork Three returned.

Denizen was also counting on knowing what the mercy looked like when he saw it. The Woman in White had looked human, right up until she hadn't. The whole thing seemed like one impossibility after another.

Of course, my other option is to go and find a nice spot to watch the apocalypse.

Denizen let out a put-upon sigh that did absolutely nothing to make him feel any better and went to look for the mercy of a god.

26

Wounds

SNEAKING UP ON people was so much easier when they didn't have perfect night vision.

Luckily, Denizen had grown up on these hills. He had played innumerable games of hide-and-seek and catch here, and it was surprising how quickly the knowledge of lines of sight came back. Crawling up the hill, his body pressed as close to the grass as he could get without actually breathing dirt, Denizen's eyes never left the now-closed gates of Crosscaper.

It took him the best part of twenty minutes to half crawl, half scuttle round to the back of Crosscaper, the huge walls of the orphanage working in his favor by hiding his approach.

There was no sign of Grey anywhere, or anyone who might be a part of the Clockwork Three. As he crept toward the rear of the building, Denizen racked his brains for any mention of the Three in the books at Seraphim Row.

She hurt them, you see. Eleven years ago, she hurt them worse than anyone's ever hurt them before.

The words went round and round in his skull. *She hurt them.* The look on Vivian's face when she heard about the Woman in White attacking Denizen in Rath-láth. The fact that if the Three hadn't sent Vivian a message luring her here, the Knights would likely never have found them.

The Three can't get her out of their heads.

Eleven years ago. Just before he'd been placed in Crosscaper. And Vivian hated them enough to put aside her duty to the Order and risk plunging the world into darkness.

Had the Clockwork Three killed his parents?

Denizen slid the last couple meters down the slope and crossed the driveway in a few quick strides. Power crackled through him, not because he had any intention of using it, but simply because it was a comfort.

People hid things. They kept secrets. They changed, or they lied, or they left. They betrayed you, or they let you down. Fire was honest. It just wanted to burn.

Angry tears stung Denizen's eyes. He blinked furiously to clear them.

The tradesmen's entrance of Crosscaper was just a small doorway set into the stone wall. Someone—the

Three?—had half torn the door from its hinges. Denizen eased himself round it, careful not to make any noise.

I'll know it when I see it. Denizen's lips moved silently as he went from doorway to doorway, freezing every time he heard a sound that wasn't his own heartbeat. He weaved through upturned furniture, stepped delicately over broken glass.

Boredom. That was what Grey had said. They liked hurting things, and they got bored easily.

He shoved the thought out of his head. The Three could return at any moment. Grey could find him and be unable to resist their orders a second time.

I'll know it when I see it. I'll know it when I see it.

He made his way through the kitchen, eyeing the hanging pots and pans suspiciously as if they might just jump free of their hooks and clatter to the floor.

How big was mercy? How much did it weigh? Should he be checking every cupboard? Peering into teapots? He didn't have time to go through the place with a fine-tooth comb. He desperately wanted to rush through the halls, looking for Simon and the others—check that they were OK, what had happened—but he couldn't. He had to find the mercy. Crosscaper was huge, and he had only so much time.

Finding it would help them too.

He tried to think where he would hide something valuable in the orphanage.

Ackerby's office? The library? There were bits of Crosscaper that were off-limits to the kids—what if it were in the basement or locked in the infirmary? Maybe the Three had been careless. There had to be *some* kind of luck coming his way.

Well, wherever it was, it wasn't in the kitchen. Denizen was about to leave when a click behind him made his heart nearly stop. He spun, his whole body tensed, his hands raised to . . . what, he didn't know. It took him a couple of seconds to work out where the noise had come from.

The pantry door had cracked open and a pair of eyes stared out, as wide and shocked as his.

Denizen's mouth worked, but it was a long time before any sound came out. Finally, he managed to choke out a single word.

"Simon?"

Unheeded by either of the boys, the door swung fully open, revealing the sorry state of his best friend.

Simon looked like Denizen felt. Somewhere underneath the shock, Denizen noted that his best friend, never the stoutest of boys, had lost even more weight. There were dark circles under his eyes, and his skin was pasty white, as if he hadn't seen the sun in weeks. He didn't even seem to recognize his best friend, his eyes darting from Denizen to the ceiling and back again with the nervous energy of a rat.

"You're not real," he whispered. "You're not . . ."

And then he *flickered*. Just for an instant, so quickly Denizen wasn't even sure it had happened at all. Simon vanished and reappeared in the exact same spot like a TV signal being interrupted or a hologram from a science-fiction story. Denizen scrubbed at his eyes and stared.

"You're not real," Simon hissed, and yanked the pantry door shut.

"I am real!" Denizen said, and then winced at both the loudness and stupidity of what he had just said.

He crossed the room and tried the door handle. He'd never been in the pantry, but there couldn't be a lock on the other side—Simon must be holding it shut. He sighed and pressed his head against the wood.

"Simon," he whispered as loud as he dared. *"Simon."*

There was no answer. Denizen let out an aggravated sigh and thought hard for a second.

"Ask me something," he said. That was how they proved these things in books, wasn't it? "Em . . . ask me something that only I could know." He fought the urge to bang his head on the door.

Finally, he heard a small voice.

"Ask you something?"

"Yes," Denizen said eagerly. "Ask me something. Anything. Come on. I can prove I'm real. Hang on . . . we'll do birthday presents." He thought for a second.

"No, wait. Something else. That's too obvious. Em . . . remember when we climbed up the Point? No—that tie Mr. Colford used to wear. His Monday tie. What if we—"

He stepped back in surprise as the handle began to turn. Simon was staring at him with tears in his eyes.

"I told you," he said, voice cracking with relief, "not to overthink stuff."

THERE WAS LITTLE time for catching up, but Simon spoke quickly and desperately. His voice was raw. It had been a long time since he'd spoken aloud.

"I stumbled right into her, Denizen," the boy whispered, his face ashen. "I'd hidden for so long, weeks of running, barely eating, and then on my birthday . . ."

He shivered, and as he did so, a pale translucence stole across his skin. Denizen could faintly see the shelves of the pantry behind—no, *through*—him. There was a lost look on his best friend's face.

"I remember this sick heat in my stomach, and wishing harder than I've ever wished for anything that she wouldn't see me, and she turned round slowly . . . so slowly, and then . . . It comes and goes. After the first time, I slept for nearly a day."

Denizen spoke carefully. "Simon . . . can I see your hand?"

"How did you know?" Simon said, holding his hand

out to show him the spot of iron in the middle of his palm.

"Happy birthday," Denizen said quietly.

A picture of what had happened was building in his mind. When Denizen's connection to the Tenebrae had bloomed, he'd been angry, angrier than he'd ever been, and it had manifested as fire. He'd lashed out at Vivian with an inferno of raw light.

Simon had been trying to hide. He'd done an incredible job of avoiding the Three for so long, and at the moment he'd nearly failed, his power had saved him. He had channeled the power of the Tenebrae unconsciously and hidden himself.

Not that it hadn't taken its toll—Denizen could see that much. Despite his relief at finding a familiar face, Simon was a shell of his former self. His shoulders trembled, his eyes darting to every shadow as if expecting to be caught at any moment.

That paranoia was probably what had kept him alive.

"Simon, we don't have much time, OK?"

The other boy nodded, thin shoulders trembling involuntarily.

"Where is everybody?"

Simon explained about the strange sleep that had kept the others frozen in their dreams.

"It *nourishes* the monsters somehow," Simon said. "That's what the man said. Misery feeds them."

Denizen's lip twisted in disgust. That's what Grey had said too. There was nothing he could do about that now, though. They were still alive, and he had to hope that by finding the mercy, he could somehow break whatever influence the Three had over them.

He asked Simon if he'd seen anything that might be called a mercy, but Simon shook his head.

"I heard them mention a cage, but that was all. I've been nearly everywhere in the last few weeks, and I haven't seen anything."

Denizen scrubbed a hand over his face. *Why is nothing ever easy?*

"Simon, you need to get out of here," he said. "Go back to the tradesmen's entrance—it's open. Find somewhere to hide where you can see the door. If I don't come back in half an hour, or if you see the Three or anyone else, *run*. Use your power if you have to. OK?"

"I'm not leaving you—"

Denizen shook his head. He could see how much it cost Simon to say that. He must have dreamt about nothing else since the Three had come.

"I'm leaving too," he said. "I just need to take a look around."

"But—"

"But what?" Denizen said.

Simon's shaking stilled. "But you came back for me."

Denizen hugged Simon fiercely, and then gave him

his best approximation of Vivian Hardwick's stare. "I did. And now I need to know that you're safe. *Go.*"

Reluctantly, Simon went. Denizen would have liked nothing more than to go after him, even just to make sure his tormented friend got out safely, but—

Duty first. Strangely, the thought came to him in Vivian's voice.

Denizen made his way to the front of the building, checking carefully round each corner before inching his way forward. There was no sign of the Three or Grey. That was reassuring in one sense, except he knew they had to be *somewhere*. It was like noticing a spider and then looking back and seeing that it was gone. Nowhere was safe.

He found Director Ackerby sprawled in Crosscaper's front hall, one hand stretched toward—but not quite reaching—the fire alarm. Denizen knelt beside him. The director's breathing was high and thready, a staccato wheeze of fear. Had he been trying to warn the children of Crosscaper when the dark sleep had come over him?

Denizen suddenly felt an absurd sort of affection for the man. A few weeks ago, Ackerby had been the scariest thing about Denizen's life—the yellow memos, the cold stare, the rules about where you could and couldn't go—

Denizen's eyes narrowed as he glanced round the hall. The basement door was open. The basement door was never open—Ackerby always kept it locked. As if drawn by some irresistible force, Denizen eased back the heavy oak door and made his way down the stairs.

A long, lightless corridor stretched away before him, the doors marked with labels like 001A—FINANCIAL RECORDS and 002A—STAFF REPORTS. If whatever the Clockwork Three had taken was small, it could take him months to find it down here.

He was just about to try one of the offices when an unearthly roar made the walls shake. It echoed down the corridor like a tidal wave, the sound as deafening as if he stood inside a massive clock striking twelve. Dust rained down from the ceiling, painting his shoulders and face in white. Denizen staggered, falling back against the wall and clutching his ears.

"All right," he said once the earth-shattering noise had faded, his voice strange and tinny in his own ears, "maybe it isn't small."

The mercy. He ran toward the source, hands pressed over his ears in case the eerie howl sounded again. Turning a corner, he found a room the size of a basketball court, the walls beige and the floor rough concrete, littered with the eviscerated remains of a hundred filing cabinets. They had all been flipped onto their backs and flung around as if they'd been swept up in a tornado. Files had slid from the rents in the metal, spilling out over the floor in great dunes and drifts of manila folders and strewn papers.

This must be where all the records of Crosscaper had been kept, but now it looked like it had played host to a fight between a pack of giant cats. The fluorescent bulbs above had been smashed from their sockets. Glass frosted the piles of paper like icing sugar.

Someone had taken great care to sweep the center of the room clean of files and folders to make way for a circle of red chalk on the bare floor.

Denizen took a tentative step closer. And in the circle's center . . .

This time the blast of sound lifted him off his feet entirely. He had time to let out a shocked yell—drowned out completely by the preternatural scream—before landing on his back so hard all the air was pounded from his lungs.

His ribs thrummed painfully in his chest, his vision swimming. Light suddenly speared from the center of the circle, as cold and fractured as the heart of a glacier.

Denizen pushed himself to his feet, head pounding. It was only then he realized that the hellish din was three words, bellowed over and over again until they bled into one shrieking assault.

LETMEOUTLETMEOUTLETMEOUT LETMEOUT!

Denizen's nose was bleeding. His ears ached.

The circle held a girl made of smoke and silver, her head thrown back to scream at the world. Her hair and eyes were knitted from storms, lightning crackling down her cheeks to bite and twitch in the air. She opened her mouth and that glacial light streamed out once again like a solar flare in polar white.

She was beautiful. The thought came from nowhere as Denizen wiped blood from his lip with the back of his hand. She had the beauty of a natural disaster, a raw and primal terror that couldn't help making him stare.

She was a Tenebrous—he had no doubt about that—but he had never read about one like this before. Tenebrous built a body from whatever they could find in the human realm, but this girl looked like she'd carved herself out of the heart of a cold and storm-riddled star.

Her fists lashed out to strike against the empty air with a thrumming concussion of light and noise, as if the chalk circle was some kind of barrier.

Or a cage.

LETMEOUTLETMEOUTLETMEOUT LETMEOUT!

"You're it," Denizen said, the words escaping before he could pull them back. "You're what was taken from the Endless King."

She spun, carving a comet trail in the air, and stared down at him with eyes of searing white.

MY NAME, the girl said, voice shaking the walls, **IS MERCY.**

27

DEBACLE

"OH," SAID DENIZEN, for lack of anything cleverer to say. "Hi."

The Tenebrous girl came apart in curlicues of mist and lightning, re-forming within the confines of the circle with her arms folded.

Her shape changed constantly, shifting from moment to moment until his eyes burned just trying to follow her. The swirling glow of her spine kinked upward, spreading into wide wings of silver-veined luminescence before collapsing into a rain of sparks that left patterns of soot on the concrete floor.

Her features were just as mutable. One moment her hair was short and ragged, the color of a summer sky, and the next a veiling shroud of white long enough to scrape soot marks on the floor. Her eyes veered between slanted fissures and shining wide orbs, their glow bright enough to blind.

There were only two constants: first, no matter what form she took, no part of her ever crossed the red chalk circle; and second, her expression was of absolute fury.

COME TO GLOAT, WHELP? COME TO MOCK YOUR PRISONER?

Denizen staggered under the barrage of sound. It was like being insulted by an artillery range. There was such *contempt* in her voice.

It was that more than anything that made Denizen lose his patience.

He'd had quite enough of every single aspect of his life right now and on top of everything the person he was supposed to rescue was treating him like a particularly disgusting type of beetle.

"No, actually," he snapped acidly. "I'm here to rescue you."

The girl of storms blinked in shock.

WHAT?

"Rescue you," Denizen said again in the same annoyed tone. "I'm here to save you from the Clockwork Three. Not"—he kicked some files out of the way—"that I'm expecting a thank-you or anything. With the kind of day I've been having, I expect you'll try to kill me when I free you. Everyone else has. It won't even be difficult. I've had about"—he half slid down another drift of folders, barely catching himself from pitching headlong into the circle—"ten minutes' training since this whole *debacle* started."

The Tenebrous girl—Mercy—stared at him with wide eyes.

DEBACLE?

This time her voice was slightly quieter, a gale that merely shivered down his spine and fluttered the paper around him.

"It's a word," he said distantly as he stared down at the chalk circle, "that means 'disaster.'"

At first glance, it looked distressingly mundane. Weren't magic circles supposed to have strange letters and runes that made your eyes hurt when you looked at them? Denizen would even have settled for a standard kind of ambient glow.

This was just . . . a circle. It wasn't even a proper one—one of the edges was slightly squashed as if it had been drawn freehand. *You wouldn't see a sorcerer in a book drawing freehand,* Denizen mused, though now that he thought about it, he couldn't imagine one using compasses either. Then again, just because it looked simple didn't mean it wasn't incredibly dangerous. That was the other thing fantasy books said about magical circles—they were supposed to take your hand off if you messed with them.

Denizen knelt, careful not to let any part of him touch the circle's edge.

WAIT.

Mercy hovered closer, but he ignored her. *You're sulking,* a part of him said. *No I'm not,* said another, *and if I am so what? I'm saving the world.*

Probably.

"Yes?" he said finally, holding a finger just shy of the chalk. If he concentrated, he could feel . . . *there,* the tiniest tension to the air, like holding your hand close to a live power cable.

YOU ARE GOING TO FREE ME?

She sounded dubious. He supposed he couldn't blame her.

"As soon as I figure out how," he said, racking his brains to try to remember if there'd been any mention of things like this in his training. Was he supposed to rub out some of the circle?

Denizen couldn't help being aware of the strong possibility that doing something wrong might cause an explosive backlash . . . and he was sitting on a pile of flammable papers with all his childhood friends asleep upstairs. Somehow, he didn't think burning the building down would improve the situation.

He chanced a quick glance up at the Tenebrous girl floating above him. She appeared confused.

JUST LIKE THAT?

"Just like that."

NO DEMANDS? NO BARGAINING?

"Should I be bargaining?" Denizen said, and now he *knew* he was sulking. "Sorry. I'm new at this. Tell you what, go back to the Endless King—tell him that it was someone from the Order who freed you and we'll be even. He can recall his Pursuivants. Everything can go back to normal. How does that sound?"

The Tenebrous was silent for a moment.

Done, she said, and this time her voice was as soft as a spring breeze. ***And done, and sworn again, Iron Knight.***

"I'm not a Knight," Denizen said. "I'm just a . . . My aunt was supposed to be here. She'd know how to free you. I don't know what I'm doing. My aunt would . . ."

Suddenly it felt like the events of the last few hours all caught up with him at once. He swallowed and sat back on a pile of folders. Why *was* he here? Vivian was the one who'd know what to do.

"He shot her," Denizen blurted. "Grey—the Three *did* something to him and he shot her and I have no idea what I'm doing and I have to stop them because if I don't then there's going to be war and I really wish—I really wish—"

Mercy's form steadied, the shifting light that made up her body coalescing into something that resembled a human girl in a simple white dress. She still glowed—her skin lit from within by a kind of chilly phosphorescence—but aside from that she might have been his own age, her hair a cascade of crackling white.

I had eluded my father's guards, she said, and a ripple ran through her, as if she were a pond disturbed by a stone. *I like exploring. Peering up at all the different worlds. They used the Boy. The Opening Boy. I heard such sobbing and I went to see, to help and . . .*

She shivered.

They took me. I'd never been in your world before. So bright. So hard. Everything staying the same shape always. How do you– She took a long breath. *The shock nearly killed me. I slept, and I dreamt, and when I woke I was trapped in this cage.*

She peered at him. *I will trust you. You are capable.*

Denizen raised his head to look at her. "How do you know?"

Her voice was soft. *Because you are all this moment has.*

Find a way to release me, and I shall return to my father. I will tell him that it was one of the Order who released me. That it was the Clockwork Three—and at the mention of their names her eyes flared, lightning seething from her lips—*and they alone that abducted me. His justice will fall on their wretched bones and there will be no war. Your aunt will not have fallen in vain.*

Denizen frowned. He wanted to trust her. At this point in the evening, he could *really* do with someone on his side. The daughter of a dark and terrible king wasn't exactly ideal, but it was better than nothing. She'd been trapped here for who-knew-how-long. She was as much of a victim of the Three and Grey as he was . . . as Vivian had been. And if he could free her . . .

"What do I have to do?" he asked.

The Tenebrous girl looked thoughtful. ***The Knight they snared to build this cage—he would come here sometimes. Talk to me. He left me books for when I woke.***

In the glare of Mercy, Denizen hadn't even noticed the stack of paperbacks piled beneath her. There were faint scorch marks on their covers from where she'd held them.

I think he was lonely. He told me that only a Malleus's hammer could break the circle. There was no pity in her voice, just calm truth.

"Why would he tell—" And then Denizen understood. *Oh, Grey.*

From the beginning, under the spell of the Three, Grey had been doing his best to sabotage their plan, getting information out any way he could. They probably hadn't told him not to speak to Mercy, and so he'd shared what he could in case it got back to someone who could do something about it. Pity twisted in Denizen's gut.

Kneeling by the circle, he noticed that it wasn't just made of chalk. Within the crudely sketched line was a second, smaller circle, almost—but not quite—touching the red. Was it dust? Some kind of black sand? He inched closer, again making sure he didn't accidentally put any part of himself across the line. It almost looked like shavings from pencil lead, but why—

Oh.

I am sorry. Distantly, he heard Mercy speak. ***The Three have dark knowledge and an overabundance of cruelty.***

Iron filings—a thick line of them just inside the circle of chalk. It was probably too much to hope for that they'd been come by innocently. Denizen thought of Adebayo Sall, Lisa O'Reilly, all Vivian's comrades from so long ago. His palms ached in sympathy.

He could get Vivian's hammer—providing Grey hadn't taken it—and use the weapon to free Mercy. Denizen wouldn't have to fight the Three at all. Instead, they'd face the justice of the Endless King.

For the first time in what felt like forever, a smile crossed Denizen's face. He had no idea what the Endless King's justice entailed, but somehow he doubted it would be pleasant.

"OK, I have to run," he said. "The Three could be back at any moment, and I'm no match for even one of them. I don't actually know any Cants. Well—I know one, but it sort of nearly killed me the last time I used it. We're screwed if they find me before I have a chance to get the hammer."

Mercy stared down at him for a long time, her body

shifting once more into an undulating nebula of light and smoke. Girl form or not, Denizen suddenly felt the age and weight behind her gaze.

The moment stretched. Denizen began to squirm. Her eyes were very bright.

"Em," he said, "what—"

Wait long enough and the sun always rises, she said, half to herself. ***Do you believe that?***

Frown No. 7—Is This the Time? There were far more pressing concerns at the moment than the most rudimentary lesson in astronomy.

"Yes," Denizen said eventually, when it was clear she was waiting for an answer. "That's how . . . suns . . . work. Right?" He thought of the bleak dark of the Tenebrae. "Oh, right, you guys don't have one. Yeah. Sure. Cool. Whatever."

Then I have a gift for you, Iron Knight. She raised hands of glittering white. ***It has been a long time since our kind has attempted to teach yours. There is much the Order has forgotten.***

"I don't understand," Denizen said. "It took me a week to even learn how to *grasp* my power, let alone use it. How are you going to—"

And she told him.

It was achingly simple, though he could have been given a thousand years and never been able to put it into words. Her voice rang out like wind haunting a ravine, like the soft music of a shoreline, and as it did Denizen's mind opened to the secret language of the Tenebrae.

It was like spending your whole life listening to someone stumble through a language they barely understood . . . and then hearing poetry. Heat bloomed in his stomach and met the chill of her voice coming the other way. They mixed in him; they swirled and combined and grew.

They spoke to him.

Her lips were chased with white fire. Everything Grey had taught him was dismantled and reforged, Cants fitting together in new and potent ways.

He saw it all with a dreamy kind of understanding—how Jack was mispronouncing the Fourth Cadence of Forging so one in twenty of his swords came out flawed; how Abigail would be more powerful than Vivian one day simply because she sang rather than snarled.

More than anything, he saw how the Cost was a terrible necessity that could not be denied.

Power always had a cost. The world wasn't built for the Cants. They infected it, wounded it, and the Cost was the scar tissue the fire left behind. *Iron . . . the most* here *thing there is*. And there was something else. Something he could only trace the edges of, something in the way the Cants fit together . . .

Denizen's head swam. Her voice was everywhere, a trilling, freezing wind. It was too much. He couldn't take it—

—and then it was over, and Denizen fell back on a pile of folders, his breath coming in short, fast gasps. Every molecule of him tingled. He felt full of light, weightless, as if he might lift off the ground if he turned too quickly in one direction. Each breath he took felt *charged,* full of potential.

He looked down at his hands. *There should be lightning crackling between them,* he thought distantly. They should shine.

Knight?

Denizen felt . . . new. He felt like he could do anything. It was like that first night the power had spilled from him—the vicious heat, the vitality of it. A feeling that you could change the world. Denizen's veins burned with it. His whole body felt energized. Inspired.

He felt like a wizard.

Denizen had no idea how long he sat there, feeling the Cants coil and slither like serpents through his mind. *Is this how Knights feel all the time?* No wonder there had to be a Cost attached; it was so hard not to just reach out and . . . change things. Speak fire and make the world his own.

KNIGHT, the Tenebrous girl said. Mercy stared at him

from behind the invisible walls of her cage. Her hair fizzled and spat in the darkness, her eyes shifting from sky-blue to storm. Denizen raised his head.

Humans and their fire, Mercy said, shaking her head. ***You need to free me. The hammer. You need to get the hammer.***

The world shook as he nodded, thoughts slowly beginning to return.

A little part of him, fueled mostly by the power churning in his stomach, *wanted* to confront the Three. Right now he felt like he could take on the Endless King himself.

Cants swarmed in him like fireflies, greedy for flammable air. Denizen took a deep and shaky breath, forcing the power down and away.

Taking on the Clockwork Three was a terrible idea. And Grey was somewhere as well—if the Three hadn't punished him for his rebellion. Denizen was outnumbered. He was untrained. He was—*so full of power that he could sing the walls of Crosscaper down; all he had to do was open his mouth, let the terrible light come free and burn the world to char*—a Knight.

Or as close to a Knight as the situation was going to get, and that meant he had a job to do.

"OK," he said, the power ignored and sulking in his stomach, "I'll be right back. Just wait—"

Mercy raised a flickering eyebrow.

"—here," Denizen finished lamely. "Sorry. Right." He maneuvered over the last of the folders and glanced back at her. Something she had said—

"Hang on," he said, "your *father*? Your father is the Endless King?"

And? Mercy said, a note of annoyance entering the crackling whisper of her voice.

"No," said Denizen. "Nothing. Sorry." He couldn't keep a silly grin from his face. "I'm just . . . rescuing a princess, that's all. Cool."

He turned to go.

Wait, the Tenebrous girl said. ***What is your name?***

"Denizen," he said. "Denizen Hardwick."

Mercy's eyes widened, her body fracturing in shock. It took her almost a minute to drag a human shape back from the murky light. When she did, there was an odd expression on her face.

Hardwick, she mused. ***Strange. I am reassured. I will trust you to return, Denizen Hardwick, because we have something in common.***

"What's that?"

The Tenebrous smiled.

Frightening parents, Mercy said, and dissolved into smoke and storm.

* * *

DENIZEN RAN UPSTAIRS. Thoughts pounded in time with his heartbeat and the slap of his footsteps on the floor.

Frightening parents.

You Hardwicks are all alike.

Eleven years ago, my aunt's entire cadre was wiped out.

Eleven years ago, I was left at Crosscaper.

Page 136 torn out.

Doors whipped by him. He vaulted over Ackerby's unconscious body. There was no telling what might be outside. The Clockwork Three. Grey, with his tortured smile and his ravaged hand. The cynical part of Denizen—which to be honest was all of him—had been wondering why things had seemed suspiciously straightforward so far, but right now there was only one thought in his mind.

The last Hardwick. The full set.

The front doors opened with a crash, and cold October air filled Denizen's lungs. He held the power tight, ready to attack if Grey or the Three were there. He could get lucky and ambush them, destroy them before they even saw him coming. . . .

He looked round the courtyard. There was no one there. The moon had gone behind the clouds, and shadows crawled across the rough gravel. Denizen's breath caught in his chest.

His aunt's body had vanished.

Denizen had enough time to register shock before

a grip of steel seized him by the back of the collar and spun him round. He almost lashed out with the power, a Cant coming to his lips—

—and then he stared up into the pale and haggard face of Malleus Vivian Hardwick.

28

C'est la Guerre

One of her hands was clamped over her stomach, her shirt dark with blood. The other held Denizen's collar in a death grip.

Her eyes burned, not with the power of the Tenebrae but with *rage*—an incandescent madness so pure you could barely describe it as human at all. You didn't call that feeling anger. You called it wrath, and when you felt it coming your way, you evacuated the villages and ran for higher ground.

Her voice was a snarl. *"Where is my hammer?"*

The words had barely escaped from between gritted teeth before Vivian's legs gave way and she fell to her knees, her fingers jerking open. Denizen nearly fell himself when that vicious grasp went away.

Vivian's eyes and mouth suddenly glowed, as did the wound behind her bloody fingers. *The Bellows*

Subventum, Denizen thought, the knowledge coming from nowhere and everywhere all at once.

It was a Higher Cant—a spell that forced your body to work overtime, repairing damage that would otherwise take months to heal. Crude, though, and hell on the patient—it was the kind of makeshift battlefield work that would keep a body upright until it could finally keel over later.

And she was saying it wrong. Denizen could hear it now—the gaps where Vivian's voice should have gone to channel the power properly. *Thank you, Mercy.* Who would have thought being a grammar nut would come in handy?

Whatever the roughness of the Cant, it was working. The rise and fall of Vivian's chest steadied and color returned to her cheeks. She took a deep breath, tentatively taking her hand away from the bloodstain on her shirt as if worried that more blood would follow it.

He had no idea how she was still alive—Denizen had never seen so much blood in his life. Her knees and the front of her shirt were filthy. How long had she lain there before dragging up the power to save herself?

"Where," she said again, her voice sounding like she'd been gargling gravel, "is my hammer?"

It took Denizen a few seconds to respond. *She was alive. Vivian was alive.*

"Uh," he said, and then flinched as she turned the

full force of her Malleus's glare on him. "Grey must have taken it. . . . Are you all right? Listen, we need to—"

At the mention of Grey's name, Vivian tried to struggle upright before breaking into a harsh fit of coughing, her head in her hands. Denizen looked around anxiously, waiting for the hacking to subside. They were too exposed out here. The Three could return at any moment.

"Back to . . ." Vivian forced each word out through sheer will. "Back to Seraphim Row. We need the others if we're to—if they're . . ."

Denizen went stiff with sudden horror. He'd been so concerned with Vivian being shot and finding Mercy that he hadn't thought at all about the wider picture.

Grey had betrayed them all, and the Three were nowhere to be found. *I was supposed to keep you here.*

"Abigail. Darcie. Oh God—we have to get back there. We have to see if they're all right!"

"Need a minute," Vivian wheezed. "I can get us back there. Just give me two seconds—"

Denizen shook his head. "You're too weak." Deep inside him, a heat built and spread. The knowledge bestowed by Mercy burned to be used, to spill out into the world. Would it work? Could he get them home?

He turned from Vivian, ignoring the shocked look on her face, and drew on the power of the Tenebrae.

The Art of Apertura—traveling between the shadows.

First, the hands must be raised, fingers stretched as if they're tearing the air. . . .

The words swam up from nowhere, and without even needing to ask, he knew them to be true. He focused on the foyer of Seraphim Row—the massive doors, the candles, the weight of a dozen painted gazes. Alien syllables slipped from his lips to part the air, and shadows spilled from a wound in the world. It would hang in the air as long as he concentrated on it, as long as he held the shape of the Cant in his head.

"Where did you . . ." Vivian pushed herself to her feet. "Where did you learn to do that?"

Denizen didn't answer. Instead, he began to jog back to the doors of the orphanage. The Clockwork Three could return at any moment, but there was no way he was leaving Simon here any longer than he had to.

"Where are you going *now*?" his aunt called after him in an exasperated voice.

Despite everything that had happened, a smile flashed across Denizen's face.

"I have someone I want you to meet."

THE SMILE LASTED until they reached Seraphim Row.

"What is this place?" Simon whispered as they picked their way through a graveyard of candles, the carpet a sea of crushed tallow, the air darkened by a thousand snake tongues of smoke.

Home, thought Denizen. Despite its darkness and secrets, that's what Seraphim Row had become.

Now it looked like a battlefield. Each portrait had been pulled from its hook and smashed against the ground, the canvas torn and the faces of long-dead Mallei smeared with wax. Frames had been stamped on until they snapped, the splinters kicked about the room with savage glee.

The chandelier sat in the middle of the floor like the beached corpse of an iceberg. Its canopy had been torn free and flung away, the once-beautiful prisms of glass that had hung from its flanks shattered and ground into the floor. The iron cage of its body had been twisted out of shape by something with incredible strength.

This had always been the warmest room in the house, thought Denizen as they picked their way across the floor, but now the cold was starting to creep in.

Occasionally, Vivian stopped to whisper the Bellows Subventum to herself, light gleaming from under the newly healed skin. The effort was taxing her, but each time she stood a little straighter, breathed a little easier.

"Can I—"

She cut Denizen off with a wave of her hand. After her initial shock at Denizen's newfound power, she hadn't even asked what had happened or who Simon was. Every iota of energy she possessed seemed to be focused on keeping herself going, one step after the other.

Weirdly, it made Denizen feel better—*Vivian Hardwick is on our side*—but the more they explored the house, the more he realized they would need all the help they could get. This was where the Three had been while he was searching Crosscaper, when Vivian had been dragging herself out of a pool of her own blood.

They had been taking their time with Seraphim Row.

No corridor had been untouched. In some places, the destruction was as mundane as the wallpaper being ripped off or the candles kicked over. In others, the entirety of the Clockwork Three's malignant fury had been released—floorboards torn up, light fixtures pulled from the ceilings to hang down like skeletal fingers, the walls riven with claw marks like signatures of insanity. Each new desecration made Denizen's anger grow.

There was no point to this. Denizen understood—in a hateful way—why they might want to isolate Vivian by attacking her cadre, but none of this had served a purpose at all. It hadn't brought the Clockwork Three any closer to their goals. In fact, it had slowed them down. They could have come back early to Crosscaper, found Vivian and Denizen when they were still at Grey's mercy.

But they hadn't. They'd tarried here, visiting little insults on unfeeling stone and wood. Denizen stopped to stare at the door to one of the broom cupboards. It had been kicked in so violently the bottom of the door had split, but that hadn't been enough for the Three—they'd reached in and crushed the handle to an unusable blob of metal.

He thought of what Grey had said, how the Three's chaotic nature meant that their plans and schemes were so often subsumed by raw hunger. This was what the world would be like if the Three had their way. The Endless King would cause untold horror if he Breached, yes, but in his wake would come the Clockwork Three—not just vicious but *petty,* piling misery upon misery until the whole world choked.

They found Jack in the Room of Swords.

In a way, it was fitting. The blacksmith used Cants in his forgings so that each weapon held special power against the Tenebrous. *Spoken steel,* weapons that burned as well as cut. With all the swords lining the walls, this room must have been agony for the Three. Perhaps it had merely spurred them on.

The huge man swayed in the center of the room like a vast statue about to topple, a relic of some ancient civilization brought low by time. Iron had spread across half his face, black under the blood.

He held D'Aubigny's crumpled shape in his arms. She looked very, very small.

"Where," he whispered in a voice thick with tears, *"were you?"*

The last word was a shout. When it left his lips, his strength seemed to leave him too, and in stiff and glacial stages Fuller Jack fell to his knees, holding the body of his wife.

"Denizen," Vivian said. "Get your friend to the room across the hall."

"What? No—"

"Now."

He did as he was told, putting an arm round Simon's shoulders, feeling them flinch under his touch. Though they had left the orphanage behind, his friend's eyes still tracked every shadow, when they weren't watching Vivian with barely disguised fear.

She closed the door behind her, but the sight of her standing there was burned into Denizen's eyes. Her voice hadn't been angry. It had been cold, all emotion once again folded behind the iron mask of a Malleus.

What must it be like? To be so long in a war that even this—a comrade fallen, her oldest friend a traitor, her home destroyed—was just one more obstacle to push past? The only reason Denizen hadn't curled up in a ball and started twitching was because so far he hadn't had time.

He brought Simon across the hall to a windowless little box bedroom he had never been in before. The single bed in the corner had no sheets or duvet, but as Simon had been sleeping rough for the past couple of weeks, Denizen didn't think he'd mind.

He was right. Simon curled up on the bed with a wordless sigh of relief. Denizen hovered awkwardly by the door.

"Simon?"

"Mmmph?"

"We're just going to . . ." He didn't know what to say. "We'll be right back, Simon. You sleep, OK?"

Simon made an incoherent noise, halfway between a snuffle and a snore.

"D'n't . . . ," he murmured. "Don't g'way again. . . ."

There was a lump in Denizen's throat. "I won't," he said. "I'm not going anywhere."

He waited until Simon's breathing steadied, and then he quietly slipped out the door.

Denizen didn't give the closed door of the Room of Swords a second glance. Instead, he made his way as quickly as he could to the foyer, stepping gingerly over the squashed remains of candle-wards.

What would happen now that they'd been destroyed? Would Seraphim Row slip completely into the dark? Did it even matter now with the Endless King poised below the horizon?

Sitting cross-legged on the floor in front of Seraphim Row's great doors, Denizen waited. Eventually, his hunch was proved right. Vivian appeared at the head of the stairs, changed out of her bloody clothes and shrugging on a thick winter coat. There was a sword hanging from her waist. She saw Denizen and froze.

"Going somewhere?" he said.

Vivian looked away. She'd been caught and they both knew it. If Denizen had just gone back to the Room of Swords, then Vivian would have been out the door and back to Crosscaper without a word.

It was a long time before she broke the silence.

"I made Jack as comfortable as I could. He's gravely wounded, but he'll live."

Denizen knew he should be relieved, but all he felt was numb. It had been a long and dark night.

"Corinne . . ." Vivian's voice was raw. "She fought them to the end."

D'Aubigny. Denizen had known; he *had.* It had only taken one look at Jack's face in the Room of Swords, but the knowledge still came as a gut punch. He remembered warm arms about him, a voice in his ear telling him to keep going, to stay alive. Her calm, steel-hard determination. Her rare smiles.

Denizen knew the answer before he opened his mouth.

"Why did they leave Jack alive?"

"So he can grieve," Vivian said simply.

Poor Jack. The builder, the forger. The man who watched his wife go out the door every night and carved creatures for her return. What would he be without her?

"And the others?" Denizen said after a few seconds of silence. Vivian shook her head.

"No sign of them. If I'd been Jack, I would have told them to run."

A flickering candle of hope lit in Denizen's stomach. The girls were smart and capable—if they had gotten clear of Seraphim Row while the Knights fought the Three, then they might be all right.

"What about your friend?"

Denizen explained what he knew of Simon's ordeal. After he'd finished, Vivian looked thoughtful.

"Bending light is a difficult art," she said, "even for an experienced Knight. It's a subtle discipline, one I've rarely had the . . . patience for."

Somehow, Denizen did not find that in the least bit surprising.

"He has a future with the Order, if he wishes it," she

continued. "We often discover lost bloodlines. Or new ones. I'd wager there's a mention of a . . ."

"Hayes," Denizen said.

"A Hayes family in our records. Something to look at if we . . . if the Order lives through the next few days."

She paused. "He was lucky you found him."

Was that approval in her voice? Denizen wasn't sure—he'd never heard it before. The thought gave him courage. He took a deep breath.

"We need to talk," he said, folding his arms.

She didn't look at him. "We can talk when I return."

"You're saying that because you don't think you're coming back."

That got her attention. She turned toward him, flashing the same look of grim disdain she always did. The Vivian Hardwick stare might have cowed him a few hours ago, but it had been a busy evening, and right now Denizen just wasn't in the mood.

There was something else too—a frayed edge to her that hadn't been there before. Maybe it was just the pain she'd been through, but she wasn't presenting the same impenetrable wall she always had. Vivian had been about to tell him something before Grey had shot her—he knew it. He just had to push a little harder.

"Denizen . . . ," she began, and then abruptly stopped speaking. "I can't—not right now. I have to go and do this. We don't have time for—"

"You haven't had time since I got here," Denizen said angrily. "And look at you—you're weak. The *mercy* isn't a thing; it's a *her*. It's the Endless King's daughter. They have her trapped, but we spoke. She . . ."

He faltered for a moment as he tried to put what had happened into words.

"She showed me the Cants. Like a . . . I don't know. A cheat sheet. I understand them now. You saw what I can do. You need me if you want to stop the Three."

"You were *taught* by her?" Vivian said, shock in her voice. "That's . . . I mean, there are stories, but . . ."

Once again, that cold Malleus control snapped back down like a portcullis, hiding her emotions from view. Her jaw tightened and she descended the stairs. For a moment, he thought she might just sweep him aside, but then she stopped, looking down on him with those ice-gray eyes.

"You can't stop me going," Vivian said acidly, "no matter what *lessons* you may have had. I am a Malleus of the Order of the Borrowed Dark, and I—"

"Have been to Crosscaper before," Denizen whispered. It was at once obvious and a revelation. "Before tonight. That's how the Art of Apertura works. You can only travel to somewhere you've already been." Mercy's words, Mercy's insight, coming out of his mouth.

Vivian opened her mouth, but Denizen cut her off. "You're right. I'm just a kid. I probably can't stop you.

But I'm going to try. And you're going to have to hurt me pretty badly if you want to get past me."

He took a purposeful step in front of the door. "So I want answers."

At this point, Denizen didn't even know if he was bluffing or not. He met that blowtorch stare and didn't look away. Would she actually fight him? Would he fight back?

The moment dragged out, so long that fear actually began to trickle down his back, and then Vivian did the one thing Denizen would never have expected.

She laughed.

It was an awkward croaking noise, as if she weren't used to laughing at all. She turned away from him, one hand pressed to her stomach as the chuckles spilled from her in rough, hacking gasps.

Denizen stood there awkwardly until she turned back to him again, wiping her eyes.

"You are so . . . ," she began, "so like him."

The smile faded from her face, and Denizen was suddenly struck by how old and tired she looked, the premature grayness of her hair, the wrinkles crowding the corners of her eyes. Her voice was hollow.

"How can you be so like him?"

"Who?" Denizen said. "My father?" Suddenly all other thoughts were driven from his head. Vivian had never mentioned him before.

"What do you remember about your parents, Denizen?"

His tongue felt heavy in his mouth. Now that she was asking him, he was suddenly nervous. What if he said the wrong thing? What if she was disgusted by how little he did remember?

"I don't remember anything about my dad," he said finally. "And my mother? I dream about her sometimes. She was small. Gentle. She smelled like strawberries, and she used to . . . she used to sing to me."

A tear ran down Vivian's cheek. The sight of it froze the blood in Denizen's veins.

"That was Director Susan Carsing," she said. "She used to run Crosscaper before . . ." Vivian took a deep breath. "I left you with her. Eleven years ago, just before I hunted down the Clockwork Three for killing your father."

Vivian Hardwick took a long and ragged breath.

"Denizen," she whispered, "I'm not your aunt. I'm your mother."

29

Malleus

"You were two," she said, "and I was just a few years into Knighthood. I worked out of Seraphim Row, but we didn't live there—we had a little house nearby. Soren . . . your father . . . wasn't a Knight, but he was a good man. So sweet. So funny. You have his hair. He hoped you'd have my height."

She gazed down at the destroyed portraits.

"The Hardwicks have always been Knights. We were born for this duty—raised for it. Soren didn't like the danger of what I did, but he loved me. He knew how important my duty was to me, and I think in a way he was strangely proud of what I did. At least at first."

Her voice hardened. "And then the Clockwork Three came. Agents of misery, nourished by suffering. We were in Galway dealing with a Breach when they took Christopher from right under our noses.

"That's how they work—jackals circling, picking you off when you're distracted. They took Christopher, and a week later Lisa went missing as well. *Missing*. The Three were taking my comrades alive, and we had no idea why."

"They were trying to make a thrall," Denizen said distantly. "Grey said it wasn't a . . . it wasn't a perfect process."

Vivian nodded slowly. "My comrades didn't survive it. When Adebayo was taken, Soren wanted me to quit. He wanted us to run."

She shook her head. "You don't quit being a Knight. *Tu ne cede malis, sed contra audentior ito*. I'm a Hardwick. We don't quit; we don't stop. More than that, though, I *wanted* the Three. After what they did to Lisa, to Chris, to dear Adebayo . . .

"And when I refused him he went to my Malleus, John Carsing. I think he thought he could convince him to talk to me. The fool. The damned, damned fool.

"The Three found them together. I don't think they even cared who Soren was. Just a toy to play with for a while. A plaything to them . . . but everything to me."

Vivian stared straight ahead, each word an effort, as if dredging the memories from some deep, unpleasant sea.

"I was at home with you when I got the phone call from Carsing's widow. She was the director of an orphanage on Achill Island. A good woman and . . . strong, to be the partner of a Knight for so many years. She'd been waiting for a similar phone call herself for a long time, I imagine. Funny. I'd always thought it would be Soren getting that call instead of me."

Vivian took a deep breath. "The man I loved was dead, and it was my fault. I brought him into these shadows—and then there was you, this sweet little child. Perfect and innocent and free of my world. I brought you to Director Carsing. I put you in her arms, I kissed you on the forehead, and I prayed that when it came to your thirteenth birthday, you would be your father's son and not mine. Then I went to my death."

"What happened?" Denizen asked.

The words had to be forced out past a lump in his throat. His eyes stung. How could she have done this? She'd walked away from her family and chosen—*chosen*—a life of danger and battle and death. He'd never had a choice. Vivian had taken that away from him.

"I became relentless," she said, her fingers curling into fists. "They would have killed you in a heartbeat just to dig the knife a little deeper . . . but I never gave them the chance. I hunted them, and in turn they hunted me. We followed each other through all the dark corners of the world, and every night they would come to me in dreams. *Oh, what we'll give you! Oh, what we'll show you if you let us in!* One night, they came too close." Her smile was grim. "And I showed them fire.

"I bled them and I broke them and I drove them back into the dark. I have never screamed Cants with such rage. I fed the power with everything I had—my hope, my love, my hate, everything. Fuel for the fire. I was young then, thought that I wouldn't need a Malleus's hammer to end them for good if I gave them . . ." She looked down at her hands. "If I gave them everything.

"When it was over . . . I wanted to come back. But I'd lived so long with this *rage,* made it such a part of me . . . How could I go back to you? You were just a little boy with *his* face and *his* smile, and I had died along with your father."

"The torn-out page in the Book of Rust—" Denizen began.

"Mine," she said. "A note to you for when I didn't come back."

"But *why*?" Denizen said helplessly. It was the only question left—the only one that mattered. "Why didn't you tell me? Why keep it a secret?"

Vivian closed her eyes. In a way, she must have been waiting a long time for this question as well.

"I honestly . . . I don't know. I've spent so long hoping that you wouldn't have a connection to the Tenebrae. You could have been anything—gone anywhere.

Walked in the light like everyone else. And with the kind of life I've been living, I really didn't think I'd get this far. The battles, the pain, the danger . . .

"On your birthday, when your power manifested, all I could think of was how I got your father killed. God, I was so *angry* that night. I thought after your training I could find you a posting somewhere safe, somewhere away from danger. Maybe even drive you away entirely. Why would you want anything to do with a cold and distant aunt?"

"*That's* your excuse?" Denizen was shaking with rage. "Protecting me? Or trying to get yourself killed so you wouldn't have to deal with me?"

"That's not—"

"That's exactly it," he snarled. "You wanted revenge, so you tossed me aside and went after the Three. What— Did you think it was *braver* to go and die instead of looking after your son? What would my . . . what would my father think about—"

"Don't," Vivian snapped. "Just don't. I did what I thought was right. The only thing I thought I could do. If I stayed, I would have . . . I would have *grieved,* Denizen. I didn't want that. I wanted to fight."

Fire. Light erupted from Denizen's eyes, howling for release, the color and sound of hate. He stared at this woman, this warrior, his *mother,* and all he wanted to do was strike her down.

And she did nothing. Just stared at him with eyes the very same shade as his.

Vivian had abandoned him. She had given in to the inferno in her soul, let it boil out and eat her until she was nothing more than an automaton powered by its heat. A life lived hunting for death—hunting for some escape from pain.

Doing her level best to get murdered rather than be his mother.

The power still coiled and flickered in his stomach. He could just feed his anger to it, let it scour him clean until he was nothing more than iron and fire lashing out at the world. Had it worked for her? Did she feel better now? No wonder she let the Cost crawl up her skin. The dead iron must be a relief.

What did you hold on to when something hurt this much?

"Duty," Denizen Hardwick said, the light fading from his eyes.

"What?"

"This is . . . this is too big for me. I can't . . ." Breath hissed from between his teeth. "You and I can wait. We have a duty to perform."

His glare made Vivian take a step backward. "That's your thing, right? Duty?"

"Denizen," she said softly. "I should go, not you. I told you, I won't—"

"No," he said. "This is what you gave me up for, right? You're weak. You're tired. *And these are the things that killed my father*. We both go, or I leave you here."

He watched her shoulders tense and wondered how long it had been since anyone had spoken to the *esteemed* Malleus Vivian Hardwick that way. It wasn't an empty threat. Right now he was just waiting for something to deserve the firestorm in his heart.

"We still need to figure out how to take on the Three and free Mercy," Vivian said. "I tried contacting the Order. Breaches are opening all over the world. It's starting. Soon we won't be able to contain it. We need to free Mercy, but we don't have a hammer."

Look at her, a cruel voice in Denizen's head whispered, *taking refuge in the work again.*

"You're right," came a clipped voice from the doorway. They both turned in shock.

Abigail stood there, feet spread, her birthday crossbow held tight to her chest. Her pajamas fluttered in the breeze from the open door. Beside her, Darcie had her hands shoved in the pockets of her coat. Both their faces were streaked with tears.

Abigail's voice was steady. "But I know where you can get one."

30

A Little More Misery

Lightning split the sky above Os Reges Point.

Denizen wondered if there were always storms here, out in the wildness of the ocean. Violence eternal in sea and sky.

The feel of the Tenebrae was everywhere—in the greasiness of the air, the staccato snarl of the thunder.

"We ran," Abigail said, and there was anger in her voice. "We ran while Jack and D'Aubigny fought."

They sat cross-legged on the stone, bundled in coats and hats. Abigail's face was barely visible behind a thick woolen scarf. Darcie had agreed to stay behind and look after Simon and Jack, but Abigail had refused to be anywhere else but at the Hardwicks' side.

"I wanted to stay, but Jack made me promise to get Darcie out. We made it to the street and just . . .

wandered until finally we circled back, hoping maybe that you'd returned or that someone had survived.

"We thought they might have followed us, but by the looks of things they were too concerned with destroying the place. They weren't even pretending to be human anymore—snapping at each other, snarling . . . *ticking*."

Denizen shivered and not from the rain. More than anything, it was the *unpredictability* of the Clockwork Three that frightened him. Maybe they had crossed over to this world with a plan, but now they were little more than beasts, destroying everything around them.

Not that it mattered if Mercy wasn't freed soon.

Denizen glanced over at where Vivian—his mother—stood, arms thrown wide to the storm. She wore the same armor she had when Denizen had first been brought to Seraphim Row. Rain glistened on the dull iron warplate. Her white cloak fluttered around her shoulders, and she'd drawn up its hood to frame her gaunt features. Power radiated off her like heat from a flame. The air was heavy with imminent threat.

"Denizen, I—" Abigail began.

With effort, Denizen dragged his gaze away from his mother. "Yes?"

"I wish we'd had a chance to get to know each other properly before all this," she said. "But just in case something happens tonight—"

Denizen cut her off. "No. I mean, I know."

He couldn't see her mouth, but he knew Abigail was smiling. She leaned over and squeezed his hand through his glove. "And besides," she said airily, "to die in the service of the Order is the greatest of all honors."

Denizen stared at her. "Seriously?"

"God, no," she said. "Are you insane?"

"Will you two please be quiet?" Vivian said, before turning back to the body of the Emissary. It was still slumped where it had fallen a few nights before, its arms flung wide, the helm empty and gathering rain.

Crossing the summit to join her, Denizen stared down at the hammer impaling the Emissary's chest. He hadn't looked at it properly before—being slightly more concerned about the giant warrior it was attached to—but now he examined the hammer closely.

Vivian's weapon had looked old. This one looked *ancient*. It bore the same resemblance to Vivian's hammer as a saber-toothed tiger did to a house cat, its head an immense block of chipped stone, its handle black wood from some long-extinct tree. It looked primeval, a weapon barely built for a human at all.

Vivian threw back her head and light speared out to burn the sky. Just as before, Denizen felt the Tenebrae intrude, called forth by Vivian's words.

He couldn't see the stars, but he was sure that they once again sharpened—points of white fire in the sky.

The wind howled louder, then died away as if afraid to touch what Vivian was bringing forth.

The Emissary rose to its feet like an avalanche in reverse, darkness threading through its joints. The great helm tilted to snuffle at the air, its fingers—fat as tank shells—reaching up to claw the sky.

Its voice was a riptide snarl.

Where is my–

"Shut up," Vivian snapped in a voice like a drill sergeant. Denizen flinched. Abigail reflexively stood to attention.

The Emissary's voice rang out again, deep and hollow and thick with rage.

WHERE IS MY–

"Shut. Up," Vivian said, stepping forward and rapping the knuckles of her gauntlet smartly on its chest. Denizen winced. "You put away your sword. You set it aside. Whatever. I don't have time for ritual today."

The giant rocked a little on its heels. Its massive hands clenched into fists.

Malleus Hardwick, it said eventually. ***It has been a while.***

"Yes," she said. "And I missed you too. Now listen. We know what was taken from the Endless King. If we return it to you, will these attacks on our borders cease?"

The Emissary nodded with a creak. ***Deliver the thieves to us. The King will want them. Want to punish. Want to hurt.***

"No," said Vivian. "They're *mine.*"

The Emissary took a step forward. It seemed like the whole world shook. ***The thieves will be ours.***

Vivian stared dispassionately into its empty helm. "No. This is the business of the Order. I have my own score to settle with—"

"Vivian!" Denizen snapped. His mother turned to him in shock. "Let him have them! Can you not just . . . just leave it? Can you not just forget about revenge for one second? What are you going to do that's worse than *him*?"

The giant stared at them impassively.

Denizen stepped forward and spoke. "Emissary."

The Tenebrous's head swung in his direction. It reminded Denizen of the bulls that had sometimes grazed in the fields behind Crosscaper. They would blink at him with deep and sleepy regard, angling giant heads to stare at him first with one eye, then the other.

He had known instinctively—even without the multiple warnings handed down by teachers—that were he to hop the fence, it would take the bulls a long time to even realize he was there, but when they did they'd hit him as hard as the world.

"You can have the thieves," he said hurriedly, unwilling to look into the darkness of the helm for too long. "Do what you like with them. We'll free the King's daughter."

Vivian's eyes bored into him, but he ignored her. With a sighing of rust, the Emissary nodded once more.

"One last thing," Vivian said. She wrapped both hands round the handle of the hammer and *pulled.*

The Emissary's roar drowned out the storm. It staggered as the hammer came free from its chest, followed by a spray of arterial dark. Metal shrieked, and the Tenebrous fell to its knees, a massive hand held to its heart. Its breath came in hollow gasps, like a tide seeping through secret caves. The hammer fit Vivian's hands as if it had always been there. She strode away without looking back.

As plans went, Denizen's was simple.

Vivian's first Cant hit the closed gates of Crosscaper like a runaway freight train. Ancient wood warped and bent, steel bands ringing like a struck bell. The night shivered in the wake of the power—echoes bouncing off the far distant hills. Denizen wouldn't have been surprised if they heard it all the way on the mainland.

The gates drooped on their hinges. Resplendent in her rain-slicked warplate, Vivian raised her gauntlets and drew in a deep breath, preparing to strike again.

"No," Denizen said, pushing past her. "Let me."

Mercy hadn't gifted him with power. She'd given him *understanding.*

The power of the Tenebrae wasn't some quick fix or bottomless well of magic to be drawn on—if it were, the Knights wouldn't need swords at all.

Mercy's gift hummed between his thoughts like static electricity. It wasn't about raw power. It was about focus. It was about placing your finger on the scales, about expending the minimum amount of effort for the maximum gain.

Denizen let the power of the Tenebrae climb his spine in a seething tide and with a muttered syllable spat fire into his hand. He rolled it between his palms, drawing it out into twin darts of light. A flick of his wrist sent both arcing toward the hinges. Metal glowed red and came apart. With a groan, the gates' own weight dragged them forward to land heavily in the dirt.

Vivian raised an eyebrow at him.

"What?" he said innocently. She didn't reply.

Beside them, Abigail Falx had removed her cap to let her black hair shine in the moonlight. Her slim rapier gleamed at her side, and her sleek crossbow was in her hands. The hammer at Vivian's waist didn't reflect the light at all.

As they strode toward the orphanage, Denizen's heart began to pound. It wasn't quite fear and it wasn't quite excitement, but some strange, headachey mix of the two.

He hadn't let the power subside—it throbbed in time with his heartbeat, prickling along his limbs, making his fingers twitch and tingle. There was a saber hanging at his waist, but he hadn't drawn it. Why would he, when he could just reach out and—

No. Not yet. When the Three revealed themselves . . . then he could cut loose. Power crackled eagerly through the vaults of his mind.

They stepped across the gates. Glancing up at the foreboding face of Crosscaper, Denizen was struck once again by that feeling of smallness, as if someone had replaced the landscape of his childhood with something just a little more threadbare.

There was a figure waiting for them in its shadow.

"I told them you'd be back."

The rain had soaked Grey's shirt to his skin and plastered his hair to his scalp. He must have been standing out there for a long time. Denizen wondered whether the Three had just left him there like a discarded toy.

Or a guard dog.

"I'm glad you're alive," the Knight said. He was holding Vivian's hammer in his hands. It didn't suit him.

"Graham," Vivian said calmly, "put that down."

"Soon enough," Grey said. "They were so *angry*. And quite specific. No more loopholes. They think it'll be fun if you kill me." He spun the hammer round him as he spoke.

"At least I think that's it. They stopped making sense a while ago. Tenebrous aren't really meant for long jaunts in the real world and . . ."

Denizen couldn't tell if there were tears on his cheeks or if it was just the rain.

"Is everyone dead?" asked Grey.

"D'Aubigny," Vivian said, stone-faced.

"Oh," Grey said in a small voice. The air trembled as he drew power to himself, his eyes consumed by pallid light. "Vivian," he said, words almost lost beneath the whirring of his hand. "I'm sorry."

"So am I," she said, and charged.

The fight couldn't have lasted more than a few seconds. Abigail and Denizen just stood and stared.

He'd seen Grey fight Pick-Up-the-Pieces. He'd watched his mentor spar with Abigail and D'Aubigny. The man moved like a conjurer's trick—blade darting faster than the eye could follow, the point of his sword never where you thought it would be.

He'd been deadly before, and now madness and the dark will of the Three fueled his blows, his mouth open in a snarl, his eyes leaking violent gold.

Denizen's mother took him apart.

At first, Vivian didn't even draw her own weapon. Instead, she caught Grey's first wild swing on the edge of a gauntlet and drove her fist into the younger Knight's face so hard Denizen couldn't help flinching.

Grey turned with the punch to attack again, other hand suddenly aflame, but his outstretched fingers caught only the head of her hammer, sizzling uselessly on the pockmarked stone. Vivian jabbed the weapon back, smashing Grey's own hand against his lips—the Cant guttering out in a cloud of sparks—and then brought the haft of the hammer around in a tight, vicious arc.

Grey hit the gravel hard, howling through a broken jaw.

Vivian stood over him silently. Her expression hadn't changed once during the fight. With a start, Denizen realized that she hadn't just beaten Grey down, she'd neutralized his ability to use Cants by the brutal expedient of breaking his jaw.

Absurdly, it was Grey's words that came back to Denizen then. *You don't rise to the position of Malleus by setting fire to coffee cups.* Everyone who had ever spoken of Vivian—human and Tenebrous alike—talked about her with the same kind of awed respect. It was only now that Denizen saw why.

"Whenever you're ready," Vivian whispered.

Grey's body arched, legs twitching ramrod straight. He clutched the stolen hammer tight, his moans of pain becoming hoarse, rhythmic—staccato sobs of mechanical hate.

Ticking.

The front doors of Crosscaper slammed open, jarring the last few shards of glass from their panes. A foul wind howled *out* from the darkness of the orphanage, bringing with it the stink of bad dreams and grease.

Denizen staggered under a wave of misery—a crawling sort of dread that made tears well up involuntarily in his eyes, like every cut and bruise and little insult he'd ever suffered all came back to him at once.

What was he even *doing* here? How could he face something like the Clockwork Three? He didn't know how to use the sword at his waist. The Cants were only his because Mercy had taken pity on him, useless rescuer that he was—and his own *mother* didn't want him. But why would she? What kind of mother would want a pathetic, cowardly, *short*—

Abigail was on her knees. Grey writhed on his back, head in his hands. His mother—*abandoner,* a part of him bayed, *absentee*—swayed, hammer planted between her feet as if she were weathering a storm.

"Yield not to evil," she snarled through gritted teeth, "but *attack.*"

And the power in Denizen responded.

He had almost forgotten its presence, but now it rose in him in a shrieking, molten wave. The terror melted before its touch like cobwebs held to a flame. Light rippled beneath Denizen's skin as he called more power than he had ever dared.

Beside him, Abigail was rising, raindrops sizzling as they hit her skin. Her eyes were the blue-white of a welding torch and whole suns flared when she smiled.

Only Grey still quaked as the Three stalked from the orphanage doors. His clockwork hand droned in sympathy.

The Woman in White came first—movements an arrhythmic prowl, her teeth bared in a gearwork grin. Pale skin and brass gleamed through the burned tatters of her coat, and her knee popped unpleasantly with every step.

Behind her walked the Man in the Waistcoat—his eyes bright stones in fleshy little pockets, his smile that of a teacher dealing with a favorite student. Half his white hair had been burned away and his left arm ended at the elbow, but it didn't appear to trouble him at all.

Despite the power blazing under his skin, Denizen shivered as their gazes met. He had seen insanity lurking in the eyes of the Woman in White. In the eyes of the Man in the Waistcoat, there was nothing at all.

Vivian, he said cordially. His mouth didn't move. Hair wafted down with each movement of his head. Grey was right. Their human forms were unraveling.

The Woman's arms had lengthened, her spine a hyena-arch straining against fabric. As Denizen watched, the skin on one of her fingers tore, a long talon of brass sliding free.

We knew you'd come back, the Tenebrous said. ***This little feud has made us both so . . . predictable.***

"Things have changed," Vivian said.

Ah, yes, it said, indicating the hammer with one bloated hand. For a creature confronting the one weapon that could properly kill it, the Man didn't seem terribly worried. ***Not much of a consolation prize, though, is it? Your husband was so pretty, and that's just a piece of stone.***

Vivian's eyes flashed with fire. For a second, Denizen thought that she was going to attack—*no, that's not the plan*—but the Man ignored her. His eyes were on Denizen.

It has been . . . trying, these last few days. We are not meant for concentration. Hold the Mercy, keep it hidden . . . so boring . . . but we can always rely on the Hardwick family for entertainment. And when you and these useless cubs are dead . . .

His smile split his cheek in a clockwork yawn.

War. War unending–a feast for all time.

Grey moaned. Denizen kept his mouth shut. He didn't trust himself to respond with anything other than flame.

So come on, then, dear girl, the thing taunted, turning his gaze back to Vivian. ***Are you going to try to kill us one more time?***

Vivian was silent for a long moment before she spoke, and Denizen could see how much the words cost her.

"There are bigger things here than you and me."

And she vanished.

Vivian hadn't lied about her lack of prowess—her disappearance was far less smooth than Simon's had been earlier. A streaky after-image hung in the air. The Woman in White flung herself at it, face twisted in animal rage—and a perfectly enunciated Anathema Bend folded her in half with a sound like cracking timber.

"Hi," Denizen said, thoroughly and inappropriately enjoying her look of shock. "Remember me?"

The Anathema Bend created a transparent curve of hard light that was practically unbreakable but carried a heavy Cost—unless you adjusted it, made it small and short lived, just a hiccup in the air. When the Woman bounded to her feet and lunged again, she only made it a little way before slamming her face off a dinner-plate-sized shield only Denizen could see.

He flung a Helios Lance at her, just to clock her reaction time, and when she bucked away from the fiery dart, he jammed a fist-sized shield into the side of her throat.

A human would have broken her neck. The Woman in White just rolled, baying like a burning wolf, and leapt at him with claws outstretched.

She swallowed Abigail's crossbow bolt instead.

Denizen didn't look to see if the Woman was dead. It would take a lot to put the Three down, and with a whole orphanage drowning in bad dreams, there was plenty of misery for them to draw on for power. He needed to wound them, keep them both distracted while Vivian did her work.

Denizen turned toward the Man in the Waistcoat, another Helios Lance on his lips—but the other Tenebrous was gone. Denizen cursed. The Three were fraying here, slowly losing their reason. They hated Vivian; they knew she wielded the only threat to their existence. But in their black and ticking hearts they were animals—easily distracted, inconsistent. Denizen had been betting on the Three's predatory nature—their desire for the prey in front of them.

Had she gotten there in time? How would they even know?

Abigail was frantically reloading her crossbow. The Woman in White was scrabbling in the dirt, choking round the bolt in her mouth. It wouldn't hold her for long.

Suddenly Crosscaper shook. A hollow detonation made the ground quake and both teenagers stagger sideways. Vivian stumbled from the doorway, visible once again in a scarlet-stained cloak, the Man in the Waistcoat driving her back with solid strikes of his pudgy fists. Her hammer was nowhere to be seen.

You think after this long I can't smell your grief? the thing cried. ***There is no running from this pain–keep it, keep feeling, keep hurting, and FEEEEEED UUUUUSSS!***

Vivian slammed him back with a howl of fire and turned to Denizen.

"GO," she snarled. "The bottom of the stairs. GO."

Denizen ran. The Man in the Waistcoat made to follow, but Vivian brought down both fists on the back of his head.

He saw the Woman draw out the bolt transfixing her and stalk toward Abigail, who drew her blade with a rasp of steel—

—and then he was pelting down dark corridors, praying he could lift the hammer when he found it.

He had moments. Just moments. His footsteps rang out against the linoleum, past Ackerby's snoring body, half falling down the stairs, and there it was—the ancient hammer, handle slick with his mother's blood.

His hands closed round it and Denizen *lifted*. The weapon weighed as much as a continent, but terror and adrenaline lent him strength and he staggered into the basement of Crosscaper, hammer clutched tight to his chest.

Mercy spun and dipped, barely more than a smear of light darting round the circle. Her glow strobed across the files and folders strewn about the floor. Could she sense the battle happening upstairs? Did she know what was being done to save her?

"Mercy," he said. "Mercy, I've—"

And then he heard the sobbing.

Oh. Right. The Clockwork *Three*. Funny how that had escaped his memory up until now.

The Opening Boy descended from the ceiling—a

patch of darkness so deep even Denizen's eyes couldn't penetrate it. The air froze in its wake, a thousand tiny particles of ice billowing behind it in a shroud of white. It looked as if someone had cut a boy-shaped hole in the universe. In its depths, Denizen could see . . . stars, or faces, or turning cogs.

The Boy is every child they've ever hurt. That's what Grey had said. *They keep him just to . . . just to make him watch.*

The Boy drifted nearer. Denizen could feel his eyebrows frost over. The folders were crinkling with the cold. Denizen drew the power of the Tenebrae close, reached for a Cant—

Do it.

Its voice was soft.

Please.

The Opening Boy closed its hands round the hammer, lending its strength to his. Smoke rose from its fingers where they touched the weapon.

All that misery. Everything the Boy had seen.

It just wanted an ending.

"Thank you," Denizen said. He didn't know what else to say.

They swung the hammer together.

31

Tock

The circle exploded.

Denizen caught a blurred glimpse of a triumphant smile before a hot slap of air spun him backward. His vision filled with falling white—thousands of pages kicked up by the blast—and he had a single moment to worry about landing on hard concrete before *something* caught him in tendrils of mist.

The darkness fled, driven away by royalty.

You came back, she said in a silvery voice.

Denizen went very still. He couldn't quite figure out what was holding him up, but at least it felt nice—like being adrift in hot water. He could sense the immense strength in it, but it held him as gently as it could, as if he was very fragile. Which, he supposed, he was.

Mercy leaned in, hair a pallid avalanche. This close, he could see every detail of her—the sapphire glow of her eyes, the translucent perfection of her skin. Every other Tenebrous he had seen was darkness wearing a form, but at the heart of Mercy there was only light.

They were very, very close.

Thank you, she murmured. Lightning climbed the distance between her lips and his.

"Ummm . . . ," Denizen began, and then she was gone, falling apart into a brocade of mist. Very gently, he bumped to the ground.

"Uhhh . . . ," he elaborated, and then just lay there, staring at the ceiling in silence.

It took a full minute before everything else that was happening crashed back into his head and he heaved himself to his feet.

The hammer lay across the circle, its head shattered into a hundred splintered shards. The largest was half the length of his forearm. It fit his hand like a short sword—an awful lot easier to carry than the hammer had been. *If I ever become head of the Order,* he thought as he ran, *everyone gets switchblades. Or tasers.*

The courtyard was in ruins. Great chunks had been ripped from Crosscaper's walls to litter the ground like lost and jagged teeth. The rain tasted like metal, sizzling where it struck burned swaths of gravel. The air stank of smoke. Everywhere, there was the chokingly alien feel of the Tenebrae.

Oh, look, the Man in the Waistcoat purred. ***The full set.***

His smile was splitting what remained of his face, skin catching on the clockwork beneath. His buttons—or were they eyes? It was hard to tell—glittered with their own unreflected light. His bulk shifted as if shapes inside fought for release.

The Woman in White had become a cadaverous thing of long scalpels and camshafts. Mad eyes glinted beneath a toothed, spinning brow. She skittered back and forth behind the Man, scarring the gravel with her touch.

Where is the Boy? The voice of the Tenebrous was mildly amused. ***Did you kill him? Did it hurt?***

I hope you've run, Denizen thought. *I hope you're far from here and free.* He stepped forward and the Man's grin returned, the Boy momentarily forgotten in the face of new prey.

Denizen's gaze flicked to beyond the Tenebrous, and anger bloomed anew. *A little more misery.*

The Tenebrous were playing.

Vivian's face was painted red from a cut near her hairline. There was another on her cheek. Her armor was slashed to pieces—the metal scarred in a dozen places, and her cloak was rags on her back.

Abigail, her crossbow long gone, had sacrificed her blade to Vivian's superior talent and held a bolt in either hand like knives. She too was swaying slightly, a bruise darkening one amber cheek.

Denizen watched as the Woman lashed out with a long blade of brass—striking sparks off the stone. Vivian flinched back, a flicker of light moving behind her eyes. With everything that had happened tonight, he had no idea how she was still standing.

"About time," she called. "Do I have to rescue you too?"

Denizen couldn't help but smile.

This is how our feast will start, the Man in the Waistcoat murmured, spitting a tooth out onto the gravel. ***An old grudge flavoring new meat.*** He padded closer, grotesquely light on his feet.

Denizen opened his fist and let the stone shard fall. What was left of the Man in the Waistcoat went pale.

"Now, I'm a bit new at this," Denizen said jauntily, "but what was it you said about the Endless King's anger?"

Thunder roared somewhere in the distance. The wind began to pick up.

"Devastating," Vivian said, her eyes narrowing. "Apocalyptic."

"An extinction-level event," they said together.

The air dropped twenty degrees. Denizen had never felt a Breach so violent, so immediate and intense. Sound distorted. Colors veered to blues and blacks. Pain stabbed through Denizen's temples at the sheer force of it. This wasn't the Tenebrae's slow intrusion—this was a sword blade through reality.

The Tenebrous *roared*. The sound shook with rage and hate . . . and loss too, the knowledge that they had failed, that the darkest of all fates was coming toward them.

They moved as one—the Man in the Waistcoat and the Woman in White—coming together in a weave of jagged clockwork, limbs winding, spines fusing, twisting into something more terrible, more *honest* than the forms they had held before. A shadow suddenly swept by Denizen, freezing the air in its wake—the Opening Boy, unable to escape, bound by misery to a greater shape.

The Clockwork Three reared. Denizen caught a blurred glimpse of something huge and spindly, a bent-spine mantis of spavined gears, faces split by shining teeth. It rose to its full height, spurs clawing at the sky, lunging for Denizen with a manic howl—and stopped a hair's breadth from his nose, talons scratching impotently at the ground.

Denizen fell back, heart in his mouth. The beast that had been the Clockwork Three writhed and snapped like a scorpion impaled on a hot needle. Its stink—rank oil and madness—made his stomach churn.

Behind it stood the Emissary of the Endless King. It pinned the Three on its spine with one great boot.

The air still shivered with the effects of the Breach. The ancient warrior towered over all of them, massive gauntlets curled into fists bigger than Denizen's skull. Rust hung about it like a cloud, jarred loose by the Three's useless struggles.

CLOCKWORK THREE, it thundered. The Three wailed and fought its grip. ***YOU HAVE BETRAYED YOUR KING.***

Gear-mouths screamed. Needle-claws dug in the dirt.

The Emissary's helm swung toward Vivian. ***You kept your word, Malleus Hardwick,*** it said in a softer voice. ***And the King will keep his. His Pursuivants will be withdrawn. And this . . .***

Its boot ground down harder.

. . . this FILTH will suffer the full justice of the Endless King.

Darkness bled and boiled through its joints. ***You are owed, Malleus Hardwick. We remember our debts, and a favor from the Forever Court is no small thing.***

Vivian said nothing. She just walked across the courtyard—stepping wide round the flailing extremities of the Three—and the next thing Denizen knew she was standing in front of him. Her eyes glittered, bright and gray and sharp as nails, and there was a question in the look she gave him.

Denizen knelt, picking up the long shard of stone at his feet, and pressed it into Vivian's hand. He nodded at her, watching as she strode back to where the Three mewled and thrashed.

The doomed Tenebrous fought to get out from under the Emissary's boot, blade-limbs straining to lash out and kill the woman they'd hated for so long, thrashing and clacking and screaming fit to burst.

Vivian stood over them, waiting until their struggles died away and they just lay there, staring up through a multitude of hate-filled eyes.

And then she brought the shard down, over and over again.

It wasn't quick, and it wasn't quiet. Maybe it would have been if the hammer had still been intact. Denizen didn't know. Maybe Vivian just wasn't taking any more chances. Either way, the impact of stone on metal went on for a very long time.

Finally, sweat-streaked and gasping, Denizen's mother flung the chipped fragment aside.

"Consider us even" was all she said.

EPILOGUE

DAYBREAK

It was a long walk to the mainland.

They found Grey still curled up on the ground where the Three had discarded him. Vivian, face expressionless, pulled him to his feet.

The madness seemed to have drained from him in the wake of the Three's death, though there was little of the cavalier rogue Denizen had first encountered with suit and scars and a cat-burglar smile.

He still grinned, though—hollowly, through a shattered jaw. "I can't hear it anymore," he was mumbling. It had taken a while before Denizen could make out the words. "I can't hear the ticking."

They picked their way across the wreckage of the gates.

"Will the other children be all right?" Denizen asked.

Vivian nodded. "Nightmares rarely last after waking. They'll have moments—faint memories—but in time they too will fade." She shrugged her cloak round her shoulders.

"And . . ." He was almost afraid to ask. "And Grey?"

"I don't know," she said simply.

Denizen didn't feel anything as he left the gates behind. There was nothing left for him here now, though he couldn't help looking back at the grim stone face of the orphanage, scarred by fire and the touch of the Tenebrae.

They had that in common, at least.

As he stared up at the architecture of his childhood, a figure appeared in the doorway. Without thinking, Denizen called a Helios Lance to his palm and held it there—a streak of jagged flame ready to be unleashed.

It was Director Ackerby. The man was still swaying, half under the spell of the Three, but as moments passed his faculties seemed to return.

"Who . . . who—is that you, Hardwick?"

Denizen let the fire in his palm go out and met the man's gaze with his own cool gray eyes.

Ackerby took a step backward.

"Go back inside, Director," Denizen said quietly, and walked away.

The rain had stopped, and though it was still bitterly cold, it was actually turning into a nice night for a walk. The wind had died down. Everything felt sharp-edged and clear, and Denizen knew that, come the morning, the world would be painted with frost.

They had barely walked a hundred meters down the road before the wet grass began to shine and spark like a reflection of a clear night sky. Moisture in the air sizzled and crackled, swirling round a starburst point of blue that guttered and wavered as stray raindrops passed through it.

Vivian raised her hands wearily, her grip on Grey slipping, but Denizen waved her down.

Denizen Hardwick, Mercy said, stepping from thin air in a cascade of sparks and gemlight.

Denizen wasn't sure what to do, so he just gave her an awkward, nodding bow. Was that how you greeted royalty?

The girl of storms drifted closer. Denizen could see the outline of the hills behind her, as if she were just an image projected from somewhere very far away. Lightning stabbed out from her lithe form, and Denizen blushed as he remembered its taste.

You'll take care of what I gave you? she asked in a voice like a waterfall.

"Oh," Denizen said, once again breaking new ground in the field of wit and charm. The Cants she had bestowed sizzled and danced in the back of his head. "Yes. No problem. Good."

She raised a glowing hand. ***We will see each other again, Denizen Hardwick.*** A smile spread across her ethereal features, and she gave both Vivian and Abigail a perfect curtsy before coming apart in threads of light. Her final words hung in the air like raindrops.

Because someday I might need them back.

"What?" Denizen said. "Uh—" But she was already gone. He turned back to see Abigail and Vivian staring at him.

"What did *that* mean?" There was a slight note of panic in his voice.

Vivian gave an exhausted shrug. Abigail was still staring at him.

"What?" he said.

"Nothing," she said, her gaze bright and sharp. "Why have you gone red?"

Denizen blushed harder. "I haven't. I'm not. Shut up."

Eventually, he found himself walking beside his mother. She was cleaning the blood off her face with a scrap of her cloak, her other hand gently steering Grey's staggering footsteps.

"Hi," he said awkwardly.

She let the scrap go, and an eddy of wind flicked it off into the night. They trudged in silence for a few moments.

"So," Denizen said, "how . . . how are you?"

Instead of responding, his mother turned to Abigail a little way back up the road.

"Do you mind?" she said.

Abigail shook her head and took over from Vivian, sliding an arm round Grey's waist. They walked on, leaving Denizen and his mother alone.

Vivian looked out over the bleak landscape—the cresting waves, the hills made silver and haunting by the moon. The view was as familiar to him as the sight of his own face in the mirror, and it was strange to see her be a part of it, though with ragged armor and sword the whole scene could have been something from a millennia-old war.

Which it was, now that he thought of it.

"What happens now?" she said.

"What do you mean?"

She looked him up and down. "Does this change things? Knowing what you know? It doesn't end here. This is just the beginning. There are years of training—for you and Simon, should he join us—there are your studies at Daybreak, a whole life of Knighthood. You could just . . . you could—"

"I'm not going anywhere," Denizen said firmly, and Vivian nodded.

They walked on a few more steps and then, abruptly, she spoke.

"I don't feel any better."

The words were raw with emotion.

"I didn't . . . I mean, I never *thought* I would, but now . . . now I know."

She swallowed. "The Clockwork Three are dead. A Malleus's hammer, even a shard of it, would make sure of that. I've been waiting for this moment for *so long*. And it hasn't changed anything. I don't feel any better."

She smiled bitterly. "I don't know what I was thinking. Revenge doesn't bring anyone back from the dead."

"I don't know about that," Denizen said hesitantly. Over the horizon, the sun was rising. "I mean, we're here, aren't we?"

THE SECRET ABOUT WRITERS . . .

. . . is that very few of us live in a driftwood cave writing soul-rending poetry on our own feet and then washing it away with the morning's first dew.

I'm not saying some don't. What I am saying is that this book would not have happened without the support of a lot of beautiful and interesting people.

First, my parents for always putting a book in my hand. It cannot be easy when one's firstborn son decides to be a writer (I could have been something respectable, like a teacher, or a human), but their love and support have always been unconditional. Thank you.

My agents, Clare and Sheila, are rock-star supernovas. That is all. The Darley Anderson Children's Book Agency has taken great care of me since the moment I was signed. Clare, Sheila, Mary, Emma—thank you.

My editors, Ben, Caroline, and Wendy, are also celestial beings of kindness and patience. To them, and everyone at Penguin Random House, thank you so much for making this happen. Onward and downward, to misery unending.

Graham Tugwell, Deirdre Sullivan, and Sarah Maria Griff—my Doomsburies. Writing is not so lonely a job when you have such fiendish and wonderful comrades-in-arms. This book would be much poorer without their advice and insight. The same goes for Sarah Jane Nangle, PhD; Arvind Ethan David; Melissa Jensen; Vanessa O'Loughlin; Roe McDermot; Kerrie O'Brien; the Arts Council of Ireland; and the staff of the Creative Writing masters program at UCD.

And to Rebecca. She read it first.

DAVE RUDDEN enjoys cats, adventure, and being cruel to fictional children. This is his first novel. Find him at daverudden.com and on Twitter at @d_ruddenwrites.

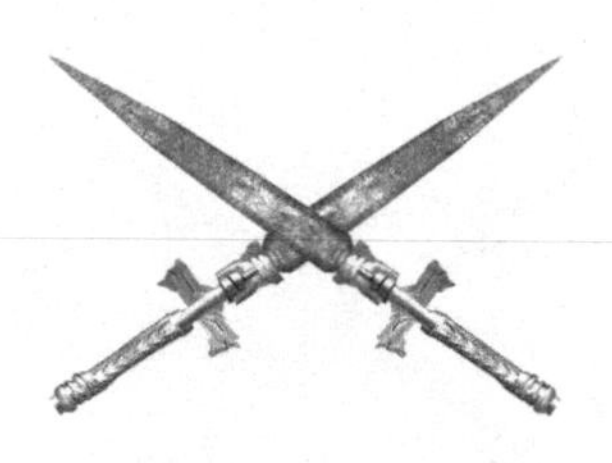